SPIDER'S QUEEN

Book 3 in the Detective Trann series

Christa Yelich-Koth

Look for other books by Christa Yelich-Koth

www.ChristaYelichKoth.com

The Detective Trann series
SPIDER'S TRUTH
SPIDER'S RING
SPIDER'S QUEEN
SPIDER'S RIFT
SPIDER'S LIE

**The Land of Iyah trilogy
(YA fantasy)**
THE JADE CASTLE
THE JADE ARCH
THE JADE THRONE

**Eomix Galaxy Novels
(Sci-fi/fantasy)**
ILLUSION (Book 1 of 2)
IDENTITY (Book 2 of 2)
COILED VENGEANCE

**Graphic Novels
(Sci-fi)**
HOLLOW

**Comic Books
(Sci-fi)**
HOLLOW'S PRSIM SERIES
(6 issues total)
Issue #1: *Aftermath*
Issue #2: *Reunion*
Issue #3: *Alliance*
Issue #4: *Trigger*
Issue #5: *Revelations*
Issue #6: *Fusion*

SPECIAL THANKS

To you, the reader: THANK YOU for wanting more from this series.

Sandra Yelich: We made it through another one. Thank GOOD-NESS this one wasn't as tough! Thank you as always for your amazing edits.

Conrad Teves: For your incredible help with the cover art.

Thomas Koth: For beta reading so quickly with my ever-changing timeline.

1

October 12th
8:00 a.m.

Wind swirled the crispy red and orange leaves around Isabella's feet where she stood, staring at the grave in front of her, tears streaking down her face. Her open coat flapped in the breeze, but she didn't bother to button it. She could barely feel the chilly air as her thoughts were focused solely on the tombstone.

"I miss you every day," she whispered into the empty space. No one else currently paid tribute at any of the other headstones in the small graveyard outside the modest-sized town in Maine. Isabella knelt down on the ground, not quite frozen in the forty-degree weather. Bare tree branches hung low over the fence next to her at the rear of the site, casting shadows like thin rickety arms reaching as if to catch her.

Except nothing ever happened here, besides the words of the living being spoken to dead ground and hard, cold stone.

Footsteps sounded behind her, steady, and unafraid to make their presence known. Isabella kept her eyes on the headstone, drinking in the simple carved words in her final moments before she had to leave.

The footsteps stopped next to her. Isabella could see the person's feet facing forward. A voice spoke into the frigid wind, its words tinged with a Spanish accent.

"You said you wouldn't return here." No accusation coated the phrase, only a sense of understanding and remorse.

"I know," Isabella said, reaching out with her fingers to trace the name on the block of granite before her. "I just. . .I really missed her today."

The woman shifted in the thick, fallen leaves, crunching them beneath her short-heeled black shoes.

"We should go," the woman said, though her words lacked conviction.

"I know," Isabella repeated, pulling her hand away. She leaned the rest of the way over towards the ground, her face inches away from the earth. "No one else will suffer like you did, my love. Like we did. I will stop them. All of them."

Inhaling deeply through her nose, Isabella forced herself to believe she could smell the hint of lilac through the scent of crisp leaves and packed earth. She then straightened, slowly got to her feet, and hastily wiped her wet face with her sleeve. With a twist, she faced her companion. A beautiful Latina woman stood there, her long dark curls flittering in the sharp breeze, her large eyes sad. She sported jeans and a black turtleneck underneath her charcoal gray pea coat. A sea-green scarf fluttered about her shoulders.

"I'm all right, Carla," Isabella lied, moving away from the grave and towards the exit.

Carla fell into step next to her. "Are you? You've come here three times since you said you weren't going to anymore."

Isabella remained quiet. The truth was she hadn't felt as sure about her mission lately and visiting the graveyard always helped.

Carla continued. "You drove all night to get here, didn't you? Right after talking to Charlotte."

"Yes," Isabella whispered. That had been another surreal experience. She'd imagined speaking to Charlotte again, but thought it wouldn't be for weeks, perhaps months. Her plans felt like they were moving so quickly she could hardly catch her breath. Revealing herself to Charlotte, asking for her help. . . everything had been exposed. If their arrangements didn't go right, they'd have to return to hiding, and possibly remove Charlotte from the equation. . .

Isabella shuddered at the thought. She really, truly believed Charlotte was the only one to help them stop the Triads, but what if she didn't join their cause?

"Do you think she won't talk to us?" Carla asked, as if reading Isabella's thoughts.

"On the contrary. I know she will." They'd reached the graveyard's wrought-iron fence with its kissing door.

Carla put her hand on top of the gate, but paused before pulling it open. "Really? Why is that?"

"Charlotte will give herself an excuse, like she doesn't know if we will harm her if she refuses to come or because she thinks she'll gain information to turn over to the police. But the truth is, she wants to know about us. About her brother. About herself. After that? I don't know if she'll actually join us." Isabella's brow furrowed at the sight of Carla's hand. Her friend's knuckles were puffy and covered with a streak of dried blood.

"Did something go wrong?" she asked, nodding at the injury.

Carla glanced at her own hand then swung the metal gate open. "The most recent target resisted."

"Badly?"

"No. Just. . .unexpectedly."

Isabella rubbed her hands over her face as they headed towards their separate vehicles. She'd felt so tired lately, and yet she still had so much work to do.

"Are all the other plans set? Any new problems?"

Carla paused. "There have been reports of fires, but no one has claimed responsibility."

"Fires." Isabella frowned. "What sorts of fires?"

"Centered around previous or current Triad activity. I haven't found a specific pattern yet."

"Can we find out about them?"

"We don't have the resources at the moment. But they'll reveal themselves somehow. Everyone makes a mistake at some point."

They'd reached Isabella's car first and she touched Carla's arm, stopping her. "Does that include us?"

"Of course."

"You say that so matter-of-factly."

Carla pursed her lips for a moment. "Isabella, the *hugeness* of what we are doing is too monumental to not blunder at times. It's one reason why we are seeking outside help. But that involves risk as well. The more players, the more secrets, the more chances for mistakes. The best we can do is the best we can do."

"We've made a difference so far."

"Yes, but we can't stop everyone. Not physically at least. There are too many of them. But we *can* make them *want* to stop."

"Not without Charlotte."

Carla nodded, then cocked her head. "What about Detective Trann?"

Isabella calculated the chance of Sean being a deterrent to their plans with Charlotte. Based on what she'd learned from him in her interview, from Carla's notes as his therapist, and Jordan's line of questioning when preparing him for the trial, she felt pretty confident he wouldn't pursue them. "I don't think he'll pose a problem."

"You don't think Charlotte will tell him you two met last night?"

"At this point, no. She won't want to put him in any danger. After we speak with her, I'll assess her threat risk and move ahead accordingly." A gust of wind whipped at her as they continued to their cars, piercing her coat as if it weren't even there. She finally buttoned it up. The weather this far north was much colder than in Boston.

Wrapping her arms around herself, Isabella let out a sigh. "What about Jordan? You said she wanted to propose a potential."

"The receptionist, Mags."

Isabella's mind circled through all the possible variables, the pros and cons of bringing in another person so soon. Mags Stinton was an unknown to Isabella. She hadn't been studied or researched like other prospective sources in the past. Like Charlotte. But if Jordan felt so strongly about it. . .the district attorney was extremely adept at reading people.

A sense of calm stole over Isabella. "We can evaluate her further when we return to Boston. If she does join us, she could be very valuable as an asset."

"I agree."

"It's settled then." She nodded to Carla's car. "I'll meet you at your new place."

Carla gave a smile and left.

Isabella glanced one more time at the grave towards the rear end of the graveyard. She couldn't keep returning here. It would be too easy to track her. She knew this.

And yet her chest hurt at the thought of finally saying goodbye to the love of her life. The woman who'd been murdered by another Triad member.

"One day I'll come here and stay, lying next to you forever, my love." She whispered her promise once more. "Then no one else will suffer like you did. Like we did. I swear."

In a swift motion, Isabella entered and started up her car, took off down the road, and headed south.

Back to Boston.

2

October 12th

9:00 a.m.

Sean couldn't find a bathroom. He'd been preparing that morning for a 10k Fun Run and the bathrooms had all been moved away from the starting line. He wouldn't be able to run unless he emptied his bladder. Why couldn't he find a restroom? Had the flying dragons burned them all down? Had the group of menacing men and women, staring at him from the stands, hidden them on purpose?

"There," he called out, seeing a Port-o-Potty in the distance. He jogged towards it, but right before he opened the door, a beautiful woman stepped out and plunged a knife right into his pressure-filled abdomen.

"The Triads are FOREVER." She pulled out the blade, the metal covered with blood. The woman looked up at him, her face a blur, swirling between beiges and browns.

"Oops," she said. "I thought you were Charlotte."

Sean woke up with a start, a shout caught on his lips. His bladder screamed at him, the feeling almost painful. Confused, he took a moment to get his bearings, and realized he currently lay on the couch in his studio apartment.

Though groggy, he pushed himself up off the cushions and ambled towards the bathroom, his feet dragging against the cream-colored carpet. On the way, his toe caught on the edge of his bed, sending a piercing stab of pain through his foot.

Either he was too tired to fully register the blow or his mind was still caught in the remaining images of his dream to voice his usual curses. Striding into the bathroom, he relieved himself for what seemed like five minutes, the pressure easing with every passing second.

Remnants of his dream sifted through his mind while he stood there. He supposed it made sense to have the nightmare. Yesterday the trial ended for Violet—a murderer who associated herself with what she called a Triad, a group of three women bent on removing people in the world whose physical flaws should have been eliminated naturally through evolution. The trial ended with Violet being found "not guilty" by reason of insanity and trucked off to Bridgewater State Hospital.

Except, when she'd arrived escorted by two guards, she'd managed to escape, steal a police van, and return to Boston. Whatever nefarious plans she may have had upon her arrival were thwarted by a random act of violence—a mugging gone wrong. Violet had ended up dead mere blocks from Sean's apartment, bludgeoned to death and tossed in an alley dumpster.

Being that close to his location should have frightened him more, but his immediate thought had been to call Charlotte, who'd just left his place around the time of Violet's murder. Luckily, Charlotte had answered her phone, and though she'd seemed a little. . .distant. . .she'd assured him she was fine.

Sean finished using the bathroom, washed his hands, and began to brush his teeth, thinking about the previous night with Charlotte. The whole evening had been such a whirlwind—they'd had pizza, talked about some of Charlotte's anxieties, which had been giving her panic attacks lately, and then they'd had the most mind-blowing sex Sean had ever experienced.

Ever.

Sean spit and rinsed his mouth, a grin instantly spreading across his face at the memory of the two of them together. She'd told him she wanted to see him again tonight and he himself could hardly wait. Though he'd known her for over a year, they'd only become friendly in the past seven months, minus the three months she'd been gone out of the country for work. Sean had worried their closeness had only been from their Triad-related experience, since they'd grown distant during her travels. However, once she returned, they both realized they wanted to spend more time together.

After being with her yesterday, he'd never felt so happy. Things were finally looking up. The Triad was finished. All three women were dead. He'd started a great relationship with Charlotte and couldn't wait to see her again. And he had the whole weekend in front of him to relax.

His life finally felt like it made sense.

In the meantime, he had a few things he wanted to do before seeing Charlotte that night: check in on Payne at the hospital, follow-up with Mags and Tay to see how they were feeling after their attacks, work out, get groceries, and do laundry so he had something clean to wear that evening.

An odor wafted up from under his arms and his nose wrinkled.

Better start with a shower first.

3

October 12th
10 a.m.

Pain. Two kinds.

A sharp, stretchy sort of pain woke Charlotte. She let out a moan and attempted to lift her head, but stopped, sucking in a breath. A kink in her neck shot through her, like a shock into her skull.

"Damn," she muttered. The second pain, sharper than the first, came from her back, where she'd been stabbed two days earlier.

With slower movements, she finished sitting up. She'd fallen asleep on her couch—something she'd never done before—with her head angled backwards and her injured shoulder blade pressing into the cushions.

With a dry mouth, she coughed a bit, then leaned forward. On the coffee table in front of her lay a folder splayed open. Its contents, including copies of medical reports, a car license plate number, the car's make and model, and some information about a woman named Betty Patrickson, were strewn all over. A few of the pages had even fallen to the carpeted floor. Some were highlighted, others crinkled slightly. Each page had notes across them in Charlotte's handwriting.

Charlotte leaned over to pick up the fallen sheets when the pain in her back flared again.

"Ibuprofen first," she said. With slow movements she rose, glancing at her digital clock on the nightstand next to her bed. The blue numbers glared at her.

10:00 a.m.

She'd slept until ten in the morning.

She'd never slept that late before, except when recovering from jet lag. How could she have slept so long?

Although, when she thought about it, she didn't actually know when she'd fallen asleep. She remembered glancing at the clock around six-ish in the morning and grabbing another cup of coffee, so she must have been up for at least another hour or two after that.

Charlotte found she didn't care. Today was Saturday. She could take a nap later if need be.

Once in her bathroom, she popped a couple ibuprofen, then a couple more for good measure, to deal with the ache in her neck and the throbbing of her back. When she went to start brushing her teeth, she finally looked at herself in the mirror.

She let out a gasp.

Charlotte made it a point to take care of herself. She ate healthily, exercised, treated her hair and skin well, and got adequate sleep. Now, staring at the gaunt face in front of her, with dark circles under her eyes, a makeshift bandage across her eyebrow which she knew covered a nasty gash, and a ripped blouse, she began to cry.

She hadn't meant to, but the tears came. Everything flooded her mind. The Triad trial. The intimate night with Sean. The attack from Violet. The conversation with Isabella. Conflicted emotions raced through her, all vying for her focus.

Charlotte always prided herself on her composure, but how could she be expected to calmly manage all these complex situations? In the past six months she'd been stabbed twice, once left for dead, kidnapped from her work, and assaulted at her car on the street. She'd spent three months traveling around the world, hunting for proof of any other Triads, and finding nothing. Then last night, when she'd felt she'd finally escaped from under the looming fear of Triad women in this world, Isabella, a previous Triad member, told her they absolutely existed.

On top of that, when she'd gotten home and opened the folder, there'd been proof that her brother's hit-and-run accident had been nothing of the sort. It had actually been a Triad-related murder.

A shudder suddenly wracked through her and the tears turned into sobs. Charlotte fell to her knees onto the pale blue bathroom rug and gripped the edge of the sink for support. Wave after wave hit her, stealing her breath, wetting the floor in front of her. Everything poured out of her: her fears, her pain, her sadness.

She didn't want to deal with any of this. Her whole life had been completely turned upside down and then, just when she thought she'd had some semblance of relief and normalcy, the whole ordeal started all over again.

Why her? Why couldn't the universe fixate on someone else?

With slow breaths, she composed herself. Flashes of literature class in college stole through her mind. She remembered when she'd read classic stories of heroes and how most of them attempted to avert their destinies. Those who tried usually self-fulfilled them anyway, and those who let go and accepted went on to become legends.

I do not want to be a hero or a legend, she whispered in her own head. *I merely want to be me.*

Really? her mind countered. *Are you sure?*

She forced the thought away. Nothing would be solved by giving into her fears or her pride. Logic would help her. It always had in the past.

Although it didn't seem to assist her when she'd been having panic attacks recently or in her decision to pursue a relationship with Sean. Her emotions, rather than logic, controlled her at these points, dictating how she reacted.

Charlotte wiped the tears from her face, fatigue settling over her. She could do this, but not right now. First, she needed to take care of herself. A shower. Redressing her wounds. Some breakfast.

One step at a time, she thought, pushing herself up off the floor. She had some decisions to make. What to do about the

Book and the file on her brother. What to do when Isabella contacted her again. And what to tell Sean about all of this, if anything at all.

Charlotte didn't like to lie, but if it meant protecting someone. . .?

All these decisions were new territory for her. She needed some time to sort each issue out.

"Shower. Injuries. Breakfast," she told her reflection.

One step at a time.

4

October 12th
11 a.m.

Sean huffed up the last few stairs with his basket of clean, dry laundry. Though grateful his building had washers and dryers in the basement, so he didn't have to go to a laundromat, the three-flight climb up and down made him promise himself he would do laundry more often so his loads weren't so heavy. A promise he made every time and had yet to fulfill.

A few feet from his door, he heard the ringing of his landline phone.

"Crap," he said, dropping his basket and fishing out his keys. He fumbled one of them into the lock, opened it, then sprinted to the phone.

"Yeah?" he answered.

"Hey, Trann. It's me, Millan."

Sean paused. It was unlike his boss to call on a Saturday, unless there was a specific case he needed help with. "Sarge?" He peered over at his open door and could see the edge of the laundry basket. "Hold on a sec." Placing the phone down, he retrieved his items and reentered, locking the door behind him. He plopped the basket on the bed and grabbed the receiver.

"Okay, I'm here. What's going on?"

"I know it's your day off, but I wanted to touch base with you about the messages you were receiving the past couple weeks during the trial. You know, the ones from an unknown caller."

"You found out who they came from?"

"Yeah, after work last night. We can follow up with it on Monday, but I thought you should know now."

A chill crept across his skin. "Who sent them?"

"The defense attorney from the Triad trial. Marina Beguilous."

The words didn't really make sense to him for a few moments. "The *defense* attorney? Why was she sending me cryptic messages about the trial and about Charlotte? Isn't that illegal as opposing counsel?"

"That'd be my guess."

Sean glanced over at his clock. "Well I'm going to go speak to her about it. Is there a way to get her address?"

"I already did."

The emptiness of Millan's words renewed the chill. "And. . .?"

"I went to her place last night, to question her myself. They were hauling out the body when I pulled up."

"She's dead?" Shock coursed through him. "How?"

"Gunshot to the head. Point blank."

Sean sunk down onto the bed, accidentally knocking over the laundry basket, which spilled its contents onto the floor. He ignored the mess, distracted by this new information.

"What happened?"

"There hasn't been an official report yet—I'm going to touch base with the lead detective at the other precinct after the weekend—but I think the killer may have been Violet. I checked the timetable of her escape from custody last night. She would have had time to stop by the defense attorney's place and shoot her before she showed up dead near your apartment. I figure there must have been some kind of connection with the attorney, a loose end, maybe, that Violet didn't want to leave hanging before she came to your neighborhood. I can't imagine she was near you for any other reason than to kill you. Thank God for that mugger."

Sean didn't want to condone the actions of the mugger who'd murdered Violet, but he had a feeling that if Violet hadn't been killed, he wouldn't be alive right now.

Sean forced his mind to shift away from thoughts about his own possible demise and rechanneled it onto the prosecutor's connection to himself and Violet. "I don't get it, though. Why did the attorney send me those messages in the first place, especially if she was in league with Violet? Why warn me at all? And why were they so cryptic? It's almost like she was barely conscious when she sent them."

"I don't know, kid. But now we can't ask her."

The defeat in Millan's voice permeated through the phone

line. "It wasn't your fault, you know," Sean said slowly. "We didn't know who she was, or that she would be targeted."

A long pause.

"Sarge?"

Finally, Millan coughed on the other end. "That's not entirely true."

Sean leaned forward, his elbows on his knees. "You *did* know she would be attacked?"

"No. But I could have known her identity before she died. I got the message from the department who tracked her number hours earlier. If I'd have listened to the information sooner, I'd have known who she was. . ."

"Yeah? And what could you have done? You didn't know Violet would escape or come after her."

"But I would have asked her to come down to the station and answer some questions. She wouldn't have been home at all, for anyone *to* kill her."

Sean hesitated. He didn't like the pain he heard in Millan's voice. "You don't know if she would have come with you," he reasoned. "She was an attorney, after all, and knows she doesn't have to. If she was an accomplice, maybe she would have taken off and left town. Who knows if she was supposed to help Violet escape or had double-crossed her or something? You can't know you would have saved her."

Another short silence.

"It's too much," Millan said quietly.

Sean shifted on the bed. "What is?"

"All of it."

A red flag waved inside Sean's mind as a warning. He'd heard statements like this before. They usually came from people who'd given up. And worse, sometimes they came from people who were suicidal.

Not being trained for a situation like this, Sean didn't want to say the wrong words, but he knew he had to say something. He pulled on some of what he'd learned when dealing with unstable people during an arrest. The person often wanted to talk, needed to know they weren't alone, and required help.

Well, he didn't know how much he could help or how well the talk might go, but he could make sure Millan wasn't alone.

"Sounds like a rough night," Sean said. "Maybe you and your wife could go out tonight, get your mind off things?"

"She's gone."

The words hung in the air. "Gone? What do you mean 'gone?'"

"She left me. She's staying at her sister's." Millan's words sounded dead.

Oh, God, Sean thought. "I didn't. . .I didn't know," he stammered. "I'm really sorry."

"Don't worry about it. Listen, I need to run."

"No wait!" Sean stood up. Frantically he blurted out, "Let's grab a beer tonight and chat about all this. I've got too many theories to wait until Monday."

"You don't need me."

"Of course, I do. You know I enjoy bouncing ideas off of you. What do you say?"

Sean waited while the silence lengthened. Finally, he heard a sigh.

"All right. There's a Buffalo Wild Wings by my house. We

can meet there at five thirty. I think there's a college football game I want to see anyway."

"Great. See you then, Sarge."

Sean hung up the phone and sat down on the bed again, satisfied with his plan.

That is, until he remembered he was supposed to have a follow-up date with Charlotte tonight.

"Awwww. . .craaaaap."

5

October 12th
11 a.m.

Charlotte's phone rang. She'd left the device on her bathroom sink.

A groan escaped her mouth and she resubmerged herself beneath the beating pulse of the showerhead. She had no idea how long she'd been standing there, letting the hot water pour over her, trying desperately to erase the pain and memories of the past few weeks. Scratch that, the past several months.

Peering down, she noted the redness of her skin. She supposed she'd been in the shower long enough. The outside world wasn't going to go away on its own.

With slow movements she turned off the knobs, hearing the

drip drip drip of the remnant water droplets plink from the faucet to the tub floor. Usually a shower rejuvenated her, but right now, all she felt was wetter, cleaner, and more tired.

Charlotte breathed in the steam of the bathroom, feeling the heated particles cling to the insides of her lungs, and then exhaled slowly. She did this a few more times until she felt a little calmer.

I can do this, she told herself. *One step at a time, remember?*

Charlotte pulled open the curtain, climbed out of the shower, and checked the missed call on her phone. The caller ID dutifully told her it had been her mother.

Charlotte had completely forgotten she'd placed a late-night phone call to her parents after reading the file on her brother given to her the night before by Isabella.

Grabbing the phone and a towel, Charlotte headed into the bedroom area of her studio apartment. She plopped the phone onto the bed, dried off her body and hair, and stood, staring at the file and Book on the coffee table across the space a few feet away.

Wrapping the towel around her, she strode over to the table, glaring at the mess. With quick movements she bent over and scooped up all the papers that had fallen onto the floor and any sprawled over the couch, arranged them into a neat pile, and placed them once again inside the folder.

The previous night, in an over-tired stupor, Charlotte had called her mother, wanting answers regarding the medical material in the file concerning her brother. The information came from their hometown hospital in Seattle, stating that her brother had a type of hemophilia. He'd been admitted several times at a young age when injuries caused continual bleeding to occur.

Charlotte had never known this. Of course, she'd been younger than her brother and only seven years old when he'd died, so perhaps her parents hadn't wanted to tell her about his condition until she'd been older. After his death, they probably no longer saw any point in mentioning it.

Still, the idea that she didn't know such an important fact about her brother had fueled anger inside her, prompting the call to confront her mother.

Luckily, her mother hadn't answered. Charlotte didn't think about the fact that her mother may ask how she'd found out about her brother's condition, and saying she'd received a medical file from a woman who'd just saved her life by murdering someone else probably wouldn't go over too well.

Now, in the light of a new day, Charlotte needed to decide what to say to her mother, if anything. Did she *want* to know if the report was true? If so, did that mean her brother was killed, not accidentally by a hit-and-run driver as her family believed, but by a Triad member because of his physical condition?

Because that was what the file implied. Isabella had given it to Charlotte to show that a Triad had known about her brother, targeted him, and murdered him.

As a bonus bit of teasing material, the name of the murderer was typed nicely and neatly above an address, just inside the outer flap. An address that happened to be about a three-hour drive away.

Charlotte had to give Isabella credit. The woman had known *exactly* the type of information to give to instill curiosity, anger, and grief. Instead of focusing on the fact that Isabella was a killer herself, Charlotte had instead focused on the detail that her brother's murderer currently lived, without having been caught, in Burlington, Vermont.

Or at least, that was what the file said. Isabella could have doctored the paperwork. Charlotte had no way of knowing if her brother's death had been simply an accident or a Triad plot. Which again, was what Isabella wanted. She knew these reports would entice Charlotte enough to pursue the truth behind the information.

Except Charlotte wasn't sure how...

Her phone rang again, startling her out of her thoughts. She glanced down onto the bed and saw the call came from Sean. A sensation of lightness stole through her body, followed quickly by the sinking feeling of dread.

They were supposed to have a date tonight.

Charlotte's hand immediately went to her cut eyebrow, as if to cover it. Her other hand gravitated towards her lower back, half of which was covered in road rash from when Violet dragged her away from her car and along the asphalt the previous evening.

The phone rang again.

She didn't want him to see her in this condition. He'd ask questions, want to know what had happened to her, but she couldn't tell him about Violet's attack and Isabella's help. If what Isabella said was true and other Triads still existed, getting Sean involved would only put him in danger. He'd want to alert the precinct, let everyone know, but know what? These women had spent years hiding. Nothing would happen except exposure, which Isabella assured Charlotte would be covered up by any means necessary. Including murder.

A third ring.

Except how could she get out of a date when they'd *just* slept together the night before? She'd have to lie, a concept which she hated. In fact she did her best *not* to lie, unless necessary or for an occasion like a surprise birthday party, but she'd already misled him after meeting with Isabella. He'd asked her if she'd felt all right and she said she'd felt fine. But fine was the furthest away from how she'd truly felt.

Her whole body tightened and she recognized the new feeling: anxiety. A recent addition to her day-to-day life was the occasional panic attack that seemed to come out of nowhere. This "tightness" in her body let her know a bout would come soon if she didn't make a decision, and fast.

Charlotte snatched up the phone and answered it. "Hello?"

"Hey, it's Sean."

A smile touched her lips without any thought. "Hello, Sean."

"Listen, I'm going to cut right to the chase."

Charlotte couldn't breathe. She had no idea what Sean's next words might be, but a thousand horrible thoughts rushed in at once, ripping through her mind like relentless overlapping rapids. Was he going to say their time together the previous night had been a mistake? That he didn't want to see her anymore? That another body had been found? Or that he knew about her meeting with Isabella and would arrest her for withholding information?

A breath forced its way in and out of her lungs. "What is it?" she asked, concentrating on keeping her voice steady.

"I have to cancel tonight. But not because I don't want to see you!" His words came quick and with a tinge of fear. "It's work. I have to meet up with Sergeant Millan."

Charlotte's knees felt weak. At least it wasn't about their relationship, but maybe Millan had heard about what had happened last night and was going to tell Sean? "Oh? Something wrong?"

"Not exactly. More like. . .loose ends from the case. And, he seems a bit down. I think he needs someone to talk to."

"You are an excellent choice for that," she said with a smile.

"Well, thanks." A beat passed. "I really want to see you though."

Charlotte chose her next words carefully. She didn't want to lie, but she needed to make sure they didn't see each other until she healed. "Perhaps it is better this way. I am feeling quite tired today. And in pain."

"Guess maybe we overdid it last night?"

"I would not take it back," she said quickly.

"Good. Me neither. I'm just sorry you feel more hurt."

"I do not think what you and I did aggravated my injury." *Getting pulled out of my car and dragged along the road did, though,* she thought. "But I am still recovering."

"That's good to hear. Okay, you take care of yourself and I'll meet up with Millan. Let's make a plan to meet next weekend instead, give yourself time to heal up?"

"Sounds perfect."

"Great. Talk to you soon, Charlotte."

"Take care, Sean." Charlotte hung up the phone. She'd both wanted to and *didn't* want to tell Sean about what happened last night. Mostly because she didn't want him to be targeted by Triads, if they truly did exist. She'd seen firsthand how these women operated. She couldn't put Sean in danger.

Yet, she also wanted his advice. What would *he* do in this situation if he were her? Ignore the women? Burn the Book and file? Call in SWAT?

Charlotte shook her head. Unfortunately, she couldn't ask him without risking his life or the lives of his coworkers. She needed to figure this out on her own.

With a whole weekend ahead of her, she had time to decide what to do. The smart thing would be to put the Book and file into the bag, never look at them again, and return the items to Isabella once she called. Charlotte had always done the smart thing. She prided herself on it. But these women had twisted logic to fit their needs. She wasn't living in a world of reason anymore, so how could she act reasonably?

No, she told herself. *You will not stoop to their level. You will take this one step at a time. You showered. Next on your list is taking care of your injuries.*

But while she mechanically returned to the bathroom and applied antiseptic and new bandages, she stared through the doorway at the folder on the coffee table.

How could she possibly let the information go? If that file *really* told her who'd murdered her brother all those years ago, how could she walk away?

A sense of purpose flooded her. One way or another, she needed to know the truth.

Finishing up, she then dressed in comfortable, loose clothing, made a smoothie, and drank it. Once finished, she took in and let out a huge breath, then strode over to the coffee table. She picked up the top page and read the typed name and address on it:

Betty Patrickson
10 Eastman Way
Burlington, VT

Folding the paper gently, she tucked it into the pocket of her khakis. She grabbed two granola bars and a water bottle from her kitchen cabinet to eat later on the road, pulled on a coat, grabbed her phone and keys, and left for the car.

6

October 12th
5:30 p.m.

Sean pulled up to the Buffalo Wild Wings in Brockton. He'd never been this far south of Boston before and didn't know this was where Millan lived. Not that he had any reason *to* know, it just felt strange to him that he *didn't* know. As close as he felt they were, he realized he really didn't know much about his Sergeant's personal life. In fact, most of their association seemed pretty one-sided at this point in time. Maybe Sean could remedy that tonight.

Once inside the restaurant, Sean spotted Millan sitting at the bar and joined him. He made his way past tables and booths, avoiding the packed crowds. Servers wove in and out of the bustle, placing drinks and appetizers in front of people with experience and ease.

"Busy here tonight," Sean said over the noise when he reached Millan.

"Pretty usual for a Saturday. They have trivia besides the football games. We can grab a booth back there," he said, nodding toward the east corner. The two made their way, Millan taking his already-ordered beer with him, and grabbed a seat across from each other.

Sean did a quick assessment of the late fifties, African-American man. He seemed all right, a little bloodshot in the eyes, but otherwise no visible stresses or strains. Still, Sean didn't believe that after years of being an undercover cop when he'd been younger, Millan hadn't learned how to hide his problems.

A server took their order, which started with a beer and ended with a burger for Sean and a basket of wings for Millan, and then settled in. Millan's gaze darted up a few times and Sean knew he was checking sports scores on the TV screen above them.

"So, the incident with the defense attorney," Sean said, trying to grab Millan's attention. "What do you make of it?"

Millan's eyes retreated from their upward stare and focused on Sean. "Like I said, I don't know anything for sure, but I'd bet my life that Violet was the one who killed her."

"Do you think we should put in a request for investigation notes concerning her murder when we return to work on Monday? We can ask the presiding precinct, see what evidence was recovered."

He shrugged. "I don't know why we should bother. Violet is dead. Can't prosecute her for a murder anymore." The defeat in his voice pained Sean.

"I guess not. . ." Sean felt at a loss. Going out for a beer sounded great when he'd thought of the idea, but truthfully, he didn't know what to say to his boss to help him out of his funk.

A young, blonde woman approached their table. Sean thought it was a different server, maybe with a question about their order, but then she called out to them by name.

"Detective Trann? Sergeant Millan?" the woman asked.

"Yes," they both answered.

"My name is Elaine McDuffal. I'm a reporter with the local news. I'd like to ask some follow-up questions about the Spider Triad Trial."

Sean was about to say "no comment," but Millan spoke first.

"You tracked us down to a Wild Wings to ask us some questions?" The heat in his words tensed the situation.

"Actually, no," she said. She pointed to a group of giggling girls in the far corner. "I'm here with my friends to play trivia. I just happened to see you sitting here and didn't want to pass up an opportunity to talk with you."

"The trial is over," Sean said. "Any statements will be made during the next press conference."

She ran a hand through her shoulder-length hair and flipped it over to the side. "What I want to ask is. . .off the record. *Way* off. This is not work-related, it's personal. Although if it amounts to anything, I'd like to eventually make it into a story, with everyone's permission, of course."

"Everyone involved is dead," Millan said curtly. "There's nothing left to talk about."

"Please," she pleaded, leaning over the table. "I think there is.

I'll only take a few minutes of your time."

Sean could see the desperation in her eyes. He didn't really care what she might ask, but he also didn't want anything to upset Millan anymore.

"Up to you," he said to his boss.

"I don't care," Millan mumbled.

Sean slid over a bit. "You can talk until our food comes," he told her.

"Thank you," she gushed. She took a seat next to him and tucked her hair behind her ears. "I've been covering this case since day one. Anything and everything that could be connected to the Triads. I thought, like most of my colleagues, that the whole situation was the work of three crazy women and nothing else."

She put her elbows up on the tabletop, her body mere inches from Sean's. She smelled like heavy floral perfume and he could see mascara caking her long lashes. She continued. "But then, before the trial, I heard about how Mags Stinton and Doctor Charlotte Salla traveled around the world, looking for other Triads."

"How did you know about that? It wasn't public knowledge," Sean said, "until their testimony."

"I know. I have. . .sources. It's my job." Her words sounded a bit defensive, but she rushed ahead. "Anyway, I did a little digging of my own and learned of the two places they'd visited in Vermont, before they flew overseas. I checked out the addresses and yeah, they looked like nothing suspicious. One was a corporate headquarters for some paper company and the other a vacation beach house that lay empty."

"What's your point? All you're doing is confirming that

there are no other Triads out there," Millan muttered.

"My point is, I asked someone I know why there would be a list of random addresses that seemed to lead nowhere. He told me, 'Well, if they are supposed to be a secret, why would they be listed where someone could simply download them? If it were me, I'd have a code.' It got me thinking. What if these addresses were written in code, so they weren't the correct places? But the code would have to be easy enough for multiple people to figure out, right?"

"Seems a bit like grasping at straws to me," Sean said.

"Oh, *really?*"

Sean started to feel a bit annoyed at the pompousness of this reporter. "Did you find something or not? Otherwise stop wasting our time. This case is closed."

Another hair flip. "Fine. Here's the deal. I tried variations on the addresses. Adding one, subtracting one, multiplying by two, etc. But since I didn't know what I was looking for, the code cracking didn't work. So, I switched tactics. I checked the surrounding area for vacancies from right around the date that Violet was arrested and the Triad was exposed. Want to know what I found?"

"Not really," Millan said with a grunt.

Elaine's face fell.

Sean's curiosity, however, was piqued.

"Here's your burger and your wings!" Their server arrived and plopped the plates down in front of each man. "Oh, hi!" she said to the reporter. "Are you joining them? Can I get you something?"

"No, I'm not staying," she said, scooting over a bit towards the edge of the seat.

"Hold on," Sean said, catching her by the arm. "We aren't quite done yet." He turned towards the server. "She won't be ordering anything, though."

"Suit yourself. Call me if you need anything!" The server bounced away towards another booth.

"I'd like to hear. Finish what you were saying," Sean said. "What did you find?"

"There were two vacancies near the original addresses on the list within a week of Violet's arrest. One apartment and one office space."

"Does that mean you cracked the code for the addresses?"

"No. I'm not quite sure how it works, but if we did this with other locations from whatever list the coroner and the receptionist used, we could probably find a trend and then crack the code for sure." Her green eyes sparkled.

Sean peered over at Millan. "What do you think?" he asked.

Millan had just ripped off a chunk of meat from one of the wings. "What is the point of this, young lady?"

"What do you mean?" she asked, her voice breathy. "This could show there are other Triads out there after all!"

"And how do you suppose we *prove* that? Vacancies aren't proof. If these so-called 'Triads' are really as secretive as you say, I doubt they left a forwarding address to lead us to their next location. And it's been six months. I'm sure there aren't any prints left, even if the places are still vacant. This first Triad never left a single one."

"But we could check!"

Millan's let out a scoff. "Who's 'we?' It's not like we have jurisdiction in Vermont. And I don't know if any law enforcement up there is going to care about looking into empty places. But you're welcome to bring your 'vacancy' theory to them. Maybe they'll waste their time. I don't care to waste mine." He sunk his teeth into a wing and ripped through it, his eyes already peering upwards to the TV above.

"But. . .!" she exclaimed.

"It is thin," Sean said slowly. "Were there any other vacancies in the state around that time? Would we have to check those as well?"

Elaine slumped against the cushioned booth. "I don't know."

Sean gave her a smile. "I. . .we appreciate you taking the time to investigate. If you find any other proof, please feel free to email me at the precinct."

Elaine just sat there, her cheeks flushed, her mouth slightly open. It snapped closed abruptly. "Fine, if you won't help me, I'll do it myself." She flipped her hair, moved out of the booth, and stalked off.

"Overzealousness of youth," Millan said, his attention still on the game.

"Yeah. . ." Sean said. "I guess so. . ." He bit into his burger and chewed, thinking. This whole situation had been insane. There were no more leads. Violet was dead, so no one could ask her. The defense attorney was dead, so there was no way to find out why she'd been messaging him. The Book was gone. . .

The Book. It may be gone, but it had been *stolen*. A jeep had plowed into Wilt the first day of the trial, the driver got out and grabbed the evidence bag from the front, which had the Book in it, then drove away. Had anyone ID'd the driver? The jeep?

Sean was about to talk to Millan about his questions, but stopped himself. The man across from him wasn't his usual boss. This man was a shell of his former self. He wouldn't care about following up on some new lead.

The problem was, Sean didn't know how to reach his boss, to snap him out of his foul mood. All he could do now was be here for him.

Sean quickly decided he would look into Wilt's accident on his own.

"What's the score?" Sean asked before taking another bite.

7

October 12th
5:45 p.m.

Charlotte parked a block away from the address on the typed sheet in front of her. The lakefront property in Vermont sat in the pre-twilight sky, its tiny outdoor yard lights just beginning to glow. Clean-cut bushes lay under the windows while a trailing vine of something, now hibernating in the late fall chill, crawled across the trellis at the end of the stone path to the front door. The dipping sun, appearing like a pumpkin hanging low in the sky, cast its orange rays towards the house, silhouetting the residence from behind.

The three-hour drive had been fairly uneventful. During the ride, she'd decided to call her mother back, but when they spoke, she couldn't bring herself to ask about her brother's medical condition. The idea of having to explain why, after all these years, she suddenly knew, stopped her. How could she explain how she'd found out? Instead, she insisted she'd called by mistake, having hit the wrong contact button on her phone. When her mother asked why she'd been up so late, Charlotte lied and said she'd been on a case. The words tainted her tongue, but she couldn't tell the truth. She wasn't even sure right now what the truth entailed.

Charlotte tried to ignore the slight tremble in her hands as she held the paper in her lap.

What was she doing at this house, confronting a woman who may have possibly mowed down her brother in cold blood? And what if the allegation was true? What could Charlotte do against a killer? Did she expect to find proof? Get a confession? Find her brother's blood on a car after 20 years?

Before she could make an actual decision, Charlotte noticed movement. A fifty-some year-old woman emerged from the front door, walked down her driveway, and hauled up the garbage can from the edge of the street. She then headed through a wooden gate behind the house, towards a lake.

Charlotte couldn't stop herself. She removed the key from the ignition, opened the car door, and stepped out. Trotting along, she followed the woman's course up the driveway and through the gate to a side path. Blood pounded in her ears as the path widened into a stunningly landscaped backyard with a gorgeous lake at its edge. A stiff breeze hit her from this angle, blowing the stray strands of hair off her face. The tops of the choppy water glinted with orange, while the rest of the lake appeared a dark steely gray.

It took Charlotte a moment to locate the woman, who stood near the end of a short dock, wrestling with a line tied to a pontoon boat.

"Excuse me!" Charlotte called out. She waved. Her heart felt like it might pound out of her chest. What was she doing?!

The woman looked up. Clearly startled, she put a hand to her bosom and gasped. Her brown hair had been pulled into a loose bun, which fought to stay cohesive in the wind. Brown slacks complimented her beige sweater, which clung to her body as if she were still in her twenties.

"I did not mean to frighten you," Charlotte continued, moving a few steps closer. "My car broke down up the block and I saw you outside. I called out, but you did not seem to hear me. My phone died. Can you call Triple A for me?" The lie felt thick in her mouth.

The woman waited a few moments, restoring her composure, before nodding. "Of course, dear. Head to the front and I'll meet you there."

"Thank you." Charlotte turned around, her breath coming in short gasps. She was glad the woman was out of earshot because she could barely breathe and knew the woman might guess something was wrong.

Relax, she ordered herself. *You can do this.*

But do what? What did she hope to accomplish? She didn't have a plan of action, which was unlike her. She just knew she couldn't leave, now that she'd seen the woman who might have murdered her brother.

Charlotte waited on the wraparound porch, its wooden

railings and planks shiny with a reddish glaze. A black mailbox hung below the address tiles and a black woven mat lay at her feet. Tiny bursts of fog appeared every so often in front of her face as the cold air frosted her breath. Several minutes later, the woman opened the front door. Charlotte flashed her a smile, her stomach in a knot.

"Thank you so much," she gushed. Charlotte pointed up the road. "That is my car. I will just wait out here, in case they want to ask me anything."

"No, please, come in. It's freezing out there."

Charlotte hesitated for the briefest of moments. "I could not impose."

"Please, dear. You'll catch your death. Triple A doesn't come quickly unless it's an emergency, and even then, it's often at least an hour." The woman moved to the left.

"All right. Thank you." Charlotte entered the house, taking several steps inside. She wasn't sure what to expect. Maybe photos plastered all over the walls of her kills or files with victim's names on them, but the house looked normal. Clean lines, airy, with lots of windows and glass doors facing the lake. The lamps around the room, tinted golden, reflected nicely against the orange glow of the sun.

What am I doing here? she thought. *This is a HUGE mistake!*

It was then she suddenly remembered something about the Triads. They worked as three women, one who orchestrated everything, one who doled out the punishment, and one who executed it. Except, according to Truth, the executioner was put into an alternate innocent persona when she wasn't killing.

Which meant this woman may not even know she was a killer at all.

How could she confront someone who may not even exist right now?

"I should go," Charlotte said, feeling foolish. She shouldn't have come here. She'd let herself get caught up in something she couldn't prove or handle.

"Nonsense, you just arrived."

"I, uh, I forgot to lock my car," she lied. "In my hurry to catch you. I should do that really quickly." Charlotte turned back towards the door.

The woman bolted over between Charlotte and the door, placing her hand against it. "You're not going anywhere, *Charlotte*." A snarl touched her lips.

Charlotte froze. The knot in her stomach twisted. "How do you know my name?"

"I got a voicemail. Two weeks ago."

A lump got caught in her throat. She did her best to clear it. "Saying what?" she managed.

"That you'd be coming. Here. For me."

Charlotte's mind raced as she took a couple steps backwards. Her instinct to run kicked in, hard, but she fought the urge to flee. She didn't want to bolt until she could get her bearings.

Keep her talking, she told herself.

"That is strange. I did not know I would be coming here until this afternoon." Charlotte watched the furrow of the woman's forehead, the confusion in her eyes.

"Then why am I *me* again?" the woman asked, lowering her hand from the door.

"I-I do not know what that means."

The woman crossed her arms. "All right. Let's start from scratch. Why are you here? The truth. And don't give me a lame excuse about your car."

Charlotte gave two short nods. "I wanted to talk to you." Her backside hit the edge of the couch and she leaned against it for support, her knees wobbly.

"About what?"

A sting developed behind her eyes as tears formed against her will. She refused to let them fall. "The death of Ferdinand Salla," she whispered.

The woman's shoulders drooped and she dropped her arms to her sides. "Oh. That."

Anger swelled inside Charlotte's chest, momentarily surpassing her fear. "Oh, *that?*" she snapped back.

The woman shrugged. "It was twenty years ago. My first kill, actually." She headed around towards the front of the couch, gesturing for Charlotte to sit. Charlotte remained standing, her gaze briefly flitting towards the door, making sure she could escape if need be. She couldn't believe this woman had just blatantly admitted to killing her brother.

The woman took a seat, sinking into the big, oversized red cushions. "The voicemail said you'd know all about me, that you were here to help, but it didn't say how or why. That you'd have questions. I thought it was a trick. It had to be. The voicemail said that you're her. The Messiah." She scoffed. "But that can't be real, right?" Her eyes widened and she sat up straight. "Except you're here. Is it you? I mean, are you the one?"

Charlotte had no idea what to say or do next. Clearly someone had set her up, but who? Isabella? But for what purpose? Maybe to make Charlotte claim the title of Messiah. Or to get the information she needed about her brother to prove other Triads exist.

But why warn this woman?

Before Charlotte could respond, she heard music coming from her phone. She pulled the device from her pocket and looked down at the Caller ID: -*Unknown number*- The ringtone was unfamiliar as well. She certainly had never heard it before.

"Sorry," Charlotte said automatically. "I do not know who is calling. . ." She stopped when she saw the rage on the woman's face.

"How do you know that music?" she demanded, abruptly standing back up.

"What?" Charlotte asked. "I do not. I mean, someone is calling me. I do not recognize—"

"That is my *trigger* song!" she shouted. "But I'm me right now, so why are you using it?" The woman strode towards Charlotte, her fists clenched.

"I-I do not understand," Charlotte stammered, retreating to the front door.

"This is a trick. It has to be. No one but my handler knows that music. You should not be playing it." She moved as if to lunge forward, then stopped. Her voice changed, a note of pleading hanging on them. "Unless. . .if you are the Messiah, do you know everyone's trigger? Do you know all of us?"

The speed at which this woman switched from anger to pleading frightened Charlotte more than anything else. She seemed to be completely unstable.

"I do not know you," Charlotte said slowly. The terror at

wanting nothing more than to leave this house prevented her from trying to think up any lies, so she merely rambled. "You were misinformed. This," she said, holding up her phone and waving it around, "is a trick. I was sent here under false pretenses. I need to leave." She turned and yanked open the door, only to have the woman snatch the back of her shirt and pull her away from her escape.

"I knew you weren't her," the woman sneered. "She's not real. This is just a test. To see if I'm strong enough."

Charlotte cried out as the woman kicked the door shut and shoved Charlotte. She tumbled head over heels over the back of the couch, landing on the carpeted floor.

"This is all a big mistake," Charlotte said, holding her hands up in defense. "I was fooled, just like you."

"So, I'm a fool now?"

"No!" Charlotte said. "That is not what I mean!" She stood and backed away, towards the glass doors behind her.

"Oh no you don't!" The woman bolted across the room, but she was too late. Charlotte had already slid open the door and raced through the doorway. She ran up the path towards the front of the house, but the woman caught up with her, grabbed her hair, and whipped her sideways. Charlotte lost her footing and skated on her backside down the short grassy hill towards the water. Her breath whooshed out of her when she landed with a thump at the bottom.

"I'm not going to fail this test," the woman said. "You aren't the real Messiah. And I'll prove it." She grabbed Charlotte by the hair and wrist, and dragged her towards the edge of the lake. "The Messiah can't be killed by us. I remember. I learned."

Charlotte fought just to regain her breath, her mind racing. As she came closer and closer to the water, she felt painful bumps underneath her from the stones which lined the path to the edge of the lake. Desperate, she clung to them, raking her hands against the ground, until one emerged from the soft mud and nestled itself into her palm.

Suddenly, she felt almost airborne as the woman grunted and half-heaved her into the water. So cold it immediately bit into her skin, Charlotte had barely taken a breath before she found herself submerged. Sputtering, she tried to push herself up into a sitting position on the sandy bottom. As soon as her head crested the surface, a hand shoved it below again.

She couldn't breathe. She couldn't see. She was going to drown in three feet of water.

The rock in her hand weighed heavy and with all the strength she could muster, she brought it up in an arc and blindly hit the woman.

The hand let go and Charlotte broke through the surface to gulp in sweet air. The woman still stood hunched over, dazed, mere inches away. Charlotte bashed the rock against her temple.

The heavy bulk of the body forced her back down as the woman fell on top of her. Charlotte struggled a bit, pushing her to the side, and emerged from the lake, gasping. She hauled herself up the bank, putting as much distance as she could manage from the water, expecting a hand to reach out and drag her down once again.

But no hand came.

Charlotte finally looked over her shoulder and saw the woman's body floating in the gentle lap at the water's edge.

8

October 12th
6 p.m.

Mags absentmindedly adjusted the bandage on her arm. Her healing wound, where she'd been sliced and diced by glass from a broken car window the day before, still stung, and would often get caught on the gauzy covering. She currently found herself once again at the hospital—not because of the injuries she'd sustained when an insane stalker had smashed her against her sister's car and wanted to bludgeon her to death—but because she sat as a visitor next to someone's bed.

Detective Max Payne.

The man who'd saved her life. Unfortunately, in doing so, might lose his own.

The blow meant for her had struck him in the head instead. Yesterday, after she'd been checked out for her own injuries, the doctors told her they'd done all they could for him—some jargon about an intracranial hematoma, which she learned meant a collection of blood putting pressure on his brain. They'd prepped him and hurried him off to surgery late last night, shooing away Mags. She'd tried to protest, but they told her to return during normal business hours the next day since she wasn't immediate family and her own wounds weren't severe enough to merit a hospital stay for herself.

Before she left, the nurse had asked for Payne's emergency contact, and Mags shrugged. Payne had moved to Boston six months ago from Texas. As far as she knew, he didn't have any family close by, but she said she'd get in touch with the precinct and find out who he'd listed and give the name and number to the front desk.

The last thing the surgeon had told her was that he was unsure when Payne might wake up, but that the staff would monitor him closely.

So, she now sat next to him, his head bandaged, his eyes closed.

She thought she'd cry. She usually did at most things. As long as she could remember, tears would well up in her eyes at anything remotely sad, from tragic book endings to a commercial about adopting stray kittens.

But nothing liquid ran down her cheeks. She wouldn't let it. She would not be sad unless he didn't wake up. In her mind, if she didn't cry, then nothing could really be wrong with Payne, right?

Soft beeps and slow rhythmic breathing were her only

answers.

Mags rubbed her face beneath her glasses, then slid her hands through her short, dark hair. She kneaded her scalp, which at this moment was, thankfully, not hurting. On top of all the chaos, she'd had another migraine last night after she'd gotten home from the hospital. The painful headaches had started about six months before, after her kidnapping by the women from the Triad. As they were infrequent—she'd only had about five or six since then—her doctor didn't think it was from that specific assault, which resulted in her striking her head against the pavement outside the precinct, but was most likely due to stress.

Mags hadn't really given them too much thought as they'd been infrequent, but the one she'd suffered last night had occurred only days since the previous episode.

The stress theory made more and more sense. Her migraine last night had begun while arguing with her ex-fiancé, Scott, who'd showed up at the apartment. She thought maybe he'd heard about the attack on her, but instead, he reminded her that he'd come to pack up his stuff, since she'd told him she'd be at her sister's. In the midst of everything she'd been through that day, she'd completely forgotten.

When he'd seen her bandaged arm and puffy nose, he *had* been concerned, but after the initial shock, and after she'd explained it had been another Triad-related incident, his eyes narrowed and he crossed his arms.

"I don't know why you stay working with the police," he'd told her. "What's it going to take for you to realize you're in over your head? You could have died, again. You're a tech nerd, for God's sake, not a cop."

She'd been in such astonishment at his outburst that she'd just stood there.

"Well I'm not dealing with getting my stuff tonight, not if you're here," he told her. "I'll come back in the morning. Just make sure you're gone. And don't forget to leave my grandmother's engagement ring."

"I don't want that ring for another *second*," she'd snapped at him. Mags stormed into the apartment, grabbed the ring from inside her jewelry box, returned, and slammed it down into his hand. "I'm glad it's over. You never understood me anyway."

"I understood you too well. You've wasted your life, Mags," he snarled, pocketing the ring. "You could do anything, be anyone, with your skills. Instead you spend your time as a receptionist and get assaulted by crazy women. You're doing this to yourself!"

"Get out of here!" she screamed at him before slamming the door in his face.

After the encounter, Mags' head almost seemed to split open in pain. She'd stumbled to her bathroom, popped two pain pills, and curled up on the floor, then blacked out to escape the agony. She'd awakened six hours later on her bed, blood on her pillow from a nosebleed.

Once she'd cleaned herself up, she called the weekend scheduler for her doctor and made an appointment for the following week. Even *she* knew a nosebleed wasn't a good sign after a migraine.

But at this moment her head felt fine and all she cared about was the man lying on the hospital bed, not waking up.

The familiar clench of her chest and slight sting of saltwater in her eyes threatened to consume her, but she refused to let herself cry. Not until she knew if he was going to open his eyes.

A soft clearing of someone's throat behind startled her from her thoughts. Mags turned, expecting to see a doctor or nurse, but instead saw a woman with short strawberry blonde hair cut to her chin. Her hazel eyes peered first towards Payne, then Mags.

"District Attorney Parker," Mags said, rising from her chair. She remembered her from the recent Triad trial.

"Please," the woman said, her words coated with a Southern accent. "Call me Jordan. We're off the case."

"What are you doing here?" Mags asked.

Jordan strolled in. "A friend of mine had an appendectomy yesterday and I'm her ride. I was walkin', on my way back from grabbin' a cup of joe, when I overhead a nurse and doctor talkin' about an injured police officer. I asked at the desk about it and they pointed me here." She took a sip of her coffee and then nodded towards Payne. "What happened?"

Mags briefly explained the attack from Jasmine, or as she called her, the "Triad wanna-be," and how Payne had stepped in, taking the blow meant for her.

"He had surgery last night to remove a blood clot creating pressure on his brain. The surgeon said everything went smoothly, but they don't know when he'll wake up."

Jordan frowned. "That's awful. Were you two close?"

Mags swallowed hard against the lump in her throat, remembering how he'd asked her out on a date right before the attack. "Not. . .close, no. He just transferred here six months ago, but I'd been on leave, so I only met him a couple weeks ago."

"Is there anythin' you need? Can I snag you a coffee or

somethin'?"

"Oh, no need to go to any trouble. There's only an hour left for visiting."

"No trouble. I'm killin' time until my friend is finished anyway."

Mags' shoulders relaxed. "A coffee would be amazing. Black, please."

"I'll be right back." Jordan left the room.

A few minutes later she reentered with an extra cup in her hand, which she passed over to Mags. The brew may not have been top notch, but it satisfied Mags' need of a pick-me-up and something hot in her belly.

"Thanks," she said.

"Mind if I stay for a minute?" Jordan asked.

A sense of relief stole over Mags at the thought of having a person there for a bit to talk to. She had to admit, sitting by herself with only the emptiness of the room and her own thoughts for company had been making her a little stir-crazy.

"Not at all."

Jordan settled into the chair across the room, which sat flush against the windowed wall. She held her coffee cup between her hands, right above her lap. "Thanks for lettin' me stay. I've never been the biggest fan of hospitals."

"I've never been in one before."

Jordan's eyebrows raised. "Really?"

Mags nodded. "Well, unless you count my birth, but it's not like I remember that."

Jordan smiled, but her eyes looked sad. "I was in too many, growin' up. As a visitor, not a patient. My mama had cancer.

Ovarian."

"I'm so sorry."

"Thanks. She hung in for a long time, went into remission for several years, but it returned even harder and eventually her body gave out. I was sixteen when she died."

Mags wasn't sure what to say. Part of her wanted to give Jordan a hug, but she barely knew the woman.

"It felt so senseless, you know?" Jordan continued, staring down at her cup. "Why did somethin' so terrible have to happen to someone so great? It's one reason I think I ended up as a lawyer—I wanted to do somethin' more, to prevent bad things happenin' to good people."

Mags nodded. "Yeah. . .my parents died when I was a baby. Car crash."

"Oh, hon, I'm so sorry."

"It's okay," she said. "I don't remember them. I was adopted right away. My adoptive parents have always been my parents. I never really think about them any differently until I get reminded."

"So I reminded you about your parents' death? Smooth move, Jordan."

Mags smiled to soften the tension. "Really, it's okay." She let out a snort. "Didn't expect our conversation to take this kind of turn."

"Neither did I." Jordan glanced at her watch. "I'm goin' to go check on my friend. If she's not ready yet, can I come back? I promise we can talk about somethin' happier."

"Sounds perfect."

Jordan grinned and left.

Mags took a slug from her coffee, feeling a little less sad. Maybe she'd made a new friend. The thought comforted her.

She refocused her attention to the man in the bed. "You're going to get through this," she said to Payne. "You know why? Because I don't think you saved my life just to die. Besides," she said, draining the rest of the weak liquid in the Styrofoam cup, "you owe me a coffee. A better one than this."

Mags had just settled into the chair, pulling a book she'd brought with her from her bag, when a soft knock sounded at the door.

Jordan peeked her head in.

"Hey," Mags said. "That was fast."

"My friend is going to be out soon, but I wanted to say bye." She pointed at Payne. "Best of luck to him, too."

"I'm sure he can hear you," Mags said.

"Well, thanks for the chat. Take care of yourself, Mags."

"You, too, Jordan." Mags watched Jordan retreat from the room. "Hey, Jordan!" she called out.

Jordan's face reappeared. "Yeah?"

"You want to grab a coffee tomorrow morning? I'll need a boost before I come here for visiting hours."

Jordan's face lit up. "Yeah?" she repeated. "That would be great!" She paused. "What if he wakes up before tomorrow?"

"Then it'll be a celebratory coffee."

"Deal." Jordan fished around in her purse. "Here's my card," she said. "My cell number is on there. Go ahead and text me where you want to meet up."

"Great. Eight thirty a.m. okay?"

"Works for me."

"Bye, Jordan."

"Bye, Mags."

Jordan left and Mags placed the card in her book to use as a bookmark before she began to read out loud.

"Okay, Payne, let's pick up where we left off last night. . ."

9

October 12th
7 p.m.

Charlotte skittered away from the lake's edge, clutching her chest. The body lay bobbing in the choppy waves about ten feet away.

"Oh, God," she whispered. The quiet lapping of the water against the shore and the stiff breeze whistling through the nearby trees were the only sounds she could hear besides her labored breathing. The sun had nearly sunk beneath the horizon and the lake appeared almost black.

Instinct to help and her medical background took over. Charlotte made her legs move and she crawled over to the woman, grabbed her by the ankle, and pulled her from the icy liquid. With a heave, she flipped over the water-logged body, scanning the woman's injuries.

A new sound emerged in the near quiet: Charlotte's chattering teeth. She pressed her mouth firmly together as she assessed the damage. A wound on the woman's temple bled freely, coating the thin layer of sand underneath her. The other injury showed as a mark on her cheek. No rise and fall of her chest. No movement of the wide-open eyes.

Charlotte ripped off her soaked gloves and checked for a pulse.

None.

She bent her head down to feel for air from the woman's mouth.

Not a whisper.

She lifted up the woman's sweater, ready to administer CPR, when a hand grabbed her shoulder and roughly pulled her away.

Charlotte let out a shriek, fearing somehow this was another attacker. When she looked up, she saw Isabella's face peering down at her, the woman's normally stunning features pinched in fear.

"What have you done?" she asked, the Italian accent of her speech strong this time.

"It was self-defense," Charlotte said. "She was trying to drown me." Charlotte knew she should be terrified of Isabella's presence, or at least ask why she was there, but at that moment, she felt relief. She wasn't alone.

Isabella peered around them. "Quick, get inside. You need to warm up. I'll meet you there shortly. Do not touch anything else."

Charlotte nodded, feeling more like a child who'd done something wrong than a grown woman who'd just killed someone. With measured movements she rose and strode to the house. Once inside, she just stood there, trembling. She could see her reflection in the sliding glass door. With drenched hair and bluish lips, she looked like a hypothermic victim.

The grandness of what just happened washed over her and Charlotte began to shake, this time not from the chill, but from the adrenaline leaving her body. She wrapped her arms around herself and held tight, telling herself she was fine.

The sound of the glass door sliding open behind her returned her to the situation at hand. Isabella entered, looking a bit wind-swept, but otherwise put together.

"Wh—" Charlotte began.

"No time for questions," Isabella said, cutting her off. "You must do exactly as I say. I will explain everything, I promise, but we must act quickly. Does anyone know you came here?"

"No"

"*No one* can know you've been here. Do you understand?"

Charlotte nodded.

"Tell me where you moved around inside the house."

"I came in through the front door. She blocked it, then charged me. I fell over the couch and onto the floor, then made it to the sliding door, opened it, and ran outside."

Isabella quickly gave Charlotte a once-over glance. "You had your gloves on?"

"Ye-ess-sss," Charlotte stuttered through her chattering teeth. "Up until I checked her body."

"All right, here is what we do. Leave through the sliding

door. Go up the path and to your car. Get in and drive south. I will message you with directions to a motel where we can meet." She handed her a key with the number 17 on it. "I will answer all your questions there."

Charlotte nodded. She glanced out at the lake. "What about the body?"

"It'll be taken care of, I promise. But you must leave, now!"

Without any more thought, Charlotte did as she'd been told, exiting through the rear and striding to her car. Once inside, she pulled off her soaking coat, placed it in a heap on the passenger seat, and cranked up the heat. A message from Isabella dinged through her phone and she used her GPS to locate the motel. It was about half an hour southeast of her current location. She put the car into DRIVE and pulled away.

The heat in the car and the past hour in the hotel room had warmed her sufficiently, although she'd laid her jacket over the hotel's heater to finish drying. She'd thought about showering, but felt too terrified to do anything or touch anything in the room. Instead, she'd either paced or sat gingerly on the edge of the bed.

Thoughts had flown through her mind too fast to even comprehend. The implications of what just happened kept threatening to overwhelm her, inviting panic. Several times she had to hang her head between her knees, trying desperately to keep herself breathing normally. The last thing she wanted was to end up having to call an ambulance because she had oxygen depletion or a heart attack.

Slowly, the most recent bout of anxiety passed, and she

returned to pacing. Several times she wanted to peer out through the curtains, but she didn't know what she would even look for. Police sirens? The woman's ghost?

Charlotte heard a knock on the motel door, and her whole body seized up. Grabbing her jacket, she peered through the peephole first, recognizing Isabella before unlocking the door.

"I killed someone," were the first words out of Charlotte's mouth, "and you got rid of the body. You destroyed evidence. You, *we*, broke the law."

"You're absolutely correct," Isabella said, walking through the door. She headed over to the heater next to the window, whose air blew gently against the curtains Charlotte had closed when she'd first arrived.

Charlotte stood there in shock as Isabella entered. "That is *it*? I am *correct*?"

Isabella rubbed her gloved hands together over the warmth. "Yes."

"This is ridiculous. I have to call the police." Charlotte didn't know why she hadn't already. This woman blatantly knew Charlotte had killed someone and didn't care. She was a psychopath, plain and simple.

"What will you tell them?" Isabella asked, her voice neutral.

"That I killed that woman. In self-defense."

"Why were you at her house in the first place?"

"I . . ." Charlotte trailed off.

Isabella's gaze flickered over towards Charlotte. "You see the problem."

"You tricked me," Charlotte seethed. "You knew I would go there to confront her. You knew this would happen."

"I didn't know you'd kill her."

"Then why were you there?!" Charlotte's chest heaved with heavy breaths. None of this could be happening. Any moment she would wake up in her own apartment, excited for the day to start, anticipating seeing Sean again, returning to work, having all this Triad nonsense behind her once and for all.

But she didn't wake up. The only things that happened instead were Isabella removing a backpack slung over her shoulders and then her coat, crossing the room, and taking a seat on the other queen bed.

"I told you I would answer all your questions. If you're ready, *really* ready, I will."

Charlotte set her jaw for a moment. "I am not joining your group."

"That doesn't matter. What I mean is, if I give you answers, then you'll know the truth, and all that pertains. I can't un-tell what I say and you will forever have knowledge about the Triads, my involvement, and possibly yours. If you choose to have this information, I cannot predict what might happen from other Triad members."

Charlotte eyed her warily. "What about from you?"

"No harm will come to you, unless you interfere or expose the Triads. You'll be free to know everything without fear of retribution. From myself and those I work with."

"But other groups may come after me?"

A sigh. "I can't guarantee you'll be safe if you learn everything and don't have my protection."

"Protection like what just happened today with that woman at the lake." A statement rather than a question.

Isabella nodded.

Charlotte rubbed her face. She hadn't thought she would need to make this decision so soon. Why had she gone to that woman's house in the first place? Why couldn't she have just left things well enough alone?

She thought about the woman's body, floating in the lake. It *had* been self-defense, but would the police believe her? And what did she plan on telling them? *Hello, Officer, I came here from Boston because a woman who killed someone who tried to kill me gave me a file telling me this woman by the lake killed my brother twenty years ago and no, I have absolutely no proof of any of this.*

She'd end up in prison. Or an insane asylum. It wasn't as if Isabella would show up and testify to corroborate. Her job was to hide all knowledge of the Triads.

Please wake up, she told herself, closing her eyes briefly. But when she opened them, she still saw Isabella's patient face, the beiges and dark blues of the hotel bedspreads, and the faded rose-patterned wallpaper of the room.

"This will not disappear," Charlotte said, "will it?"

"If you walk away right now and never speak of any of this to anyone, I will leave you alone, I promise. Those who I work with will leave you alone. But I can't guarantee no one else will come after you. Your name is out there, Charlotte, as the Messiah. Truth sent out an alert about you. You are on their radar. There is a chance that if you keep your head down, maybe you'll escape their notice." She paused. "You can even consider relocating and changing your name. We may be able to fake your death, but without a body. . .some Triads may not believe. Still, it could give you a fighting chance to live on the run. It would definitely be safer than returning to your current life."

Charlotte's head spun and her stomach lurched. Denial kept insisting that this couldn't be happening. She kept trying to rationalize the situation or figure out a way in which everything could not. . .be. . .*real!* "I do not want this," she whispered.

"I know, but—"

"I do not want this!" she yelled. Tears slipped down her cheeks and she hastily brushed them away.

Isabella's face softened. "*Others have greatness thrust upon them. . .*" she quoted. "I'm so sorry, Charlotte. You didn't ask for this, I know. But whether you like it or not, you are a part of it. You have choices. Not necessarily ones you'll like, but you do have them. You can always do nothing and hope for the best, but I can't promise you'll be safe. Regardless, the choice is yours."

Charlotte couldn't quite deal with thinking about that choice yet, so she stalled. "What did you do with that woman's body?"

"I staged it as an accident. The police will think she slipped on the dock, hit her head on the edge, and fell into the water, getting caught up in the boat's rope."

"Are you sure there will be no connection to me?"

"As sure as I can be. I've done this for many years, training others to do the same. We are very cautious and thorough."

Charlotte's stomach rolled and she told herself she would *not* throw up. "All right. I accept that my name is now out there and that other Triads are aware of me. I did not fully believe it, but that woman in the lake house knew my name. She knew I was coming." *Even before I did,* she thought.

Isabella's eyes narrowed. "What do you mean she knew you were coming?"

"When I tried to leave, she blocked the front door, and called me by name."

"Was this before or after your phone rang?"

"Before."

Isabella's whole body stiffened. Charlotte could feel the tension spike in the room.

"Why?" Charlotte asked. "Is that significant?"

Isabella stood up and paced. "Hm…"

Charlotte could feel her temper rise. She was in a strange hotel, had just killed a woman, was sitting with someone who covered everything up, and felt more confused than when she started.

"Enough," Charlotte snapped. Isabella stopped and turned towards her. "Sit," she ordered.

Slowly, Isabella sat.

Charlotte felt a bit better, now that she'd reclaimed a tiny amount of control. "Unless we are in danger right now, you will sit there and answer my questions. *All* of them. I do not want to answer yours. Understood?"

"Of course."

Pleased, though not quite sure why the shift of power happened, Charlotte began. "Who are you, Isabella, if that is even your real name, where are you from, and what is your connection to the Triads?"

Isabella crossed her legs. "My given name was Imelda, named after my father's mother, who was Spanish. My mother was Italian, which is the country where I grew up. It is there I was introduced to the Triads and received my new name, Isabella. I was the principal position, the one you associated with Truth."

Charlotte found it interesting that Isabella still chose to go by her Triad-given name. "You chose the victims."

"Yes, and recruited the second and third positions."

"How long were you with the Triad?"

"Seven years."

"Is that normal?"

"A principal is supposed to change every ten years. The second and third can be replaced at any time, if the principal deems it necessary. The new principal may also keep a second or third on if they choose."

Charlotte waited a few beats, thinking. She had so many questions, but wanted to make sure she didn't miss any critical information. First, she needed to determine what was true and what wasn't.

"Truth told me many things about the Triads. Last night you said some of them were not true. Which parts?"

Isabella uncrossed her legs and leaned forward. "When Truth's Triad was revealed, protocol went into place. Triads knew to scatter immediately at exposure. They were to reconvene, if deemed safe, after six months. This is why I didn't contact you until now. The Triads would not have reemerged until this point in time, six months after the notice went out.

"When Truth died," she continued, "I investigated. I was fascinated when she put out an alert regarding the Messiah and began researching you right away, as I'm sure many other Triads had as well. But because I wanted to invite you to help me, to use your status as Messiah for an advantage against the Triads, I also got access to your file at the precinct and read your report about what she'd told you in the underground bunker."

Isabella reached into the backpack she'd brought with her, pulled out a water bottle, and took a swallow before continuing. "The bunker was the main key. Truth had decided to utilize it again. I used every resource I knew and even found new people to help me determine why."

"What did it matter?"

"Because Truth's focus had been on restoring the Triads to their 'original' glory, except that model had died out decades earlier. She tried to cling to a belief that no longer exists. This showed me that these stringent believers were still out there, corrupting new women. I couldn't allow this to happen any longer. The Triads need to be stopped."

Charlotte scowled. "I find it unlikely that you could stop so many *or* that the number of women you claim are part of Triad groups can be so high. Truth told me there were five hundred thousand Triads all around the world. I cannot believe somehow one point five million women exist without ever being caught."

Isabella cocked her head. "No? Think of it this way. You live in an apartment building, right?"

"Yes."

"How well do you know your neighbors? Can you guarantee that none of them have ever killed someone? Do you even know their names or occupations?"

"Well, no but—"

"There are more than eighty cities worldwide that have over five million people living in them and you can't even account for the couple dozen or so people who live in one building."

"But. . .one and a half million. That number is so high."

"It is, but it's not inconceivable. Don't forget, either, that only one member of the Triad commits the crimes, not all three. So out of eight billion people, would it really be that hard to hide half a million killers scattered around the world?"

A sense of defeat washed over Charlotte. "Then there really are that many Triads out there?"

Isabella pulled at the edges of her gloves. "Well, that's where I think one of Truth's facts fell flat. I believe she projected that number from where the Triad count *should* be, not where it actually is. With our current population, that number would be correct, if the Triads had continued to expand based on the number of people alive in the world."

"But you do not think there are that many?"

"No. My research shows the number to be much lower."

Charlotte recalled what Isabella had mentioned the previous evening. "After the Internet."

"Yes. Our true numbers were revealed at that point, and afterwards many Triads disbanded, combined, or fled."

"So what do you think the real number is?"

"I would say closer to twenty thousand Triads still exist, though I'm not sure of the exact total."

Twenty thousand seemed a lot easier for Charlotte to swallow than 500,000, but it made the next question come easily. "How can you possibly think you can stop all these Triads? You are just one woman."

"I've asked myself that question almost every day since I began this effort." Isabella closed her eyes for a moment. "First, I am not alone. I am part of a very small group and we often have outsiders help us who aren't even aware of the big picture. The total remaining number of Triad groups is daunting, but we've already made significant progress. We've confronted several groups, eliminated others, and offered a way out to even more. Except for the third position. They are allowed the chance to turn themselves in for their crimes, without mentioning the Triads, of course, or they are killed."

Charlotte felt appalled at the casualness of the woman's words which nonchalantly spoke of killing. "How can you be so blasé about this situation? These are people, killers maybe, but still people. They need to be brought to justice."

"I just told you, they are given that option. They aren't jumping at the chance to take that opportunity."

"Then force them to be arrested! Who cares if the Triads are revealed?"

"The Triads care. Don't you understand?" Charlotte noted a sense of pleading in her voice. "The faith of these women is unwavering. They will stop at nothing to protect themselves."

"How do you know that?"

"Because I've already stopped three of them from killing you!" Anguish filled Isabella's words.

Charlotte's chest tightened. "What?"

Isabella ran a gloved hand over her short, dark hair. "I didn't plan on telling you unless you decided to help us. The severity of this situation is so much higher than what you think. They know who you are, Charlotte, and what you represent. You are either a prize to be collected or a target to eliminate because you have the power to instigate change."

The gravity of the situation sliced through her like a scalpel across her chest. Charlotte stood and ran past Isabella into the bathroom. She gripped the edges of the sink, turned on the faucet, and splashed cold water onto her face. After several minutes of deep breathing, she patted her face dry with a towel and returned to the main area.

"This is really real."

"I'm afraid so. You can still leave, right now, and take your chances. Or, move and change your name. It'll be like witness protection. You can have a regular life somewhere else."

Images passed before her eyes: her apartment, her office, Sean. She'd worked so hard for this life, her job, her relationships. She wanted to open up and explore life more, not run away and worry that every move she made might reveal her, every picture plastered onto social media would expose her.

And yet, 20,000 Triads. . .how could they ever get rid of them all soon enough so she could have her "normal" life again?

"I will not kill anyone, nor will I allow you to kill anyone on my behalf."

Isabella folded her hands on her lap. "Then I can't help you."

Charlotte stalked across the room. "You cannot ask this of me!"

"I can't stop them any other way. The other Triads, if they get wind of what's going on, of what I'm doing, will eliminate *everyone* involved. You think there's never been a cop who hasn't died because of this? Or a precinct bombing? Or a government building targeted? Over the centuries these types of crimes have been committed because people kept investigating. It's no different than a battle fought for religion, beliefs, territory, or pride. You can't change their minds, you can't convince them to stop.

They will always believe they are right and they will continue to kill because they *want* to."

"And you? Have you gotten to the point where you enjoy killing these murderers?"

Isabella's lip quivered. "No. I do it because I have tried all these other ways. I've tried reasoning, explaining, turning them into the authorities. And do you know what happened? I got officers killed. I got journalists murdered. And a bomb that went off in my apartment, set to kill me, killed my girlfriend instead. She didn't even know about any of this, but they didn't care. They only cared that I died and included her on the chance that she *might* know about it."

Charlotte wanted immediately to say she was sorry for Isabella's loss, but stopped herself. She didn't want to care about this woman, to sympathize with her. But this woman was also the only one so far protecting her and giving her options.

Tears rimmed Isabella's eyes. "After that incident, I left the Triads. I knew they were corrupted. I need to make sure you know, that when confronting these women, I've always given them the chance to stop or pay the price in prison, but they've *never* taken it. Not once in four years."

"How many women?" Charlotte whispered.

"One hundred and twelve."

Charlotte slowly sank back down onto the opposite bed. Isabella could be lying, or think she knows these facts, like Truth did, but had been misled. Except Isabella had done her own research, not just following what someone told her beforehand.

"Is that why you started all of this? Because of your girlfriend's death?"

"Yes. Before they targeted me, I had stumbled across a file I shouldn't have found, from another Triad. They'd been recruiting many more than just three women for their group. They'd basically formed a cult. When they found out I knew, they planted the bomb at my apartment. After that, I tried to go to the police, to journalists, whoever I could. They tracked me and killed anyone I talked to. Once that happened, I fled the country."

"And then?"

"And then I started doing my research, quietly. I discovered another woman who'd been wronged by her Triad and had killed her principal and second."

"What happened to her to make her do that?"

"She made the mistake of falling in love with her husband, so they had him killed."

Charlotte's brow furrowed. "What?"

"You know about the alternate personas created, the ones that fill the time between murders?"

"Yes."

"Well, this woman, when she'd wake up as her true-self, she found she liked her boyfriend, who eventually became her husband. She asked her principal if she could stay in her real persona and live her life with him. She promised she'd still kill for them every month, but she didn't want the alternate persona to exist anymore. They told her they would, and then triggered her created persona anyway. When she woke a month later, her husband had been murdered."

A pang of sympathy hit her, but then Charlotte pushed it away and shook her head. "That woman was a killer. She should not get to live a happy life with some husband."

"I thought that at first as well, but I found out her Triad had been modified over the years. They only eliminated mentally imbalanced individuals, like child molesters, rapists, and murderers. They never killed anyone innocent. I eventually tracked her down and told her of my cause and she joined."

"Who is she?"

Isabella cleared her throat. "I won't tell you that unless you're going to help us. The less details you know, the better."

Charlotte's head spun with all the new information. Even though she still had so many questions, she didn't know if she could absorb much more. She did, however, want to get a few things straight.

"Let me know if I missed anything so far. I have been exposed. These women know about me, and apparently, are after me, for either positive or negative reasons. You believe I can help flush these women out and find them, offer them a way out, and then eliminate them if they do not."

"That's all correct so far."

Charlotte rubbed her temples. "I do not feel like I have much choice here."

"Not ones you would like, sorry, no."

"I cannot condone killing people."

"Do you wish Violet was still alive? Do you think she would have stayed in a mental institution for long? Or what about the woman at the lake? If you hadn't killed her, do you think she would have left you alone?"

Charlotte had completely forgotten that mere hours ago she'd killed someone. What had her life already become?

"I need some time to think," she said. "I need to go home and sleep and think about all this."

"I understand." Isabella bit her bottom lip. "Charlotte, I have to ask you something."

A dull ache began to form at the base of Charlotte's skull. "One question. Then I am leaving."

"You said that Betty knew your name, and that you were coming. Did she say who told her?"

Betty. Charlotte realized she'd never even asked the woman's name, to find out if it was the same as on the piece of paper. Even though it had been given to her, she wondered if Betty was her birth name or her Triad name.

"No," Charlotte answered. "She said she'd received a voicemail, which triggered her into her current persona, then told her I would be coming, but not why."

Isabella's eyes darted around the room.

"You seemed nervous about this before," Charlotte said. "Why?"

"Because I planned to trigger her by calling your phone while you were in the house. I wanted you to see her transform, to prove that all of this was real." She clasped her hands together, as if praying. "I promise, I had no idea she would become violent. I believed you would leave after you saw her change. That's why I was there, to make sure you left."

"So, if you did not alert her two weeks ago, who did?"

"Two weeks—"

An explosion right outside the room rocked them both. Heated energy knocked Charlotte off the bed and onto the carpet. The door to the room had been blasted open, the wood splintering around her. Black smoke filled the small space and burned her throat and nose.

Within seconds, she was yanked to her feet, ears ringing. Isabella pulled at her, dragging her towards the bathroom. Instead of going inside, she flung open the rear window and shoved Charlotte through it.

Landing awkwardly on the ground, Charlotte skidded across the tiny pebbles beneath her. Tears stung her eyes from the acrid smoke that now billowed through the same window. She skittered to the side, the noise in her ears subsiding a little, and took in a deep breath of fresh air.

Barely a second later, Isabella slid out feet first, her hands gripping the frame. She looked around, spotted Charlotte, then hauled her to her feet. She pointed at Charlotte, moved her index and middle fingers as if they were a person walking and mouthed "Can you run?"

Though a little wobbly, Charlotte's legs felt okay. She nodded.

Isabella didn't wait for any other response. She took off and Charlotte followed close behind, her lungs burning. They raced through the adjunct lot and Isabella cut east into an alley. Once they reached the end of it, she slowed her pace, and walked normally down a side street.

Charlotte clutched her side, pushing against a stitch that had formed. Isabella seemed completely at ease as if they hadn't just sprinted several hundred meters. A bird sounded above them and Charlotte realized her hearing had returned.

"What happened?" she said, her voice a bit rough from the soreness in her throat.

"Bomb, most likely," Isabella said. Charlotte watched her eyes flitter around, as if searching for someone following them.

"A bomb? Meant for us?"

"Again, most likely. Judging from the blast range, I assume they put the bomb on your car. That would explain why it blew in the door. I had parked mine several doors down."

"But why? If they knew I was not in the vehicle, why blow it up?"

"Sloppy planning."

Charlotte coughed for a moment. "Sloppy? It seemed pretty spot-on to me."

"They were unaware of the rear window. They meant to trap us."

"How do you know?"

"Because if they wanted us dead, they could have kicked in the door and shot us. Or put the bomb next to the door to make sure we'd be killed. No, they targeted your car so you couldn't escape, and made sure we couldn't leave the room without them seeing us." She paused as if thinking. "Although they may not know I was there. . ."

Charlotte tugged on Isabella's arm and stopped walking. "Who are *they*?"

"I don't know. Yet. Someone who wants you alive, at least, so that's good." Isabella started walking again.

"Where are we going?" Charlotte asked, catching up.

"There's a family restaurant nearby. We can breathe a bit, let things cool down. Although I don't know how to get us out of this one. If they figure out it's your car. . .Damn!" she cursed, loudly.

They approached the restaurant. Isabella glanced at Charlotte. "I'll get us a table in the back. Go get cleaned up."

Once they entered, Charlotte turned towards the restroom first and went inside. She cleaned off her sweat-stained face and scratched palms. She stared at her reflection, usually so calm and collected, now fearful and pale.

You could leave, her mind told herself. *Just walk out of here, find the nearest police station, and confess to everything. Even if you go to jail, at least you'll be safe.*

But would she? Inmates had been paid off before to kill other prisoners. Would she ever be safe from them anywhere? Even if she moved and changed her name, how could she know what city didn't have a Triad in it, where one of them might recognize her. *She* hadn't even known she would go see Betty, and yet someone else had. Someone who'd publicly bombed her car in front of a motel to flush her out.

Charlotte took in a shuddering breath, then let it out. She repeated the process five times.

She wasn't going to get time to think. She couldn't just go home and hope everything would be okay. She needed help. Protection. A way to keep herself safe.

Charlotte squared her shoulders. Her decision had been made.

With sure steps, she left the restroom, headed into the restaurant, and joined Isabella at the table.

10

October 13th
8:30 a.m.

Mags arrived at the *The Friendly Toast* and saw Jordan wave her over. They'd planned to meet for coffee, but Mags' stomach growled as she entered the restaurant. People occupied every table and a short line had formed outside. The funky artwork and fun color scheme always made Mags feel comfortable. She loved this place.

Sidling up to a small table, she joined the district attorney and smiled when she sat down.

"Morning!" Mags said.

"Mornin'."

"Have you been waiting long?"

"Nope. I've only been sittin' here for a few. Haven't even seen the server yet. I told them I was waitin' for another person."

"Good. Then they should come soon once they see me here. I'm *starved.* You don't mind if I eat, do you? Do you have time?"

"Sure thing."

Their server arrived shortly and Mags ordered an omelet and espresso while Jordan asked for a cup of coffee.

"Any change with Payne?" Jordan asked.

"Nothing yet," Mags replied. "But he'll wake up. I know he will."

"I'm sure he will, too," Jordan said. "We're tough from the South."

"That's right. Where are you from again?"

"Tennessee."

"Ah. Payne's from Texas."

Their drinks arrived and they each spent a few moments sipping.

"So how do you like Boston?" Mags asked.

"I'm likin' it. Wasn't sure I would with the colder weather, but it's been better than I thought."

"Well, it's not quite winter yet. You may change your mind in a month or two."

"True. I guess I'll just play it by ear." Jordan added more sugar to her coffee. "What about you? You live here all your life?"

"Nope. I'm originally from Canada."

"Talk about cold!"

Mags laughed. "Yeah. Boston is a piece of cake to me."

"So why move here?"

"Put my finger on a map."

Jordan coughed into her coffee. "Seriously?"

"Yep. After college, I wanted to live somewhere I'd never lived. So, I pulled up a globe, spun it, closed my eyes, and pointed." Mags remembered the rush of exhilaration when she'd performed the task. She could have ended up anywhere in the world. It had been such a thrilling feeling.

"I don't know if I could do that, go somewhere without a plan. But then again this is the first place I've lived outside Tennessee. I'm not sure I ever thought I'd leave there."

"So why did you?"

Jordan's stare stayed on her coffee as she continued to stir it. "For work."

"'District Attorney' must be a tempting position."

"That's not the only work I moved here for." Though Jordan never raised her gaze, Mags felt a heaviness to her words.

"No?" Mags asked.

Jordan shifted in her chair and Mags felt a wave of tension from across the table.

"I don't mean to pry. . ." Mags began.

"It's all right." She let out a sigh. "There's somethin' else that enticed me to move to Boston."

"What's that?"

Jordan lifted her gaze and locked eyes with Mags. "Can I ask you somethin' first? Since you were part of the Spider case, I don't want to seem like I'm imposin'. . .but you're the only one I can think would know the answer."

"You already grilled me to prepare me for cross-examination. Not sure what else you could ask me."

Jordan waited a few moments as the server arrived and

placed a plate of food in front of Mags. Once the server moved out of earshot, Jordan continued, her voice low.

"What I'm goin' to ask is less official."

Mags separated a bite from her omelet, focused on her food. "Go ahead." She shoveled the forkful into her mouth. Warm egg, leafy spinach, and tangy sundried tomatoes hit her taste buds. She sighed with contentment.

"How hard was it for you to work through those files you found in the underground bunker? You know, the ones that gave you the addresses you and Doctor Salla went to search for around the world."

Mags coughed on her bite of eggs, her face warm. "How'd you know about that?" she managed to squeak out.

Jordan added more cream to her coffee and stirred, the spoon clinking against the sides of the mug. "It came up durin' the trial. It wasn't as if it were secret."

"No, I mean about my involvement with the files? *That* didn't come out at the trial." She could feel her heart race a bit. Would she somehow be brought up on charges for having hacked the computer in the bunker? She couldn't see how, since the police commissioned her to do it, but she didn't know where else this conversation might go.

Jordan half-smiled. "You do know I did my research on you as well, before the trial, right? You and all the witnesses. You have degrees from MIT, Cambridge, and Stanford. You used to work for a security firm for several years, developin' new software. And when I checked into it, the precinct never requested an outside source to view the files. So, I made an educated guess and assumed they'd been given to you."

"It wasn't illegal, what I did. It was evidence," Mags said quickly.

"Don't worry. I know that. I'm not here as a lawyer. I'm here because. . .well. . .I *do* like the idea of gettin' to know you. I don't know that many people here. But besides that, I thought. . .never mind. It's silly. I shouldn't have even brought it up."

Now that her blood pressure had returned to normal, Mags prepared another bite of food. "Well, you already figured out everything now, so I can't possibly guess what else you could want to know."

"All right. If you're sure?"

Mags nodded.

Jordan hesitated. "This can't go anywhere outside the two of us. Not your coworkers or friends or anythin'."

Mags frowned. "Jordan, you're starting to weird me out."

"I'm sorry, it's just. . .okay. Here goes." She pushed her cup to the side and leaned forward. "I think I may have found a file. Another one. Connected to a different Triad in Tennessee."

Mags blinked several times. "What are you talking about? You found another underground bunker in Tennessee?"

Jordan shook her head. "Nothin' like that. The file was recovered from a laptop found at an office site which burned down. The case was. . .well. . .odd, for lack of a better word. Somethin' felt strange about it from the start." She propped her head up on her hands, elbows on the table. "Now, mind you, I've seen off-the-wall cases before. You can't be in my line of work without seein' some, but this one kept naggin' at me. It felt too. . . professional."

"What happened in the case?"

"A young woman was murdered in her apartment. Strangled. No DNA found. No fingerprints. The cops determined the killer was the food delivery person, but the young man swore up and down it wasn't him. He told the cops that he delivered the food to a blonde woman, but she'd been alive and well when he'd left."

"So?"

"So, the woman who died in the apartment was a brunette."

Mags thought about it for a moment. "Maybe he misremembered."

"That's what the cops thought. Since the food was there, all over the ground, as if the woman struggled when he'd come in, they assumed the man was lyin'."

"What made you think this was a Triad killing?"

"Nothin'," she replied. "I didn't know anythin' about the Triads. Never heard of them. This was three years ago."

Intrigue tickled her insides. "Then where did the laptop come from? Was it in her apartment?"

"Nope. The hotel next door."

Mags furrowed her brow. "I don't understand. How are the two connected?"

"A fire broke out at the hotel later that day, spreadin' to four rooms. After the firefighters put out the blaze, the contents were sifted through. The items from one of the rooms never got claimed, as in no one ever returned to try and pick them up. The manager gave the name of the person who'd checked into that specific room at the front desk, which was Alex Jackson. He said he couldn't even remember the person specifically, not even gender or race, as the hotel had been busy that weekend."

Jordan hailed a nearby server who carried around a pot of coffee and tapped the side of her mug. After it was refilled, Jordan added several tiny containers of cream, stirred, and sipped.

"What ended up being on the laptop?"

"Encrypted files. They were sent out to a lab to break through their codin'. When they returned, there were a list of addresses."

"One of them was the brunette's apartment," Mags guessed.

"No, but very close. The address in the file was 1133 W. Illinois Ave. The woman's apartment address was 245 W. Illinois Ave."

"What was at 1133?"

"Nothin'. It doesn't exist."

Mags frowned, her omelet forgotten for a few moments while she listened to the details of the case. "Then why did you think it was connected?"

"I didn't. Not until the Triad trial here in Boston. I just thought it was strange that an unknown address on the same street was on a laptop with other addresses a day after that woman was killed."

"Okay, so what makes you think it's a Triad case now?"

"You found a list of addresses at the underground bunker, right? That led nowhere?"

Mags methodically put the last bit of eggs in her mouth and chewed slowly. "Yeah. . ." she said.

"What if the addresses are encoded?"

"A code? Really?"

"I just thought. . .if on your own time, you could check out a couple of the addresses from the file I have. See if there are any properties nearby, like on the same street or same neighborhood, that had anythin' criminal happen around the time of Violet's arrest."

Their server arrived, cleared away Mags' plate, asked if they wanted anything else, then left the bill when they declined.

"Look, Mags, I know we just met and I know this sounds insane, but I guess I've just seen too much in my line of work to think this is all nothin'. You don't have to look into anythin' and I hope this doesn't mean we can't meet up again another time. I just wanted to throw it out there right away, not let you think I was only interested in your friendship for this."

"I wouldn't even know what to look for."

"I don't know either. But if you'd like, I'll get you a copy of the list I found on that woman's laptop, see if it sparks any ideas?"

Mags wanted to decline. She felt she'd had enough of Triads to last three lifetimes. But then Scott's words resonated inside her head: "*You're a tech nerd, for God's sake, not a cop.*" She may not be a cop, but she used her skills to help solve cases. After her security job, she swore she'd never work for another huge company again. She wanted to help people, and working for the police department let her do that.

Maybe these "lists" wouldn't lead to anything Triad-related, but maybe they would. And if they did, she could prove once and for all that she was worth something to the department.

"Why don't you see if you can get that file and we'll meet up later in the week and go over it."

Jordan's eyes lit up. "Really? Oh Mags, you don't know what this means to me. Anyone else I ever talked to about it thought I was wastin' my time."

"I know the feeling," Mags muttered. "It may be nothing, but heck, why not? It'll give me something to occupy my time during my awful breakup."

For the next hour they sat at the restaurant, drinking coffee and chatting. Mags talked about Scott, about growing up in Canada, and about loving being at the precinct. Jordan told Mags about her time on the beauty pageant circuit, about law school, and about *her* worst breakup, which involved catching her boyfriend of two years with not one, but *two*, of her friends in their dorm room.

After Mags left, she headed towards the hospital, feeling better than she had in months. It was refreshing to have a new friend, and especially one outside work. No longer having access to her sister's car, she walked the couple blocks to the hospital from the bus stop, the late October wind whipping her face.

About half a block away, she heard her phone ring inside her bag. Grateful she'd heard it now, she would remember to put it on vibrate inside the hospital. Reaching inside, she retrieved her phone and checked the number.

Scott's Mom popped up on the Caller ID.

Though the two of them weren't very close, they'd spoken a few times over the past couple years, once about setting up a surprise birthday party for Scott, but she knew his mother liked her a lot. Maybe she wanted to talk to Mags about the breakup?

Mags hesitated for another ring, unsure if she wanted to deal with this now, but she figured she should just get it out of the way.

"Hello?" she answered.

A sniffle came through first and then, "Oh, thank goodness you picked up!"

I guess she does know about us splitting up, Mags thought. "Hey, Kathryn. So, you heard?"

A wail emitted from the other end.

Mags had gotten to the hospital and stood near a far corner, resting against the side of the building. "It's okay, Kathryn. It's for the best." She absentmindedly watched an ambulance arrive. Two orderlies rushed out to assist the EMTs in unloading a stretcher.

The sobs halted and Kathryn said in a breathy voice, "For the best? How can you say that!"

Mags was surprised at the intensity of her reaction. "I just mean, Scott and I both sort of knew it was coming for a while."

The phone went silent. "You *knew* he was going to DIE?" Kathryn screeched.

Numbness hit her. "I'm sorry. What?"

"He's dead!" A few more wails.

"He's. . ." The world swam and her legs gave way. She fell to the hard, concrete sidewalk, her ankle twisting underneath her. She barely felt any pain. "What do you mean he's dead?"

Kathryn seemed to be getting herself under control as the crying turned into hitched breaths and sniffs. "Wait, you didn't know?"

"I had no idea," Mags mumbled. She noticed one of the orderlies glance over at her, his head cocked.

Silence again, and then with quick words Kathryn said, "Oh my God, Mags, oh my God, I'm so sorry, oh no, no, honey I got a call this morning from the police. He's dead. I'm coming up to Boston to identify his body. I was calling to see if you were okay, if I could stay with you, you know, keep each other company through this, oh God I didn't know you didn't know. . ."

Mags didn't hear anything after that. Her eyes rolled up into her head and she passed out.

11

October 13th
9:40 a.m.

Sean groaned and rolled over in bed. Light streamed in through his window. He winced and quickly turned away from the sunshine, his head pounding. Memories of why his skull throbbed filtered in slowly as remnants of his dream slipped away. He'd drunk *way* too much at Buffalo Wild Wings last night. Even though he'd sufficiently sobered up before he'd driven home, apparently his body thought the amount of alcohol he'd consumed had been too much.

He and Millan had stayed until closing, yelling at different games that Sean didn't care about, but Millan seemed intensely invested in. Intermittently, they cheered their own victory at finally being done with Violet and the Triad trial, and they spoke at length about difficult cases they both had dealt with over the years. By the end of the evening, Sean felt like Millan had cheered up a bit about his life and that he'd done a decent job of being there for his boss.

Now, through bleary eyes, he glanced at his clock, which read. . . 8:40 a.m. He blinked. Nope, 9:40 a.m.

Running his hands over his face, he wondered if he could go back to sleep when a thumping sound coming from below him caused his eyes to open wide. Several more thumps followed, along with strong footsteps and loud voices.

Movers, he thought. *Someone must be moving in downstairs.* Sean had a slight pang at the thought of Gerald and Nell no longer being his downstairs neighbors, since he'd just learned how to deal with them. A new tenant could bring new issues.

Sean shook away the thought. He didn't want to anticipate problems. He wondered if that line of thinking was a trait from being a cop, or maybe having so many things go wrong in the past several months, that he just expected complications.

A yawn escaped his mouth and he stretched. He tossed away the tangled sheet, and without his consent, Charlotte popped into his mind. He wondered how she'd slept and if she felt better today. He knew they weren't going to meet up—to give her time to heal—but he thought it would be all right for him to check in on her.

Before he could do anything, the buzzer to his door sounded. The noise drilled through his brain and he groaned again. Rolling slowly off the bed, he dragged himself to the intercom and clicked the button to talk.

"Yes?" he rasped. Dryness filled his mouth and throat.

"Detec—ive Trann? It's E—"

He *hated* his broken intercom.

"Who?" he asked.

"Elaine, the repor—."

The reporter? he thought. "Nope," he said into the box. "It's Sunday and too early. Call me at the precinct tomorrow."

"Please, De—, it's impor—"

"No." Sean turned away from the door.

The intercom buzzed again. His head screamed at him.

Sean turned back and slammed his finger onto the intercom. "Go away!" he said.

"I think I found a con—ection."

Sean let out a sigh. He really wasn't in the head space to deal with this right now, but he figured she wouldn't leave him alone otherwise. "I promise, I will talk with you first thing tomorrow morning."

"We won't have time. It'll be cle— by then. They will –ave co—red it up."

What the hell can't wait one day? Sean let out a growl. "Fine. You have five minutes." He buzzed her in, found and put on his pants and a T-shirt, and opened the door for her when she knocked. He watched her eye his place and his disheveled state.

"One word about me or my place in an article and I'll sue your ass," he warned.

"Trust me, I don't care about any of this." She flipped her hair from one side to the other, the same tinge of arrogance in her words. It disappeared with her next statement. "But I need police help and I doubt very many others would believe me."

He took a seat on his couch, not offering her a place to sit. "Talk," he ordered, doing his best to ignore his growing headache.

"Okay," she said quickly, smoothing away an imaginary wrinkle on her white sweater. "I did some digging. All night, in fact, after I left BBW's, about the places in Vermont near or related to the addresses I had from Doctor Salla and Miss Stinson's list. I thought about what you said, that vacancies weren't enough. So, I also looked up equivalent places that were moved into within the same week as the vacancies." She took a deep breath, as if she'd only realized the requirement of oxygen to stay alive.

"I, um, did something *very* off the record," she continued with a slight waver in her voice, "and obtained information on the tenant of the vacant apartment and crossed-referenced that with new rentals from that same week."

Sean's eyes narrowed. "What does 'very off the record' mean?"

"Nothing technically illegal. I just lied. . .a little. Anyway, the less you know the better."

Sean had worked with some journalists in the past, intent on getting, or creating, a story any way possible. He had no desire to help this woman sensationalize a case that should be over. "You can't break the law to get information."

"I didn't." She rolled her eyes and let out an exasperated sigh. "Fine. I pretended I was doing a survey about apartment tenants, gender, age, etc. No names or anything personal. I just wanted general descriptions. I told them I was part of a service that wanted to know if the 'general type of apartment-searching individual' had changed over the past year."

"I take it you found something?"

"Did I ever! One of the tenants who'd vacated their apartment the week Violet was arrested had the same description of someone who rented a new place across town within that same week. A fifties-something woman."

"So?"

"So, the woman is dead. Died yesterday."

Sean sniffed in doubt, a slight furrow appearing on his forehead. "Murder?"

"I don't know. I haven't been able to get ahold of anyone at the local police department. This was where I hoped you could help."

"To what end? Even if she was murdered, it doesn't prove anything."

"Right. Okay. I forgot one thing. This woman who died lived in a lake house. However, the other address on the list in Vermont, the office space I mentioned yesterday? There was *another* office space rented during the same week by two women. That place burned up, with two bodies in it. I checked it out and it was deemed accidental because of 'electrical problems,' but, Detective, that's two places now that were rented within the same week and the tenants are now dead. It just feels like this is something to look into."

Sean didn't want to admit it yet, but he could feel the curiosity climbing inside him. "What would you need from me?"

"I'd like to look through the files with the other addresses on them, start digging around, see if this is a pattern anywhere else. But I'd like your help to do it. And, as a cop, you can access files and pictures from the crime scenes of both the office fire and this woman's murder. You know, a reporter can only get so much."

Sean rubbed his hands over his face. "All right. Look, maybe I can help you with some of this, but there is no reason why it can't wait until tomorrow."

Her face hardened and Sean was forcibly reminded of what she must look like when she reported the news. "Actually, there is. The office building crime scene was 'cleaned' within twenty-four hours of the initial burning. The bodies disappeared. I'm afraid this woman's death, if it is indeed a murder, will be 'cleaned' as well, to cover anything up. If this happens, the cops there won't understand what's going on. I'd like you to come with me, today, to check the scene. If we wait until tomorrow, it may be too late. I'd like to drive up there with you and investigate."

Sean wrinkled his brow. "Look, Elaine, this sounds like way more than you learned from just looking up addresses. What's really going on?"

Elaine shifted back and forth on her feet. "Okay, full disclosure? I've been working with a few other journalists on this for the past six months. We've been compiling our research, trying to find connections between other possible Triad killings. A reporter I know in Vermont got wind of the story of the dead woman yesterday and messaged me last night. I've been up mostly since then checking facts and figures."

"I don't have any jurisdiction in Vermont to investigate a crime scene."

"No. . .but you could just ask some questions, right? Maybe say you're trying to see if this connects to a Boston case?" Elaine crossed her arms. "I know how you cops work."

Sean found her haughty attitude irritating. "Oh you do, do

you?"

She must have noticed his tone because she dropped her arms and the scowl melted from her face. "Listen, I get it, you want your life back. After all this Triad stuff, I don't blame you. And this may be nothing, even though I don't think it is. But if it's true, if there are other Triads, then these women have been getting away with murder for decades, centuries even." She took a seat on the arm of his couch. "I know that Book you had in evidence was super old, like thousands of years. I don't know if Triads have existed that far back, but I interviewed some of the women who'd been in the bunker and *they* said they didn't know, either, but they knew the Triads had been around at least several hundred years."

Sean's head throbbed. Whether from trying to think or being hungover, he wasn't quite sure. She was right. He *didn't* want anything to do with this anymore. He wanted his life back.

Or did he? He vaguely remembered that last night he'd wanted to investigate the jeep that had plowed into Detective Wilt the week before. Did he perhaps think there was more to this as well and he just didn't want to admit it?

If someone was trying to cover up the crime scene, he should let the local police know about it. Except, what would he tell them? Elaine was right. Only someone who believed there could be a Triad connection would look into this woman's death.

"What time did the woman in Vermont die yesterday?"

Elaine's shoulders rolled backwards, as if she were releasing the tension she'd been holding this whole time. "Time of death was about six in the evening."

Though protesting, he made his brain work. "And how far

away is the crime scene?"

"About three hours."

"You really think someone will try and 'clean' the scene within twenty-four hours?"

Elaine nodded. "I do. My friend is currently staking out the house. She said she hasn't seen anyone approach it yet, but I planned to head up there and take over her shift, so she could go to work on the Sunday night news. I was hoping to convince you to join me before I left."

Sean really hadn't anything else planned for the day. He'd originally thought he might spend it with Charlotte after she stayed over last night, but when that didn't happen, he figured he'd just relax.

What would be the harm in going up there? If nothing else, it would put to bed any thought of other Triads existing.

"If I do this," he said, "and there is nothing suspicious, you can't come back to me, ever. I mean it. I don't care if you find a bloody knife that a woman from a Triad used to kill someone in front of you. You tell someone else. I'll be done."

Elaine nodded vigorously. "I totally understand. Agreed. You got it."

Sean glanced at the clock, surprised that only twenty minutes had passed. It felt like they'd been talking for hours.

"Give me an hour to get ready."

"Do you want to drive separately?"

"You might as well drive us there. That way I'm just along for the ride." He paused. "But you're buying coffee along the way. A lot."

"Deal!" She practically skipped towards the door. "Just call me when you're ready and I'll pull up out front. Yellow Kia." She exited.

Sean let out a groan then went to his bathroom, turned on the shower, and let it heat up. He took those few minutes and tried to call Charlotte to check in, but she didn't answer. He then phoned Mags to see if she'd heard any news on Payne, but she didn't answer either. His last call went to Millan to see how he'd fared after the previous evening, but it went straight to voicemail.

Guess it's a busy day for everyone, he thought.

Sean then cleaned up in the shower, got dressed, grabbed what he needed, including his badge, and headed downstairs. He joined Elaine in her sporty yellow car and they took off.

Before she could say one word he butted in with, "Coffee. Before anything else, coffee."

"You got it," she replied, detouring slightly to the nearest drive-through coffee-related window.

12

October 13th
10:30 a.m.

Detective Juliette Tay had spent the whole weekend in shock, staring at the TV screen in disbelief. Violet had been killed on Friday night. Right here in Boston.

It was over. The three women associated with the Triad were all dead. The strange stalker who had delusions of being in a different Triad, Jasmine Stower, was also dead.

But Juliette didn't believe a word of it. How could she?

On the coffee table in front of her lay her prosthetic ear—a replacement for the real one which was shot off six months previously by Violet. She hadn't been able to make herself reattach the fake ear since she'd pulled it off two evenings ago in the courthouse after the verdict against Violet had been announced.

While she'd been getting up to leave the courtroom, a song began playing from her ear, blaring loudly enough for everyone there to hear. She'd unclipped the prosthetic and made a dash to leave the building, but before she could exit, the tune stopped.

There appeared to be no reason for the music. Nothing changed in the room. Spectators all seemed as surprised as herself. So why had it happened?

That evening, when she arrived home, she'd inspected the ear. She'd found a hole on the back, unnoticeable while she'd been wearing the piece. It appeared as though the hole had been burned into the silicone. Upon closer inspection, Juliette determined that the hole had been seared from the *inside* out. So, something had been inserted into the ear, which then burned up, creating the cavity.

Juliette had a pretty good idea when her ear had been implanted with the musical device. On the same day as the trial, she'd been attacked and sedated by two figures in her garage. She could pretty much guarantee they'd been responsible. And then, either designed that way or triggered, the hidden device had been scorched away after the song played in the courtroom. But to what end?

After discovering the hole yesterday, she'd immediately called her partner, Detective Cam Wilt.

"Jasmine is dead," he'd replied. "Whatever her intention with putting that thing in your fake ear doesn't matter anymore. She's gone. It's over, Juliette. Let it go." He didn't want to listen when she reminded him that she'd been attacked by two women, not just one, or that she wondered about the timeline of Jasmine's location and if she'd actually been one of the assailants.

"Maybe you imagined things?" he'd said. "You *were* knocked out and drugged. Some of those sedatives can mess with short term memory. Besides, why are you always trying to make cases more complicated? You never know when to let things go."

After a night of fuming, Juliette hadn't woken up any less angry.

And now she sat on her dark blue couch, still in shock at the news about Violet's death.

It may have been a crazy notion, but she'd wanted to visit Violet at Bridgewater Mental Institution, to see if she could find out why Jasmine would have implanted this device in her ear, how it could be connected to the Triads, or if it even was.

But now Violet was a corpse, unable to talk to anyone.

The problem was, Juliette's assault didn't add up. No matter what Wilt said or what they used to drug her, she *knew* there had been two attackers, one definitely a woman. And this had been right around the same time that both the coroner and Mags had been attacked. It would have been difficult, if not impossible, for Jasmine to plan and execute all three occurrences, especially when she must have been lying in wait for both Charlotte in the parking garage outside the courthouse and Mags outside the precinct as they both headed towards their vehicles. How could Jasmine have gotten all the way to Juliette's house in such a short time span?

Then there had been the issue with the bomb planted on her front door. Why attack and sedate her if they planned to kill her?

The final thought which needled its way through her brain all night had been the question about the music itself. What had been the point of it? Why did someone plant a device on her so that music blared throughout the courtroom?

Nothing about the situation made sense. And the more she'd discussed it with Wilt, the more he'd dismissed her.

Juliette turned off the TV and reclined into the sofa cushions. Wilt had been right about one thing: she'd never been satisfied letting things go. She kept copies of her unsolved cases and once a year brought them all out, hoping maybe she'd find something with fresh eyes.

The idea of this case, possibly unfinished, nibbled at the edges of her mind. She wouldn't be able to let it go. She knew this.

"Where do I start. . .?" she said out loud, rubbing at her real ear. "I start with the evidence I have and see if it connects to any-thing else. See if there is a pattern. But first, I need to know what was done to the prosthetic. . ."

A fire of determination rumbled in her belly, matching the intensity of her fiery red hair. Without another thought, she snatched the prosthetic off the coffee table. She grabbed her phone and called the number of the one woman who could help. As a genius with computers and technology, Mags may be able to identify the device used.

Ring. Ring.

"Hi, this is Mags, let me know who you are!"

"Hey Mags," she replied to the voicemail message, "it's Juliette. Give me a call back when you get a chance." Juliette hung up the phone and frowned. Well, if Mags wasn't around to help her, she could start digging into things herself.

Juliette got ready and left for the precinct, the prosthetic in her purse, her hair down underneath a hat to cover the missing ear.

13

October 13th
11 a.m.

Charlotte rolled over in bed, somewhere between asleep and awake, and turned straight into a tiny slice of sunshine. Squeezing her eyes further shut, the light remained persistent, so she pulled the cover over her head. Expecting the fluffy softness of her duvet at home, she felt surprised at the heaviness and stiffness of the comforter in her hands.

A sense of clarity returned to her mind, pulling her from her dreamy haze into fully being awake. She slid the blanket from her face and opened her eyelids. Brown and rusty-red striped wallpaper greeted her eyes.

A motel room. A different one than yesterday. Right.

Suddenly, a flash of panic raced through her as the memories from the previous day flooded her mind: the killing of Betty, the explosion at the last motel, the decision to work with Isabella.

The thought of her companion made her sit up fully. Aches and pains filtered through her body. A bruise had bloomed around her right elbow, and the back of her legs felt a bit raw from being dragged across the rocky lake bed. Including her previous injuries, she imagined her body looked like a beat-up ragdoll.

Charlotte stretched a bit and checked around the room. She could hear water running in the bathroom and assumed Isabella must be taking a shower. Glancing over, she saw a plastic bottle of orange juice and an apple on the bedside table with a note, "*In case you're hungry,*" written next to it. A dark sweatshirt lay near the end of the bed. Charlotte's stomach growled, as she hadn't eaten anything since the restaurant yesterday afternoon, and even then she'd only managed a few spoonfuls of soup.

Charlotte drank down half the bottle of OJ and chomped into the apple. When she reached her final bite, she heard the water turn off. Chucking the core into the garbage can next to her, she saw Isabella emerge, white towel wrapped around her head, a few beads of water still on her face and neck. A fitted black T-shirt hung over dark jeans.

"You're up," Isabella said.

Charlotte pulled the cover tighter around her body. "Just barely." She reached for the sweatshirt and pulled it on over her tank top.

"I'm not surprised. You said you hadn't really slept the night before."

"What time is it?"

"Eleven."

Charlotte couldn't believe the lateness. "*What* time?"

"Eleven," Isabella repeated. "You'll have to stay here, just for a few hours. I need to call someone and take care of some things, including my car, which we left at the last motel."

Charlotte recalled that after the restaurant, they'd rented a vehicle—Isabella assuring her they wouldn't be tracked. Since Charlotte's car had been the one blown up by the bomb, they didn't want to alert anyone who may be following her by using her ID, so bus and train were out. A rental car allowed Isabella to use one of her many aliases to keep up their anonymity.

The previous night had been another whirlwind of information, which eventually caused Charlotte to become so exhausted she'd fallen asleep in the middle of one of Isabella's explanations. Now that she was "in," Isabella opened up about multiple things, including her time on the run, the tricks she'd learned, and her plan for Charlotte.

"You really believe these women will come out of hiding for me?" Charlotte had asked the night before.

"I do."

"And then what? You kill them all?" Charlotte had shaken her head. "I cannot allow that."

A sigh. "I understand. We will give them the same opportunity: if they are the third, to come forward and admit to their crimes, without exposing the Triads, and serve their time. If they are a primary or second, they need to shut down their operation and we must be allowed to keep tabs on them moving forward, to make sure they never start up again. If any of them disagree. . .we will figure out a plan at that point."

"I do not think they will listen to me."

"Yours is the only voice which can convince them that the time of the Triads is over. And no, I don't expect, well, almost any of them to discontinue, but at least they will be exposed. I have done the math. We could never stop everyone, not without them revealing themselves somehow. This is a chance for you to issue a command, as the Messiah, and get them to change, or at least reveal them to us so we can find as many of them as possible. We'll use the same alert system Truth used when she announced to everyone about your Messiah status. So, have you made your decision? Will you help us stop the Triads?"

Charlotte couldn't remember if she'd agreed or disagreed because she'd fallen asleep at that point, but she did remember having multiple dreams of being a queen bee and ordering her worker drones to cease working. Several of them did, but then died on the spot when they stopped. Others rose up against her in a buzzing haze, racing towards her, while Isabella broke off her own human-bee hybrid stinger and fought them off, one by one, using the stinger like a sword.

Now, in the reality of her surroundings, the dream seemed silly, but Charlotte couldn't shake the unease that came with it.

Isabella brought her out of her thoughts by pointing to the wastebasket with the apple core lying inside it. "Here is an example you'll need to learn once we are on the road. You can't leave any evidence of yourself behind."

Charlotte nodded and removed the debris from the can. "What about DNA or hair?" As a medical examiner, she knew how difficult it would be to keep all physical traces of themselves from a scene.

"There are some tricks to help with that, although most things are pretty easy to cover and clean up. I'll go over everything with you when we leave tomorrow morning."

Charlotte froze. "Leave?"

"Yeah." Isabella finished towel-drying her hair, reached for a large, black trash bag from a backpack she'd picked up the previous night, and placed the towel inside. "Remember? We need to keep you on the move while we do this. You have a giant target on your back. You can't go back to your apartment now. Or your job. Not until we make our plan work."

Realization sunk in. Apparently, she'd agreed to help. The previous night still felt a bit like a blur.

They both jumped as Charlotte's phone rang. The caller ID showed Sean calling.

A warmth flooded her and tears stung her eyes. She wanted more than anything to answer the phone, have him come pick her up, and spend the rest of the day with him, forgetting about everything Triad-related.

But then her gut tightened. What if someone went after him to get to her? What if they were using his phone right now, trying to get ahold of her, preparing to threaten violence against him if she didn't comply with their wishes?

She automatically reached over to answer, wanting, no *needing* to hear his voice, to know he was okay, when Isabella snatched the device away. Anger flared up inside Charlotte, but the emotion dissipated at the look of sympathy on Isabella's face.

"I'm sorry," she said, "but you can't answer your phone. If they tracked your car, they may be tapping your phone. It's unlikely it has a tracer on it, but truthfully, we should get rid of it as soon as possible."

"Throw away my phone?"

"We can retrieve any contact numbers you may need to cover things on your end. Then I'll have someone bring it back to your apartment and leave it there. If anyone *is* tracing the phone, they will think you're at home."

Charlotte could see the *Missed Call* message on the screen of her phone in Isabella's hand. "People will start to wonder about me. . .Sean, coworkers. . .I cannot stay away for long."

"I know." Isabella turned off the phone and slowly handed it back to Charlotte, as if not wanting to take it again unless given permission. "Charlotte, you still may not grasp this, but I've been planning this for months, ever since your name was announced to the other Triads. I'm ready to send out our message, to receive communications back, so I'm hoping none of this will take too long. A week, maybe."

"A *week*?"

"Yes. Ask for a leave of absence. Say you need some time off after your attack."

"No one knows Violet attacked me."

Isabella gave a weak smile. "I meant when Joslyn. . .I mean Jasmine stabbed you in the back at the parking garage."

Charlotte sat in shock. She'd already forgotten. In the past few days she'd been attacked three times. Was she somehow already used to the trauma or had her brain simply had enough and blocked it from her mind?

"Of course," she said softly. "But Sean. . ."

"You can tell him you'll see him next weekend, that you want some time to recover."

Charlotte shifted on the bed. She'd actually already told him that. The timing was perfect. She looked down at her darkened phone. He'd probably just been calling to check in. "He may worry if I do not let him know I am all right."

Isabella tousled her wet, dark hair. "Don't worry. We'll deal with that, too. I promise." She placed a hand on Charlotte's knee. Even though this woman was a killer, or at least confirmed murderer, Charlotte didn't feel afraid of her. So far, this woman had been the only Triad member, current or former, that wasn't trying to kidnap her or kill her. "I know how much he means to you," Isabella continued. "I'll do everything in my power to make sure he stays off anyone's radar.

A vibrating noise came from Isabella's jacket, which hung off the back of one of the chairs. "She must be here." Isabella answered her phone. "Yes?. . .I'm ready. . .I'll be right out."

"Who is it?" Charlotte automatically asked.

"Someone to help." Isabella slid a forest green sweatshirt over her own head and then pulled on her coat. "It's noon now. I'll be back in three hours. Feel free to shower, watch TV, sleep, whatever. If you're still hungry, there are some granola bars, some peanuts, and an orange in my backpack. Just don't leave, no phone calls, and don't answer the door. Even if it's the hotel manager." She slid a small black phone into Charlotte's hand. "If there is any trouble, hit *01 and this phone will call me."

Charlotte tried to take the phone, but Isabella held it for a moment.

"I'm sorry, for all of this," Isabella said, her eyes sad. "You don't deserve it." She let go of the phone and strode to the door. "Lock this behind me. I'm the only one with a key."

With that, she left, and Charlotte immediately broke into tears.

14

October 13th
11:30 a.m.

The first thing to filter into Mags' foggy mind was the sound of calm, continuous beeping.

A heart monitor.

She recognized the noise and assumed she must have fallen asleep while reading to Payne in his hospital bed.

Opening her eyes, confusion stole over her. Why was *she* in the bed?

A young nurse, maybe mid-twenties, sidled over.

"How are you feeling?" she asked.

Mags took a few moments to assess her condition. Should she be feeling something? Pain? Headache? Queasiness?

"I feel. . .fine?" She uttered the statement like a question, as if she weren't sure it was the right answer.

"Good," the nurse said, giving Mags a broad smile.

"What happened? Why am I here?"

"Someone found you on the side of the building, unconscious. We weren't sure if you'd been coming to the hospital for help and maybe you'd collapsed?" She adjusted one of the monitors nearby. "Can you tell me your name? Do you remember why you were coming here?"

Flashes hit Mags like sharp darts to her brain. She'd met with Jordan for breakfast. She'd been coming to see Payne. And then the phone call from her almost mother-in-law.

Scott was dead.

"I need my phone," she said, reaching randomly around her.

"All your belongings are over there," the nurse said, pointing across her. A stack containing her shoes, a jacket, and her bag all sat neatly on a nearby chair. The nurse tapped the bed, bringing Mags' attention back to her. "Can you tell me your name?"

"Margaret Stinson," Mags said, realizing she hadn't answered the nurse. "I was on my way to visit someone here in the hospital when I got some bad news and. . .I guess I passed out."

"That makes sense with the fact that we can't find anything wrong with you. When we found you outside, you did seem to become conscious for a little bit, but seemed disoriented, so we thought maybe you'd hit your head. Then you passed out again so we submitted you, just in case," the nurse said, plastering on another broad smile. "As soon as the doctor comes in, if he gives the okay, you can leave." The smile faltered a bit. "I'm sorry to hear you had bad news."

"Yeah. . ." Mags said softly. "Me too."

The nurse left and a few stray tears slid down Mags' face. She brushed them aside. This couldn't be real. Scott's mother must have been mistaken. Mags reached over and with a grunt, grabbed her phone, and pulled it onto her belly.

Six missed calls and three messages in one hour. All of them from Scott's mom except one from Juliette and one from Sean.

Did they know, too? Were they calling to check on her, see if she'd heard the news? Had Scott been murdered nearby and so they'd been assigned to the case?

With trembling fingers, Mags held the phone, unsure of who to call first. She supposed Scott's mom, if nothing else than to reassure her she was all right.

Mags dialed and Scott's mom answered after the first ring.

"Oh, Margaret," she gushed. "Are you all right? Where did you go?"

"I'm fine, Kathryn," Mags reassured her. "I. . .dropped my phone," she lied. "Into a sewer grate. I had to have someone help me get it out."

"All right, then." Kathryn immediately broke into sobs. Mags waited a few minutes for the woman to compose herself. "David and I are in the c-car, on our way up to Boston t-to identify Scott."

Mags' throat tightened at the awareness. It was real. He was really dead.

"We rented a hotel room," his mom continued, "but if you'd prefer I stay with you tonight. . ."

"I don't know," Mags said, her words quavering. "I can't. . . let me know when you get into town and we can talk about it then."

"Of course, dear."

"Hey, Kathryn?"

"Yes?"

"Did they tell you what happened to him?"

"They said they aren't sure, that maybe it was a mugging. They found him in an alley next to a bar."

"Where?"

"I don't remember. The place had a woman's name. . .Lola or something like that."

Mags' heart pounded in her chest. "Lolita Back Bay?"

"Yes. Yes, I think that's right."

A sense of dizziness swept over Mags, but she mentally told herself she would not pass out again. The bar was only a couple blocks from the apartment, one of their favorites. "I'll see what I can find out. That bar is inside the jurisdiction of the precinct where I work. Maybe they have more information about what happened."

"Oh, thank you so much, Margaret."

"You're welcome. I'm. . .I'm so sorry about Scott."

Kathryn broke into a fresh wave of wails.

Mags waited for her to calm down, they promised they'd talk soon, and Mags hung up. She immediately called Juliette.

"Hello!" Juliette answered, her British tones clipping the word. "I tried to call you earlier."

Tears sprung into Mags' eyes and streaked down her face. "Oh, Jewels!" she exclaimed. Her chest tightened and her body shook as shock melted away into grief.

"Mags, what's wrong? Are you okay?"

"It's Scott. He'd dead!" Her voice broke.

"Oh my God."

Mags wiped her nose and forced a few quick breaths. "I just heard from his mom. Juliette, I saw him only two nights ago. I can't believe this."

"What happened?"

Mags explained about his body being found near a bar and the apparent mugging.

"We loved that place," she said. "He must have gone there after we fought. Ugh, it was so nasty between us." Mags used the hospital blanket to wipe her cheeks, but the tears continued to come.

"Don't worry, luv. I'll help you figure this out."

"Can you call the precinct and find out what they know? Kathryn, that's Scott's mom, is on her way up to ID the body."

"Not a problem. I'm actually already here."

Mags sniffed. "You are?"

"Long story, but it can wait. This is more important. Are you okay where you are?"

Mags was about to tell her how she'd passed out, but she changed her mind. "Yes. I'm at the hospital, about to visit Payne."

"I'll call you back as soon as I find out anything and then I'll come pick you up. All right?"

A sense of relief stole over Mags. "Yes, that'll be great. Thank you so much."

"Of course. I'll give you a call soon."

Mags saw the doctor stick his head in and nodded to him. "Talk to you then," she said into the phone and hung up. She quickly rubbed the rest of her tears away.

"Good to see you awake, Miss Stinson," the doctor said, coming the rest of the way into the room. He looked young, with large dark eyes behind thick, black, square glasses.

"Good to be awake," she replied.

"How are you feeling?"

"Embarrassed."

His eyebrows raised.

She quickly explained about the phone call regarding Scott. "I was on my way here to visit a patient," she concluded, "when I got the call and I guess I passed out. I just saw him. . ." she added, a lump forming in her throat.

"I'm very sorry for your loss," he said. He checked her chart. "It doesn't seem like you bumped your head or anything when you collapsed, and your vitals look fine. Has anything like this ever happened before?"

"Nope."

"Any other issues you'd like to discuss? Otherwise as far as I'm concerned, you're free to go. I'm sure you have a lot of things to take care of."

The lump grew a little. "There's nothing else." She paused, recalling her bloody nose after her migraine. "Well. . .never mind."

"You sure?"

"Yeah. I have an appointment with my own doctor to-morrow, so I'll just ask him."

"All right. My condolences once again. Feel better."

He left and Mags got out of the bed, put on her shoes and coat, and went to check in on Payne. He lay there, still unconscious. He looked so helpless. What if he didn't wake up?

What if he ended up dead, like Scott? Before she could stop herself, she flung herself onto the bed and cried into his chest.

"Everything is so horrible!" she exclaimed, her words muffled against him. "I don't know how to deal with this!"

She felt a gentle pressure on her shoulder and heard a slow, Texas-twanged voice say, "Hope these tears aren't for me, cuz I ain't gone yet."

Mags' breath caught in her chest and she slowly lifted her face, mere inches from Payne's.

"Hey," he said.

A smile broke across her face as a few fresh tears of relief slid down her cheeks. "Hey, yourself," she managed.

15

October 13th
11:45 a.m.

Juliette hung up with Mags and picked up the copies she'd made of the Triad trial evidence from her desk. A sadness stole over her. Even though she believed it was better for Mags to have broken off the unhealthy relationship with Scott, she knew his death would hurt her friend immensely. And to have it happen in a possibly brutal way. . .

The papers in front of her could wait. She needed to find out what happened, for Mags' sake.

A half hour later, she'd learned all she could about Scott's case, at least, everything that had been determined so far. It had appeared to be a mugging. Scott's wallet had been found near the body, empty of any cash or credit cards. Any other personal effects that he may have had on him, like a phone or car keys, were nowhere to be found. A knife wound in his gut had been determined as the cause of death and the body had been haphazardly left in the middle of the alley without any indication it had been moved or dragged. There'd been no sign of a struggle.

Juliette had been oddly relieved at the information. *Finally,* she thought, *just a normal murder case.* The thought made her queasy afterwards, thinking that any death should be better than others, but at least it didn't have to do with any crazy Triad women who carved words in walls or went after someone just because they weren't physically fit.

The only thing that prickled under Juliette's skin revolved around the fact that Scott had a few droplets of blood on his face. The detective overseeing the case hadn't made any extra note about it.

It's probably just Scott's blood, Juliette thought. Still, she decided to check with the officer assigned to the case.

"Doesn't look like there was a struggle," the officer from the weekend shift said. "It's probably the vic's. There was blood pooled all around him. But it'll still get tested."

"Thanks. I appreciate it. I know the victim."

"You do?"

"Yes, indirectly through the full-time receptionist, Mags. I'm following up for her."

"That's too bad. I've never met her, seeing as how I'm not nine-to-five, but I heard nice things about her." The officer patted her on the arm. "I promise, I'll keep you updated."

"Thanks, Rick." She'd then gone back to her desk to gather her things and head over to the hospital to meet up with Mags.

On her way out, she heard a familiar accent—another Brit. Glancing around, she noticed a tall, good-looking fellow standing at the reception area, speaking with an officer. His dark skin stood out against the collar of his pale green men's dress shirt, which lay under a charcoal gray suit coat. His long, black outer coat hung over one arm.

Juliette smiled, always happy to hear a voice from her home country. She'd just passed by him when she stopped at the sound of her name.

". . .Detective Juliette Tay. Is she available?" the man asked.

"I'm sorry, she isn't here until after the weekend." The officer working the front desk paused. "As in, tomorrow." Juliette realized the officer must not have seen her come in.

"Ah. It's still Sunday," the man said. "Apologies. Jet lag. I will check back tomorrow."

Juliette cut off his exit. "Excuse me, I'm Detective Tay. Can I help you?"

The officer behind the desk chimed in first. "Detective! I didn't know you were here today."

"I stopped in to pick up some files," she said, lifting up the bulky objects in her arms. She gave the officer a smile and turned back to the gentlemen.

"Detective Tay," the man said, cocking his head. "That's right. British."

"Grew up there, yes. Outside of London."

"I'm from London proper myself. Wonderful to meet you." He smiled, his teeth white and shiny. He pulled something from his jacket pocket. "My name is Inspector Omani Woods." He flipped open his wallet and showed ID. "I'm from Interpol. I was hoping to speak to you, but I've been traveling and didn't realize it is still the weekend. Can we make an appointment for tomorrow?"

She frowned. "Interpol? What are you doing here?"

He cleared his throat and moved a few feet away from the desk. Juliette followed suit. "I'd prefer to speak about that in a, um, more private location."

Juliette chewed her bottom lip for a moment. "Of course, but I'm curious as to what this is about."

He reached into his inside breast pocket and handed her a card. "Unfortunately, I'll have to insist it waits until we can meet. Feel free to reach me here in the morning and we can set something up for tomorrow, perhaps lunch? I'll explain everything then. It's not urgent, necessarily, but this would be a collaborative effort and we are interested in working with you in particular."

Juliette's skin tightened. She lowered her voice. "Does this have anything to do with the Triad trial that just took place?"

He waited a beat. "That's classified until our meeting."

Excitement grew inside her. She *knew* it had something to do with them.

"Would you be able to meet then?" he asked.

"I'll make it work."

"Smashing." He slid on his coat. "I look forward to speaking with you. Good day."

"You too."

They both exited and, once outside, went in different directions towards their own vehicles.

Juliette's brain swirled with thoughts. If Interpol was involved, there must be more to the Triad story. She did wonder why she had been singled out; perhaps it had been because she'd also been a witness to Triad activity and not just assigned to the case. But then why not Trann?

Either way, she planned on getting some answers at lunch tomorrow.

First, though, she needed to be a friend to Mags.

16

October 13th
1:30 p.m.

Sean snorted himself awake. He glanced over and saw Elaine still at the wheel, humming to some song that played softly in the background of the car. A shift in his gaze to the clock on the dashboard revealed that about three hours had passed since they'd left his apartment and about a half hour had gone by since he must have dozed off.

"I was just about to wake you," she said. "We're almost there."

Sean shifted in his seat, stretching the slight kink that had formed in his neck. "I still can't believe you talked me into this."

"I get the rules," she said, her voice tight. "If there's no proof,

I leave you alone. You've made that clear."

He noted the whiteness of her knuckles as she gripped the steering wheel. "Is everything okay?" he asked.

"That other reporter I told you about? The one waiting at the lake house? I called her right after you fell asleep, to let her know we would be there soon. The call went to voicemail. I've tried a few times more times, but nothing."

"Maybe her phone died? It's happened to me before during stakeouts. It's not like you want to leave the car running to charge up your battery. It would bring attention to you."

"Maybe. I'm just ready to be there. I don't like that she isn't answering."

Though Sean wanted to dismiss the idea that her friend was in danger, he couldn't. The insane events that had happened to him during the past six months kept rearing their ugly heads inside his mind.

"There's a big curvy road coming up," she said. "My friend told me she would be parked just past it, where she could see the house, but not be too close. She wanted to stay out of sight."

The road turned into its bend and Sean could see the shimmering of a lake behind a few of the houses. Trees dotted the edges of the lake, their fall leaves sporting patches of reds and oranges. He'd never thought too much of where he might want to live if he had an actual home instead of an apartment. He and Angellica had rented, but never talked about a house. And currently being a bachelor, mortgage payments and mowing a lawn weren't exactly top priorities. He was too much of a city boy, but the sparkling water and well-crafted homes they passed even caused him to take a long look.

As they took the final edge of the curve, the scent of smoke filled his nostrils.

"It's a bit cold for a bar-be. . ." he trailed off as they rounded the bend.

"Oh my God," Elaine exclaimed. She slowed at the scene in front of them.

One of the lake houses billowed gallons of black smoke. Two firetrucks were parked nearby, with firefighters hosing the place down as best as possible. Sean strained his neck and could just see around one of the trucks, into the front yard. The outline of a blackened, crispy-looking car sat wedged in the entranceway of the house, as if the driver had mistaken the front door for the garage.

"Gloria!" Elaine cried out. She made a move to pull over, but Sean put his hand on the wheel.

"Wait. We need to find out what happened here. Drive closer and we'll ask someone." Sean nodded over toward a group of people standing across the street. Elaine took in a shuddering breath and did as he said. They moved along, but before they could get close enough, a firefighter, minus his helmet, came running over, waving his hands.

"You gotta turn around!" he shouted. "The street isn't clear!"

Sean rolled down his window. "What happened?" he asked, holding up his badge. "I'm a detective with the Boston P.D. Is anyone hurt?"

The firefighter lowered his hands and continued walking over. "Sorry, Detective. It's a mess. Someone plowed into the house and then their engine blew up. The fire on the car is out, but it looks like the driver didn't make it."

Sean heard Elaine gasp and he shot her a look, letting her know to keep quiet. She gave the tiniest of nods.

"Awful," Sean said, returning his attention to the firefighter. "We'll turn around and head another way. Thanks for your help. And stay safe."

The firefighter gave a quick nod and moved off, back towards the truck.

"It's Gloria, I know it," Elaine said. Her hands shook against the wheel as she stared at the burning house.

"You don't know that for sure," Sean said, but even he thought it would have to be a pretty big coincidence that the exact house they'd plan to check out had been burned down by a random driver, especially since Gloria was supposed to be here and hadn't answered her phone in the last half hour.

Elaine gave Sean a scathing look. "I've been a journalist long enough to put together facts, Detective." She roughly swung the car around and headed away from the house.

Sean's irritation at her attitude spiked. "Maybe so, but assumptions don't prove anything. We can obtain details later from the fire department or the coroner's office if they recover a body."

"No."

Sean let out a scoff. "No? I thought you were all gung-ho about finding out about this place and now your friend might be dead and you don't want to investigate?"

"Of course I'm going to investigate, but not with your help. It was a mistake bringing you here. It was a mistake letting you talk to anyone. They might have been watching. They might know to connect this to you or me."

The notes of paranoia in her voice scared Sean. "Elaine. . ."

"Don't," she snapped. "I told you, I've been a journalist long enough. You know what that means? Sometimes people die for a story. I've seen it happen. You poke your nose into the wrong mob scheme or corporate takeover or governmental cover-up and suddenly you've 'mysteriously' disappeared. Uh uh. Not on my watch."

She slid back onto the freeway and Sean waited a few minutes before chiming back in.

"Elaine," he said.

He saw her lips purse.

"Elaine," he said again, his tone gentler.

"What?"

"I know you're scared. But. . ." He took a deep breath. He couldn't believe what he was about to say. He remembered having just told himself that if there were any other Triad crap out there, he would leave the problem to someone else. He didn't want to deal with it anymore.

Then he remembered the dream he'd had the other night, about a Triad woman stabbing him, saying she thought he was Charlotte.

If these Triads still existed and they believed Charlotte to be some kind of important figure to them, she could still be in trouble. He couldn't let that happen. He'd just gotten her into his life.

"But what?" Elaine asked, her own voice softer, almost hopeful.

"If we confirm it really was Gloria, then I will help you with all this. You, and she, obviously believed something bigger was going on. If Gloria lost her life for it, don't let them win. Don't let them get away with this."

Elaine stayed quiet for quite some time. Eventually she said, "I don't want to die."

"I know."

A few more minutes of silence. "They are really real, aren't they? The Triads, I mean."

Sean stared out the window, not really seeing the landscape, buildings, and billboards fly by. His mind returned to the memories related to the Triad—the underground bunker he'd been in six months ago, the Triad-stalker-woman from last week, the look of Charlotte as she lay almost dead on the floor, a knife in her chest. The fact that Violet escaped custody and died a few hundred feet from his apartment. The defense attorney's death. The other women in the bunker. The missing Book.

"Yeah. . ." he said slowly. "I think they are."

17

October 13th
2 p.m.

Charlotte heard the key turn in the lock of the motel room door. Snapping to attention, she slid to the end of the bed. Isabella had been gone about two hours, even though she said she wouldn't return for three. During that time, Charlotte had showered and tried to nap, though her eyes kept popping open. Giving up on sleep, she'd decided to eat, and found a granola bar in her purse. The whole situation felt like a strange warped vacation.

The door opened and Isabella walked in, followed by another woman.

This must be the other woman helping their cause Isabella

had referred to earlier.

Charlotte frowned at the worried expression on Isabella's face. "Is everything all right?" she asked.

"I'm not sure," Isabella replied, closing the door behind her companion.

Charlotte could feel the tension in the room. "What happened?"

Isabella took a seat on the opposite bed. The other woman remained standing. Charlotte took a moment to size her up. Attractive, once again, with a lot of curves, and black hair pulled back into a loose bun at the base of her neck. Charlotte could sense the strength of this woman and immediately knew she was not someone to cross.

Isabella let out a sharp sigh and Charlotte refocused her attention. "I can't keep any more secrets from you, Charlotte. From this point on, you have the ability to help us or destroy us, and possibly yourself. I'm willing to put my faith in you because. . ." She took a beat, glancing over at the other woman. "Because we don't have a choice."

Charlotte swallowed against the dryness in her mouth. "I am listening."

"This is Carla. She is the woman I mentioned before, the one I met up with whose husband had been killed by her own Triad members."

Charlotte noticed out of the corner of her eye how Carla twirled the ring on her finger.

"I called Carla to meet up here for damage control," Isabella continued. "We went back to the previous motel where the bomb had been placed, retrieved my car, and checked to make sure there were no traces that could lead back to you. The explosion demolished your vehicle, but we found where it had been taken and made sure the VIN number, license plate, and any personal items of yours could not be identified. The bomb did a thorough job on its own and there wasn't much left for us to cover up."

"Okay…" Charlotte said slowly. She couldn't believe she was sitting here listening to a woman tell her that her car had been bombed and that all trace of its connection to her was gone. A sense of surreal-ness washed over her and she reminded herself that this was her reality now.

"We then headed up to the lake house, where Betty lived," Isabella continued. "I thought it would take us a bit of time to clean things up, but. . ." she trailed off.

"But what?" Charlotte's stomach tightened. Had someone seen her go into Betty's house? Was she still alive? Had they found Charlotte's fingerprints and already knew she'd been the one to kill Betty?

"The house was up in flames."

Charlotte had not expected that. "A fire?"

"Not just a fire," Carla chimed in. Charlotte noted a Spanish lilt on the ends of her words. She remembered Isabella had said she'd found Carla in South America. "The house had been set ablaze. According to the preliminary report from the first responders, a car had driven into the house and the engine exploded. Plus a few of the neighbors said they heard a loud bang and raced outside, only to see the place engulfed in smoke."

"Another Triad?" Charlotte asked.

"We don't think so," Isabella said. "It's too. . ."

"Sloppy," Carla finished. "Incendiary devices are tricky at

best if you don't know what you're doing."

"Like blowing up your car at the motel," Isabella continued. "It draws a lot of attention, isn't well contained, and it's difficult to make sure any incriminating items at the scene are properly destroyed or disposed of."

"But you stated some of the Triads are different now, after they split into factions. Could this be the result of that?"

Carla shook her head. "Every Triad member knows the consequences of exposure. It would make no sense to create such a public spectacle."

"Also," Isabella added, "this now makes two explosions that we know of. We don't have proof yet, but I believe someone outside the Triads is doing this on purpose."

"To what end?"

"Our best guess? To force the Triads into the limelight." She crossed her legs. "Charlotte, when you and the Boston P.D. uncovered that bunker and a Triad, a light shone on a construct we've all worked centuries to keep quiet. There have always been conspiracy theorists or loved ones of victims who did not accept the official explanation given by the authorities in some of the murder cases. All primaries, such as myself at the time, were also tasked with keeping an eye out for these types of variables."

"How?"

"Before the Internet, we would track rumors in bars, follow-up on witnesses from police reports, sometimes even tap phone lines. Once the communication became global, most people thought they could say anything they wanted online, anonymously join any group, and no one would find them. Honestly, it made them so much easier to track."

Charlotte let out a deep breath. She wished she was home. She felt so tired, all the way into her bones. "What does this mean? I mean, if the Triads are revealed, *truly* revealed, would that not be helpful? Keep them on the run, on the ropes, so to speak, so they can no longer kill?"

"They already were exposed, remember? Six months ago. And all that happened was a shutdown of procedures until everything cooled off. A lot of Triad members didn't even move their operations or their operatives, but if they needed to, they did. They know how to make new lives, move to new cities or countries, terminate the current Triad members and recruit new ones. Whoever is trying to expose them right now with these fires will do nothing except cement the notion that these women will disappear even more thoroughly until they can pop up some-where else."

"And you expect me to stop all these trained women?" Charlotte laughed, hard and sharp. "This is ridiculous!"

"Maybe," Isabella said gently, "but I can't think of another solution right now. And these women, they are vulnerable. After the factions split apart, many of them want to be led or told they're done with their missions or be instructed that their missions have changed."

"But these women are killers!"

"Yes," Carla spoke up. " *We* are."

The statement hung there for several moments and Charlotte felt the smallness of herself in the presence of these murderers. *But you killed someone, too,* she reminded herself. *Self-defense or not.* Still, that hadn't been by choice. These women decided to end the lives of others based on their own rules.

"Our goal," Isabella continued, shooting a fleeting glance at Carla first, "is to give these women a way out."

The theoretical noose felt tighter around Charlotte's throat. Though she'd agreed to help, she now felt trapped. Maybe they hadn't thought of every possible scenario? There had to be another way out of this. "You have the ability to create new personality constructs. What about if we make them all into an innocent persona and let them live out their lives peacefully?" Charlotte bargained.

Carla shook her head. "It wouldn't last. They have to be monitored, often drugged, and reconditioned at least every six months. The project would be massive and we don't have enough people to help with the upkeep."

"You saw what happened with Joslyn," Isabella said. "Her Triad members abandoned her in her innocent persona, planning on reinstating her when they'd been instructed to continue with their mission. After being left on her own for too long, she began to break down, slip back and forth between her personalities without anyone's control. It drove her insane. She became broken into two women."

"How do you know that? If she was from another Triad, how did you know her condition?"

"I spoke with her," Carla said, clearing her throat. "At the end. She thought I was there to bring her back into her Triad."

Charlotte stood and paced the room—whether to alleviate pent up energy or give her the sense that she could run if need be, she didn't know—but either way, the movement relaxed her.

"Let me get this all straight. You want me to magically tell a group of hidden women to show themselves, stop murdering, and the thirds to turn themselves in."

Isabella nodded.

"However, some of the Triad women already know about me. Some want to kidnap me, others to kill me, correct?"

"Correct."

"And now, you are telling me there is a *different* group out there trying to expose the Triads by setting bombs in and around Triad members, and myself, to shine a light on what we are doing?"

"It seems so."

"Also that I cannot call anyone, go home, or return to work, but instead live on the run until this can all be accomplished, assuming it ever will."

"Right."

Charlotte's head ached. "This is insanity. You must see this."

"Insane or not," Isabella said, "it's happening, and you're a part of it. I've tried to keep you shielded, but it's become too difficult. Like I said, if you want out, we can help you disappear into a new life. But even that? I don't know how long we can keep up the façade. They will need to see a body, to prove you actually died." She shook her head. "I can't see another way out of this for you, to return to your life, and keep your loved ones safe. Unless you help us. But like I told you before, it's your choice."

Charlotte plopped onto the bed, exhaustion rearing its ugly head once more. Her eyes felt grainy and dry and the ache in her skull intensified. "What do I need to do to get my life back?"

"I told you about the emergency alert that was set up after the Internet began, so we could connect with all the other Triads in case of impending exposure, needed assistance, etcetera. It was how Truth broadcasted about you as the Messiah in the first place. We'll use that alert to contact the remaining Triads."

Carla added, "It will also give us a chance to discover the true remaining numbers of Triad members, to see what we are actually up against."

"And it'll give us locations so we can start tracking them," Isabella finished.

"It still seems like an impossible task."

Isabella uncrossed her legs and leaned forward. "Honestly? I have no idea what the outcome might be. This is completely uncharted territory. It may backfire, causing a backlash. It could get us all killed. Or, fingers crossed, it will actually work. I just know I can't sit back anymore, knowing they are killing people simply because of a physical abnormality."

"Or because someone gets in the way," Carla said, her voice low. Once again, Charlotte could feel the power in this woman, like a tiger constantly poised to spring.

"And if this does not work?"

"We have a contingency in place, but it's a secondary option at best," Isabella said.

"Which is?"

Carla spoke up. "We are working on a way right now to decipher the remaining list of addresses from Truth's computer files."

"You have that?"

"Yes. The files were corrupted, as the woman you worked with discovered, but she didn't know what to look for. The partial list you two followed up on was uncoded through a glitch."

"Those addresses led nowhere," Charlotte reminded her.

"The addresses were also coded. A primitive code, but one that worked well enough."

"Which was?"

"To add the number of letters of the street from the address to each number in the address."

Charlotte's forehead wrinkled as she tried to follow the logic.

"For example," Isabella said. "If the actual address was 123 Green Ave, the coded address would read 678 Green Ave, because there are five letters in 'Green.'"

Charlotte blinked. "That is it?"

"Simple, but effective. You and Mags couldn't find any of the locations, right?"

"No." Anger flared up inside Charlotte. They'd spent *months* searching for those places, and to only be off by a few lousy numbers? So much time wasted on such a simple tactic.

"It's just enough to throw anyone off who doesn't know the code."

Charlotte took a deep breath, forcing herself to calm down. She realized the light in the room had lessened. The sun must be setting. She couldn't believe a whole day had already passed. The stitches on her back itched. Her head throbbed. Her body felt heavy and tired. Resignation began to steal over her. At this moment, she could not win, escape, or survive on her own.

Still, every thought in her mind rationally screamed at her to leave. Except one.

Where can you possibly go unless you give up your whole life and become someone else? You are their Messiah. Whether you believe it or not, they *believe it. And they will never leave you alone unless you help stop them.*

Charlotte made one last stab at getting out of this whole situation. "What if we just tell them all I am not the Messiah? Tell them there's been a mistake. Find a loophole in the Book that makes me *not* fit the 'profile' given."

Isabella and Carla exchanged a knowing glance. "Unfortunately, we already looked for that. When Truth declared you the Messiah, I searched for a way to prove you weren't. I'm sure a lot of Triad members did. I couldn't find any way you *didn't* fit. Since you already matched all the parameters, there was only one way to prove you aren't the Messiah."

Charlotte's bottom lip quivered, remembering all too well. "I would have to die."

No one spoke for several moments as the words hung in the air.

Charlotte inhaled deeply, knowing that her next words would fully commit her. "What is our next step?"

18

October 14th
9 a.m.

Sean arrived at work Monday morning with a completely cluttered mind. So many events had happened over the weekend he could barely keep his head straight. With so many incidents taking place one after the other—the trial ending, Violet's murder, he and Charlotte sleeping together, his attempt to pull Millan out of his rut, the trip to the lake house with Elaine, and his decision to start looking into other Triads—he'd hardly slept. When he did, he had a swirl of nightmares that continually overlapped each other, making him feel like he'd run a marathon in bed.

The one thing that made him smile was the idea that Mags

might bring him a cup of her specially blended coffee. She always seemed to know when he needed it the most. But when he entered the precinct, he saw Judy behind the desk, the temp who'd been here while Mags and Charlotte had gone searching the globe for other Triads.

"Morning Judy," Sean said. "I'm surprised to see you back again."

"I'm surprised to be back," she answered. He noted her attire, similar to what she usually wore: beige slacks, a navy blue sweater, and her hair in a bun.

"Do you know where Mags is?"

"No."

"They didn't tell you why they called you in?"

"I just show up."

Once again, though nice, Judy's comments held no real emotional feeling. Also, she never seemed to like saying more than the fewest amount of words necessary to get by in a conversation.

"All right. Thanks." Sean walked away and headed towards Millan's office. To his surprise, the door was closed and locked.

Frowning, Sean turned around and spotted Wilt at his desk. He headed over.

"Hey, Wilt."

"Hey, Trann. Happy Monday." Wilt's trademark toothpick hung from his mouth.

"Yeah. Do you know where the Sergeant is? Or Mags for that matter?"

Wilt glanced over at their boss's office. "I'm not sure. I haven't seen Millan come in yet and Judy was here when I got here."

"Hm." Sean wondered if he should call them both to find out what was going on. Just as he wondered who he should call first, Detective Juliette Tay entered the precinct and strode over.

"Morning, Tay," Wilt said.

"Morning, chaps." She plopped her purse onto her desk. "It's getting quite frigid out there." She pulled off the purple scarf wrapped around her neck.

Sean thought about how close Tay and Mags were. "Tay, do you know why Mags isn't in today? I called her on Saturday, to check in, but never heard back."

She stopped in the midst of removing her jacket. "You didn't hear?"

"Hear what?"

Tay lowered her voice. "Scott was killed. Over the weekend."

Sean's stomach dropped. Wilt stood.

"What?" Sean asked. "Her ex?"

Tay nodded. "Yeah. Mugging gone wrong, it looks like. Happened right after they saw each other Friday night. She didn't find out about it until yesterday."

"Oh my God. How is she doing?"

Tay finished removing her coat. "Pretty terrible. Scott's parents are in town. Apparently they ID'd the body yesterday. Mags said she wanted to take the day off to spend with them." Tay's face pinched. "She told me they didn't know yet that she and Scott had broken up."

"Yikes," Wilt said. "That's an awkward conversation."

"I'm not sure she knows if she'll tell them or not," Tay said as she took a seat at her desk. "I don't know if I could do that."

Wilt sank back down in his chair. "Poor Mags."

"Yeah. At least the whole weekend wasn't bad news. Otherwise I think she'd be in much worse shape."

"What do you mean?" Sean asked.

Tay's face brightened. "Payne woke up!"

"Really?" Sean asked. Relief washed over him. "Is he okay?"

"He seemed pretty good, considering. I got to see him when I went to pick up Mags from the hospital. He's talking a bit slowly and seems to get confused every once in a while, but the doctor seemed optimistic that he could make a full recovery."

"I gotta tell Millan," Sean said. He glanced over at the office, then realized his superior wasn't there. "Well, when he gets in."

"It's about time there was some good news around here," Wilt added. The phone at his desk rang. "That Triad stuff is finally over and we can all move on." Wilt left the two of them to answer the call.

Sean noticed Tay pat the edges of her hair, which she wore down.

"Hey," he said, noticing the difference. "Your hair looks nice."

Tay rubbed her mouth. "Well, the truth is—"

The phone sounded in Sean's office. "Hold that thought," he told her and bolted over to answer it. He hoped that maybe it was Millan for some reason, or even Charlotte. He'd tried to call her yesterday after returning from his trip with Elaine, but had secretly been relieved when the call went straight to voicemail. He hadn't left a message because the truth was, he'd *wanted* to tell her about everything: the lake house, the inconsistencies with the Triad case, and his new partnership with the journalist.

But then he remembered Gloria had been killed just for staking out a house. That these Triad women had already gone after Charlotte on more than one occasion. He couldn't get her involved in all this again. The less she knew, the safer she would be.

Still, he wished he could hear the sound of her voice, ask how her weekend went, and make sure she was feeling better.

"Detective Trann," he answered.

"Morning, Detective. It's Elaine." She sounded as though her nose was stuffy.

A wave of disappointment washed over him. "I wasn't expecting to hear from you so soon."

"I wasn't expecting to call so soon either. But I got confirmation that it was Gloria who died in that car."

"I'm really sorry."

A sniff. "Thanks. I'm sort of numb about it now. I cried for like an hour when I found out."

"Are you still planning on following the story?"

"Yeah. Like you said, no one should get away with killing Gloria."

Sean eyed the area outside his office, making sure no one was in earshot. "Did they rule it a homicide?"

"I don't know. I checked in with the news station where Gloria works, erm, worked, last night to see if she went on the air, and they told me she never showed up. Then I went online to check the local news this morning and they had a story on her. They said it looked like an accident, but an investigation was underway and they'd have more information soon."

"I'll see what I can do on my end. I'll get in touch with the lead detective and let you know what I find out."

"I'd appreciate that. It's not like Gloria is going anywhere. . ."

"Sorry again," Sean said awkwardly and they both hung up. He wished he could say more, but didn't know how to make any difference, except help catch Gloria's killer.

Sean turned to head out of his office and finish his conversation with Tay when Millan walked by and went straight to his own office, his head hanging low. He unlocked it, entered, and shut the door behind him, which was unusual. He most often kept it open.

Sean headed over, knocked a couple of times, and waited.

"Yeah," Millan said from inside.

Sean opened the door and went inside. "Morning, Sarge."

"It's light out, so I have to agree with you."

Sean cleared his throat. He wasn't certain if he should ask how Millan was doing or how his weekend went or why he was late. They'd had so few personal times together and even though Sean felt like he could come to his boss with a problem, he wasn't sure if Millan felt like he could reciprocate.

"Good news," Sean said, taking a different tactic. "I heard Payne woke up."

Millan finally raised his head. The bags under his eyes looked even thicker than usual and his eyes appeared tinged with red. For the first time since he'd met his boss, Sean thought he looked. . . old.

"Really?"

"Yeah. Tay just told me. Looks like he's going to be all right."

"That's great to hear. Guess you'll just solo or team with Wilt and Tay again until Payne is back to full status."

"Sounds good to me." Sean paused. "You all right, Sarge?"

A long sigh. "Laila left me. For good."

Sean stood there, stunned. "What?" he finally said.

"After you and I went out, I came home. As you remember, it wasn't exactly early. She'd been waiting for me. I guess I forgot that she said she'd be home that night, to talk. We didn't really talk, unless you call fighting talking. Anyway, the next morning I woke up after sleeping on the couch and found a letter from her."

"God, Millan. That's rough."

He shook his head. "Everything she wrote in the letter was right. I never got over Daniella's death. And then all this Triad stuff. . .too much loss, too much pain."

Sean swallowed. He'd remembered how happy Millan had been when he learned he had a daughter from a previous relationship, as he and his wife never had children. Then, to learn less than a year later about how she'd been killed by a drunk driver. . . Concern crept into his chest. "Are you going to be okay?"

"I made a decision this morning, after rereading my wife's letter." Millan dropped his gaze. "I'm retiring."

A numbness stole over Sean. "No. No you can't."

"It's already done. I called in my notice before I came to work. That's why I was late. The phone call wasn't. . .easy. I'm planning to give my written notice today."

Sean closed the door behind him and pulled up the chair across from Millan. "You are so great for this precinct, though."

"That may be, but it isn't good for me anymore. If I'm gonna get past Daniella and try to save my marriage, I can't be here anymore. Too many losses from too many directions."

Sean leaned forward, putting his elbows on his knees. "Is there anything I can do to change your mind?"

"If you respect me, you won't try."

Sean nodded, stood, and extended his hand. "Then I won't try."

Millan shook it. "Thanks, kid. I don't want to leave this team. You're all an excellent bunch of detectives, but it'll be good for me to move on. And if you don't mind, I'm not planning on announcing until the end of the week."

"Not a problem." Sean swallowed against the lump that just formed in his throat. He thought about how he'd planned to talk to Millan about Mags' absence or what he'd possibly discovered with the journalist over the weekend, but decided against it. "I'm going to go check what new cases are up for grabs."

"Sounds good. And Trann?"

"Yeah?"

"Thanks for everything."

Sean gave another nod and left the office. He remembered how he'd felt just last week, how he'd never wanted to deal with anything "Triad-related" again, and here he was, starting the investigation up once more.

These groups of women had wreaked havoc on the people in their precinct and it had only been one Triad. How was he supposed to take on possibly hundreds of thousands more?

He took a breath. *Do what you always do. Follow the evidence, think outside the box, and see what comes up.*

He decided to call the Vermont precinct in charge of the house fire on his lunch break and do some detective work. Step one: confirm that Gloria was the one who died in that fire. Step two: find out if it was accidental. Step three: if it wasn't an accident, see if they have any leads.

For now, he just had to pretend that the only thing he cared about were the cases brought into his own precinct. He strolled over to Wilt and Tay's area.

"Guess it's the three of us again," he said with a smile. "Let's see what's up for grabs today."

19

October 14th

11 a.m.

Mags awoke to the sounds of hushed talking and the occasional clink of silverware on plates. Pulling herself from her slumber, it took her a few moments to pinpoint her location.

The couch. Of her apartment.

The room appeared slightly blurry so she reached over and found her glasses perched on the coffee table. Placing them on her face, the room became clearer. As it did, so did the previous 24 hours.

She remembered meeting up with Scott's parents yesterday outside the apartment, bringing them inside, and setting them up in her bedroom for the evening. They then drove to the coroner's office to ID Scott's body.

The experience had been unreal. Mags felt a strange sense of being outside herself as she peered through a window into the room. She couldn't bring herself to go inside and yet she knew she had to see him, to know he was really gone.

He'd looked so pale, and yet perfect. He'd always been attractive. Death hadn't taken that from him.

But it will eventually, she'd thought morbidly. *He'll decay and rot, just like everyone else when they die.*

Pain started throbbing in her head at the distressing thought and she'd excused herself to take a pain pill, waiting afterwards in the main lobby until Scott's parents finished.

Once the three of them returned to Mags' apartment, her next step had been to call the temp agency, asking them to send a replacement at work for the next couple days as she needed some personal time off. Then they all sat around the kitchen table and drank a few glasses wine, reminiscing about Scott throughout the years.

Mags found herself becoming more and more uncomfortable the longer they spoke. She could feel him in the room—plopping on the couch to watch his History Channel documentaries, racing with Mags to get the first cup of coffee from the pot, playfully tackling her and carrying her into the bedroom. His ghost haunted each room, each piece of furniture.

On top of those unpleasant images, Mags hadn't been able to bring herself to tell Scott's parents about the breakup, or about how the last words he and she had spoken to each other had been in anger. But this morning, in the light of day that shone through her slatted blinds, Mags finally realized she wanted to tell them.

The moment had happened right before bed. A throw-away sentence that normally would have brought warmth to Mags' heart only filled her with more sadness. As she'd said goodnight to Scott's parents, his mother said, "I'm glad you've got the next few days off from work, sweetie. This is a time for family."

Family. The word cut into her and she'd tossed and turned on the sofa for hours before finally falling asleep from exhaustion. She wasn't family. She wasn't ever going to *be* family.

Mags sat up, said the cursory "good morning's" towards the kitchen, and headed to the bathroom.

Quick and to the point, she thought to her reflection in the mirror. *You can say you still love him and will be there for the two of them, but they need to know that you and he were no longer involved.* The last thing she wanted was to have them always call her and check in, or invite her to family outings or something. This definitely needed to be taken care of.

Mags headed back towards the kitchen when she heard her phone ring next to the couch in the living room. She detoured and answered it.

"Hey, Juliette," she said into the phone after checking to see who was calling.

"Morning, luv. Just wanted to see how you are."

"Good timing. I just woke up."

"Well at least you got some sleep."

"I suppose I did." She paused. "It's so strange, being here. I thought it would be hard enough without us being together, but *without* him?" She glanced around her place. "I can remember everything about him here."

"That sounds awful." Juliette paused. "Is there someone

there?"

"Yeah. His parents."

"For how long?"

"Just in town for the funeral. They wanted to stay with me. I want them to as well—I don't want to be alone—but I also don't really want to be here at all." She'd hoped the feeling of Scott would have dissipated after sleeping, but she felt him just as strongly.

"Can you tell them that? Maybe they'll go to a hotel. Maybe you should, too. Just until you can catch your breath."

Mags gulped and peeked a glance over at the couple in the kitchen. "I think after I talk to them *they'll* suggest they go to a hotel."

"Why is that?"

"I'm about to tell them about me and Scott. About the breakup."

A moment of silence. "Wow. Good luck."

"Thanks."

Another few beats of quiet. "Say, Mags, I don't know if you'd be interested, but. . ." Juliette trailed off.

"What is it?"

"Well, I know you said your lease was up soon anyway. . ."

Mags' brow furrowed. "Yeah? What are you driving at, Jewels?"

"What would you think about moving in with me? You know, being flatmates and all that?"

Mags frowned. "Into your house?"

"Yes. Truth is, the explosion that blew out the front of my house has cost me more than I expected."

Mags thought for a moment. "Didn't your parents buy you that house?"

"They did. Unfortunately, I recently spent a lot of time back in England with my mum and she berated me for having such a dangerous job. I feel. . .uncomfortable, to say the least, in asking her to fix a giant hole in the place due to a bomb. So, truth is, I could use the extra rent help."

A smile crept across Mags' face. "Just for extra rent, huh?" she teased.

Juliette laughed. "Not just that. My house has always been too big. My parents were convinced I'd be married and have at least two children by now. Honestly, with three bedrooms and two floors, it's always been too much. But it's just a suggestion. No pressure."

"Jewels, that would be amazing!" Mags said. "My lease is up in two weeks. Would that be too soon? How much would you charge for rent? Can I get a kitten?"

Juliette laughed harder. "Hold on! I don't know any of this yet. The idea just popped into my head this morning. Maybe we can meet up in the next day or two when I'm done with work and chat about it more."

"Sounds great. Who knew getting kidnapped with you would end with us being roomies?"

"I sure didn't. Well, I need to run. Hope things go well with Scott's parents. If you need me, I'll have my cell on me."

"Thanks. I appreciate it."

"Take care. We'll talk soon."

Mags hung up. She peered into the kitchen and her stomach tightened. Straightening her shoulders, she took two steps towards Scott's parents.

Her phone rang again.

She let out a grateful sigh and answered it. "Yeah?"

"Oh. Hi, Mags. It's Jordan. I didn't expect you to pick up. I was goin' to leave a message. Figured you'd be at work."

A sudden swell of emotion hit Mags and her eyes welled up with tears. "Personal day," she muttered. "Funeral."

"Oh no! I'm so sorry. Was it the detective you were visitin' at the hospital?"

"No. He woke up actually. I'm so grateful for that at least. It was my ex. His parents are staying with me. We just ID'd the body yesterday."

A long silence. "Someone you know just died?"

Mags' forehead wrinkled. "Yes, like I said, he is, *was,* my ex. I saw him the night it happened. He went to a restaurant nearby. Guess it was a mugging gone wrong." A tear spilled down her cheek and her lip quivered.

"That's awful. Well I won't bother you with my stuff then."

Mags wiped her face and ventured a glance over at the kitchen. "No, it's okay. What is it?"

"I was goin' to see if you wanted to meet for lunch. Some-thin' happened I want to talk about, but I think in person is best. Obviously you have a lot goin' on right now. It can wait if it needs to."

Mags watched Scott's parents, his dad reading the paper, his mom wiping the counter. They appeared so normal, most likely just going through the motions, letting time pass by between bouts of grief. She hated that she'd have to possibly bring them more pain about the breakup. "Actually. . .I could use a distraction in a little while. I have to tell Scott's parents that he and I broke up. They didn't know."

"Oooh. Ouch."

"Yeah. Might be nice to have an excuse to get out of the apartment after I tell them. Can you meet at about one?"

"Sure. I can take my lunch break then. You remember where I work, right?"

"Yeah. I'll see you then."

Mags hung up, cracked her neck from side to side, and gritted her teeth.

Just get it over with.

With measured steps, she walked into the kitchen.

20

October 14th
Noon

Juliette met up with Inspector Omani Woods at a small Cambodian restaurant called *The Elephant Walk*. It wasn't normally her type of place—she tended to be a meat and potatoes type of girl—but she didn't plan on eating much anyway. Her stomach roiled with both nerves and excitement at the idea of finally getting some answers about the Triads.

Juliette stared across the table at the attractive Interpol agent. He'd laid his charcoal gray suit coat over the back of his chair and his crisp, pale yellow dress shirt complimented his dark skin. They'd begun with the normal pleasantries and while Juliette sipped her tea, he'd switched topics, reminding her that the following information was classified and couldn't be repeated. For the full ten minutes he spoke, the original balance between nerves and excitement inside her tipped completely to the latter side.

"It's really true, then," she said. "Other Triads exist."

He nodded. "I've reached out to multiple other countries around the world, digging into mysterious circumstances and odd cases. For over three years I've been collecting evidence, but now, after what occurred in Boston? I believe it all connects."

"So, what comes next? And why do you need me?"

"I'd like you to help us expose the Triads, once and for all. It will be difficult, because they already work in secret and can seemingly disappear at will, but I believe there is a way to find them all."

"How?"

"Oddly enough, through arson."

That got Juliette's attention. "Arson?"

Woods nodded. "A rash of fires have been reported in several countries over the past six months. Based on our research, we believe whoever is setting them is either trying to cover up or expose Triad movement, agents, and crime scenes."

"But which is it, a cover up or exposure? I mean, setting fires is very public, but it can also be a thorough way to dispose of evidence."

Woods settled into his chair, one arm draped loosely onto his lap. "That's what I'm not sure of. The fires have definitely made headlines in the news, but they seem haphazard. They are drawing attention, but not necessarily destroying the area they burn. However, there has been no claim from any group concerning these fires, either about why they are being set or trying to bring any Triads to light."

A frown touched her lips. "It sounds sloppy."

"It does, but the attacks are also coordinated. Whoever is igniting these fires must have contacts all over the world. They know their exact targets and not one of the perpetrators has been caught."

Juliette absentmindedly twirled the noodles on the plate in front of her with a fork as she mulled over the information, pulling on her time as a profiler. Arsonists often used fire-setting as a way to express anger or revenge they felt couldn't be expressed in any other way. Vengeance would be next on her list of "why's" if these fires weren't being used to cover anything up *or* as exposure.

She cleared her thoughts. "This still doesn't tell me why you'd like to work with me."

Woods moved forward, elbows on the table, hands clasped under his chin. His gaze bore into her, but instead of feeling intimidated, Juliette felt admired. "You are the only detective who actually has first-hand experience with any of these Triad members and has a profiling background. I'm hoping you will want to help us with a composite personality and psychological profile, or any other tidbits, to create a clearer picture of the type of criminals we're dealing with."

The flattery hit her hard. Juliette fought the urge to shyly tuck her hair behind her ears, since she still wasn't wearing her prosthetic one. Being a detective was often a thankless job. And also, if Interpol could really help, then perhaps she could shed light about her attack and the strange music that had come from her fake ear.

Her ego deflated a bit when she voiced a thought which crossed her mind. "What about Detective Trann? He was a witness as well and helped solve several of the clues left by the Triad."

Inspector Woods placed his folded hands down onto the table. "We debated about Trann and decided against involving him."

"Really? Why?"

His words came out with a slight edge. "Trann's connection to the case became much more personal than anyone else's. He had been romantically involved with one of the Triad members—"

"He didn't know Angellica was a killer," Juliette said, immediately coming to Trann's defense.

"Even so, that relationship could cloud his judgement, as well as the fact that he'd been targeted personally. We feel he may seek interest in this case out of a personal vendetta, which is exactly what we are fighting *against*."

"Trann is a professional."

"I'm sure." Inspector Woods rubbed his hand over his shaved-down scalp. "Detective Tay, I'm not trying to belittle him. However, as I mentioned, this project is classified. We can't afford any missteps on the *hope* that he'll help us, even if he would be an asset. And besides, when comparing the two of you, there is no contest. You are a better fit to work with us."

Juliette's chest purred at the compliment, then realized the implications. "So, I can't let my coworkers or boss know about this?"

"Correct. This will have more of an 'undercover' feel. We

learned the hard way that the more people involved, the more mistakes happen." His forehead wrinkled. "We've already lost two Interpol members to this because they were exposed. I won't lie; there is risk involved. I realize you've already been through a lot of grief because of these Triads, but we seem to be running out of time."

"How come?"

"The fires are escalating. It's as if the Triad trial set off a sequence of events and we are scrambling to catch up." He took a sip of coffee. "So, Detective, what do you say?"

A sense of purpose flowed through her. She'd been right. There had been more to the attacks than just three crazy women and a stalker. And there was nothing Juliette liked more than solving an unsolved case.

"I'm in."

21

October 14th
12:30 p.m.

Charlotte woke up in an unfamiliar room. Rubbing the sleep from her eyes, she glanced over to see what time it was, but her familiar blue-numbered clock wasn't there to greet her. Confusion clouded her mind.

Where am I now? She reached around to find her phone, the familiar shape comforting in her hand, but then remembered it had been taken away, to prevent anyone else from tracking her. With that thought, more of the previous day washed over her.

They'd vacated the hotel the night before and headed for a "safe house." Charlotte had fallen asleep in the back seat of the rented car, unable to keep her eyes open. After the stress and information overload, sleep had overtaken her without her consent. Her head had bobbed when she exited the vehicle. She vaguely remembered being half carried into the house, with oddly bright yellow daisies along the walkway, before her head hit the pillow in the room she currently inhabited.

Wrestling with the covers, Charlotte felt around and found a side table, on which sat a lamp. She turned it on and blinked repeatedly, letting her eyes adjust to the room. Though sparse, with pale sunshine walls, drawn golden curtains, a dresser in one corner, and a bookshelf in the other, the space felt inviting. Not exactly what she would have thought of as a "safe house," which was what Isabella had called it the previous day. She'd expected some sort of seedy, abandoned place, unclean and unkept. But this house felt lived-in, cared for, and comfortable.

Before they'd left the motel yesterday and arrived here, the three of them worked out a plan.

First, it was imperative to get supplies—food, water, whatever necessary to live on the run for a while.

Second, Charlotte had to inform work about her leave of absence. They also figured she should let Sean know she wouldn't be available to talk to him or see him, since he would most likely worry if she didn't check in with him. She'd pulled all the contact numbers she'd deemed important from her phone before they'd taken it, but she couldn't make herself call him on the burner phone yet. She was told to incinerate the list as soon as the phone calls were completed.

Charlotte was *not* looking forward to speaking with Sean. She didn't know how she *couldn't* lie to him. The thought sent waves of nausea through her belly.

And third, they needed to access Charlotte's apartment to a) retrieve the Book and b) leave her phone there, to keep any other trackers off her scent.

This seemed to be the trickiest step. Both Isabella and Carla were worried about going back to Charlotte's place. They didn't know if it was being watched or perhaps rigged with a bomb.

Charlotte had suggested leaving the Book and simply destroying the sim card.

"Do we really need either?"

Isabella had said, "I think we will. I think your message to the Triads will be stronger if we show you also contain the Book in hand. It'll give it a more 'Messiah' feeling."

"And what about the sim card? If anyone has been tracking me, they will know I have not been home for two nights."

"But they may be waiting for you to come back. We can capitalize on that. We can plant listening devices as well, in case you have any unexpected visitors. The more information we can get about whoever is setting these fires, the better."

Since Carla had the most experience with stealth, they decided she should be the one to retrieve the Book and leave the phone. She'd set off that evening with Charlotte's keys.

At that moment, as she watched a woman leave to infiltrate her apartment, Charlotte had two realizations: one, she was completely at the mercy of these women and two, she was completely in on their plan.

The notions caused fitful stretches of sleep during the night, punctuated with dreams about running from hordes of angry women to a dream where she sat on a throne, a crown on her head. When she looked down at her subjects, they all appeared as spiders.

She'd become the spiders' queen.

From that dream she'd awakened this morning, disoriented and sweaty.

Now, she did her best to go through any motions of normalcy: brush her teeth with a newly-bought toothbrush and toothpaste, shower using cheap gas station bar soap and shampoo. And dressing in a pair of jeans and a grey T-shirt they'd picked up from Goodwill. She added to that a hooded, navy sweatshirt and stared at herself in the mirror.

She barely recognized herself. Normally in khakis, black dress pants, or blouses, she looked. . .so. . .regular.

Charlotte returned to the bedroom and rechecked her packed backpack. It contained two more sets of clothes, similar to the ones she already wore, all greys, blacks, and blues. Materials to take care of her healing wounds. The rest of the supplies were in another bag with Isabella.

Charlotte stared at her new burner phone. She needed to call Sean, let him know what was going on *without* letting him know what was going on. Calling him now, while he was at work, would be her best bet. She could be brief, knowing he was at the precinct and wouldn't be able to talk long.

At least, she hoped.

Isabella had procured two more burner phones to use, each to last only three days. From one of these Charlotte had made the call to work the previous day. Now, she took the same phone in her hand, inhaled deeply, and dialed the number she'd written down for Sean.

Ring.

Ring.

Maybe he will not answer, she thought.

Ri—

"Hello, this is Detective Trann."

"Hi Sean, it is Charlotte." She hoped her voice sounded steady.

"Oh hey, Charlotte! Perfect timing. I'm just finishing up my lunch break. Are you at work? I don't recognize the number."

"Actually, I am not. I decided to take a few days off," she said, using the dialogue she'd rehearsed to herself the day before. "After everything that happened over the past week, I am not feeling very well. It may just be a reaction to the antibiotics from my injury. If it gets worse, I will check in with my doctor, but mostly I am very fatigued. I think it will be better to rest."

"Oh wow, yeah, of course. You should take care of yourself."

"I wanted to make sure you knew. Also," she said, swallowing hard, "I dropped my phone into the toilet accidentally last night. It is unusable."

"That sucks. You just got that new phone. So then where are you calling from?"

"A neighbor's phone. I had a feeling you might worry if you did not hear from me."

"You'd have been right," he said, laughter in his tone. His voice then grew serious. "Are you sure you're going to be okay?"

"I. . .I believe so," she said. She'd just looked up and saw Isabella in the doorway, gesturing that they had to leave.

"Do you want me to stop by and bring you anything?"

Her hands shook. "No. Thank you, but no. I stocked up on some things last night, just in case I did not feel better."

"When does your new phone come?"

"I am not sure. Hopefully a few days. My current type of phone is on backorder."

"Well I'm really glad you called me and told me. And if you need *anything*, please call me again on your neighbor's phone. I wouldn't mind stopping by, if you're up for a visit."

"I will. Thank you, Sean."

"Feel better."

"Thanks. And Sean?" she asked, emotion welling up inside her.

"Yeah?"

"I am really looking forward to when we can see each other again."

"Me too. Bye, Charlotte."

"Bye, Sean."

Charlotte hung up, her chest tight. She hated this. All of this. She'd wanted nothing more than to tell him everything, see if he could help, or maybe to talk her out of it.

But that was just it. What could he do? Anyone else included would only draw attention. If a Triad member went after him, he'd not only be in danger, he'd be a liability. Any spies needed to think Sean wasn't interested in searching for the Triads anymore. That had been Isabella's purpose in the first place, to reduce and remove any interest from outside parties who may try to follow-up on their organization.

Charlotte couldn't be the one to drag him back into all this.

"We have to go. Ready?" Isabella asked, her tone soft.

Charlotte clenched then relaxed her hands. "No. But let us do this anyway."

22

October 14th
12:45 p.m.

Sean hung up the phone, happy he'd gotten to talk to Charlotte, but sad he wouldn't get to see her. Not that they'd planned anything earlier than the weekend. Still, he didn't mind the idea of bringing her soup or something while she recovered, just to spend time with her.

Wind whipped at him, piercing his thin jacket. He'd just reached his car in the hospital parking lot after visiting with Payne. When Tay said she had something to do for lunch, Sean figured he could use his own lunch break to visit his partner. Though Payne was a bit slow to speak sometimes and stumbled on a few of his words, he seemed all right. Although whatever changes he'd made to his personality before getting smashed on the head with a crowbar appeared to have stuck. The man seemed more polite and attentive. He didn't leer at any of the female staff attending him, didn't crack any dirty jokes, and spoke softly about how happy he'd been to wake up to Mags' presence.

"I hear there has still been quite a bit going on the past couple days I've been out of it," he'd said to Sean.

"Yeah. I guess that's life. It doesn't always let you catch your breath. But you waking up really helped offset all the other crap."

"I'm glad you're happy about that." Payne paused. "Look, I'm not good at this kind of stuff, but I was an ass. You deserve a better partner."

"You *were* an ass, but you're a great cop. You just weren't the best guy to be around." Sean's words felt a bit blunt, but he wanted to make sure he got his point across.

"I get it."

Sean mentally let out his breath.

"They pairing you up with someone else until I get out of here?" Payne asked.

"Nah. I'm going to work with Wilt and Tay."

Payne seemed to sag with relief. "That's good."

"Were you worried they'd replace you?"

"I'm not exactly up and running at the moment."

"Hey, I was shot six months ago. It took a while before I was back at full duty as well. We don't give up on our detectives that easily."

Payne grinned. "Good to know."

Sean had stayed a few more minutes, filling the time with small talk, before heading out. He hadn't thought he'd spend so much of his hour-long lunch break there. He'd wanted to touch base with Elaine before his break concluded, but when he went to call her, his phone rang and he'd spoken with Charlotte instead.

Now, sitting in his car, he felt as if his team members were dropping like flies. He couldn't blame Charlotte for needing some time to recover. He supposed she'd pushed her limits since she had literally been stabbed in the back a few days ago. Payne had only just woken up from head trauma. Millan felt like he needed to quit to find peace. Tay, who he'd been surprised to see at work, just had a bomb blow up her front door, which killed two officers on duty in her yard, right after she was attacked and drugged in her garage.

Even Mags, who wasn't actually an officer, had dealt with an attack from a stalker. Not to mention adding Scott's death to the mix couldn't have helped her stress levels.

Sean shook his head, started up his car, and cranked up the heat. As he drove away from the hospital, he found himself amazed at what they'd been through the past six months. All of the people he knew were pretty incredible.

The idea made him even more determined to discover the truth behind the possibility of more Triads. If he could, he'd make sure none of his coworkers or friends or Charlotte ever had to deal with a Triad member again.

Taking a left, he put his phone on speaker and called Elaine.

"Hey, Detective," she answered, her voice a bit high. "I was just about to call you. What's going on?"

"I think we should meet up as soon as you can and go over everything you've discovered so far about the vacant homes, the address list, etcetera. As a detective, there may be something I see that you don't."

"That's a good idea. Because I found out something else."

Thick raindrops fell from the sky, pelting his windshield. He activated his wipers and watched as they streaked like thin black bird wings in front of him. "What's that?"

Elaine cleared her throat. "There was accelerant in Gloria's engine. The police are claiming it wasn't an accident. Her car had been rigged to explode when it hit the house."

23

October 14th
1 p.m.

Mags got off the bus at the stop near Jordan's office. As District Attorney, Jordan worked in the Suffolk County Courthouse, a place which Mags had now been to twice in the past couple weeks. She hustled the extra two blocks, tightening the scarf around her face. A brusque wind whipped at her and stung her eyes, even behind her glasses. Gray clouds dotted the sky, currently blotting out the sun. Dark spots speckled the concrete sidewalks, indicating the rain had briefly stopped a few moments before. The sky threatened that the drops would fall again soon.

During her walk, Mags tried her best not to think about the past hour with Scott's parents, but that proved impossible.

They'd been devastated, of course, to find out about the breakup.

"I wonder why he didn't tell us?" Scott's mom had asked.

"I don't know," Mags had replied. "Maybe because it had just happened. Maybe because he didn't know if we'd reconcile. I know for me, the first time I told someone, it made it real. That was hard."

"Well, what *did* happen? I mean, you two seemed so happy, so good together."

Mags didn't want to get too personal, or put Scott in a bad light, so she stayed as vague as possible. "Things got strained between us and then I went out of town for a few months for work. I think the little things just added up and the distance didn't help."

"Well, little things can be worked on," Kathryn had said, wringing her hands. "I'm sure that's why he didn't tell us. The two of you would have worked things out. Now we'll never know."

Mags had given a weak smile and let Kathryn hug her. Scott's father stood in the background, shaking his head slowly. Mags felt he may have known more than Kathryn did about what Scott and Mags had been going through.

They'd parted ways after that—Scott's parents going to a hotel—and told her they'd be in touch about the funeral scheduled for later that week.

Afterwards, Mags had found a seat near a window on the bus, hid her face as much as she could in her scarf, and let the tears come. She didn't sob or make noise, she just let them fall, as much for Scott and for his parents as for herself.

Now, the recently shed tears felt cold against her face in the sharp wind. She knew she'd better stop before she saw Jordan and assess the damage—puffiness, redness, mascara streaks, etc.

Once inside the building, she made her way to the bathroom and cleaned herself up as best she could. Her eyes still looked red, but that could be blamed on the wind and chill outside. However, since Jordan knew what had happened to Scott, Mags realized the district attorney probably wouldn't need to be lied to.

Mags let out a sigh, watching her own reflection do the same. She'd been extremely glad she hadn't attempted to make it through work today. All she wanted to do was return home, curl up in bed, put on a stupid goofy movie, and fall asleep until this whole ordeal was over.

Except her apartment had been *their* apartment for a long time. Memories of Scott lingered in every room. He'd never even gotten the chance to remove his belongings. Given the circumstances, she could use something to distract her. But without work, what would keep her mind occupied and away from morbid thoughts?

Mags made her way to Jordan's office, knocked on the door, and entered when prompted.

"Hey," Jordan said. "Please, go on and sit."

Mags took the seat across the desk, a sense of déjà vu flooding over her. The only other time she'd sat here was to go over her testimony for the Triad trial. It felt like a lifetime ago and had really only been about two weeks since that whole ordeal had begun.

"Hey, Jordan."

"I'm glad you could come in," the district attorney said, "especially with everythin' goin' on. You don't have to, though, I hope you know that." Jordan once again looked very professional in her fitted charcoal suit. Mags had always prided herself on her unique and funky sense of style, but maybe it just showed her immaturity? She'd always thought it displayed her independence, but maybe Scott had been onto something—that Mags projected her desire to stand out as a way to feel important at the precinct instead of merely being the receptionist.

Mags dismissed her negative thoughts. She didn't want to let her grief make her question her whole lifestyle. "I could use the break," she said, meaning it. "I need to feel useful. I don't feel like I can do anything right now."

"I understand. Well, I'm glad I can provide some distraction. Unfortunately, I wish I had better news."

Mags frowned. "What do you mean?"

Jordan held a pen in her hand and tapped it against her desk. "We talked about how I'd planned to give you the files from Tennessee, remember? Well, I called down to my old law practice, because we had copies of those files put aside." The tapping stopped. "They're gone."

"Gone?"

"Yes. The computer files have disappeared."

"Huh." Mags wracked her brain. "How?"

Jordan let out a sigh. "An intern did it by mistake."

"Just those files?"

"No. All files timestamped from the previous week and the followin' week. Accordin' to my old coworker, it looked like they selected a timeframe and deleted everythin'. Apparently they were supposed to be copyin' the files and erased them by mistake. When the error was discovered, the intern was immediately let go. I guess the young woman cried and all, but they couldn't keep her on after such a huge blunder."

"Were there any paper files?"

Jordan pursed her lips. "No. We don't keep paper files for finished cases, only digital copies."

Mags let out a low whistle. "Well, where does that leave us?"

"That leaves us with nothin' and no way to trace the addresses. I'm so sorry, Mags."

Mags pushed her glasses a bit up her nose. "I guess that's a dead end then. I'm sorry, too, Jordan. I know you really wanted to look into that case."

"Yeah. . ." Jordan said. "You know, maybe I was just makin' somethin' out of nothin'."

"Really?" Mags' mind started sifting through ideas. "I don't know. . ."

"What do you mean?"

Mags leaned forward. "Don't you think it's a little convenient that the only files deleted were the ones that included the case you think was related to the Triads?"

Jordan didn't answer for a few moments. "I didn't think about that. I mean, other records were deleted by mistake as well, so. . ." She shook her head. "You think these specific files were erased just to cover up the focus on the possible Triad-related files?"

"It's possible, isn't it?"

Jordan scoffed. "I can't believe these women would wreck a bunch of other documents just to cover their tracks."

Mags remembered all too well being kidnapped and taken by one of these Triad groups. She didn't think a few extra files would bother them that much. "Can you find out who the intern was?"

"Maybe, although it may seem sort of strange to ask about her without a good reason. I don't exactly want anyone to know I'm investigatin' this."

"Totally understandable. Jordan, you do realize that the same evidence you discovered vanished? Imagine if any of these women knew *you* were looking for this same stuff. They could come after you, too."

A short pause. "That means they could come after you as well."

Mags' stomach dropped. She hadn't thought of that. She'd been so excited to do something important, to prove she could be helpful, it was as though she'd completely forgotten about how easily these women would kill if they deemed it necessary. Why was she playing with fire? Had Scott been right about her?

Mags stared across at Jordan, silent.

"It doesn't matter anyway," Jordan said. "Without that evidence, without those addresses to analyze, we can't prove anythin'."

Something went off in Mags' head. Perhaps she had something else that could be used instead. "What about the list of addresses Charlotte and I searched through? I found a partial list in the underground bunker. We could go through those, see if we can find a pattern based on what you found out from your case?"

Jordan's eyes lit up. "Oh yeah! Do you think you can get copies?"

"Of course." She grinned, but her smile faded. "Okay, I just let myself get caught up again." She chewed on her lower lip.

"Jordan, this is serious stuff. If we do this and someone finds out. . ."

"I know. If those files were removed by that intern on purpose. . ." her eyes widened. "Maybe the Triads already know I wanted to look at them." She shook her head. "This was a big mistake, Mags. I shouldn't have started this and I can't have you be a part of it. These women already went after you. You know firsthand how crazy and dangerous they are."

"I do." Mags wanted to back out. Every part of her logical brain told her to leave immediately. Jordan was right. If these women were already covering their tracks in Tennessee, they may connect things back to Jordan, since she'd been asking around. Who knew how far the influence of the Triads went? They could be anywhere, impersonate anyone. They could obviously get into corporations, law files, and who knew what else?

A thought crept into her mind. The documents she'd compiled with the addresses . . .what if one of these women had gone after those files as well? What if they'd been expunged somehow from the Boston P.D. database?

"Okay. Before we do or don't do anything, let me check on the files at work, make sure they are still okay, and make backups."

Jordan raised her eyebrows. "But if someone knows you are lookin' into those, they could come after you. If you even access them, it may put you in danger."

Mags rubbed her forehead. A mild pain began to throb. The last thing she needed was a migraine. She had a doctor's appointment that evening to go check about the increasing pain and nosebleed. Maybe she should call it a day until she talked to her physician. Regardless, she couldn't get access to the files until she returned to work.

Unless...

"You know what? I think I have a way to keep us safe and still access the files."

"How?"

Mags grinned again, the pain in her head receding. "Let me worry about that. I'll let you know when I retrieve them, assuming they are still there."

Jordan's forehead furrowed. "Mags, are you sure? Once we go into this, we may not be able to get out again if we are found out."

Mags thought about all the things these women had gotten away with: shooting Juliette and Sean, kidnapping her, trying to kill Charlotte, the attack on Payne, the three months they wasted looking for these women, so close to finding them, but off by some sort of code...

"I'm really tired of being scared. I'm tired of being sad. I've nearly lost everyone close to me, potential friends, and a possible..." she trailed off, thinking about Payne. "I thought everything would be over once I heard those Triad women were all dead. Then that stalker woman came after us, again. And now you have noticed other discrepancies."

"But that doesn't prove anythin'."

"No, but I think these women are showing their hand, if we know where to look for it. We may not be able to stop them, but if we can expose more of them? If we can show that we know how to find them? Maybe they'll stop or go away or mess up and we can catch them."

"If you're really sure..." Jordan nodded. "Then I'm in, too. I need to know if these patterns I'm seein' are real or not. If not, I can drop it. But if they are. . ."

". . .we can help save lives."

"All right. You do what you need to do and let me know about the files when you can. I think meeting in person will probably be safest. Just call me when you're ready and we'll find a time to meet up."

"Sounds good." Mags shook with a mixture of excitement and fear. "Talk to you later."

"Bye, Mags. Good luck."

Mags left and headed for the bus stop, yawning. With so many mixed emotions flooding through her, she stopped for a moment and rested against the wall of the building. The list of things to do threatened to overwhelm her. She needed to hack into the precinct archives and find the files while not allowing anyone to trace anything back to herself, she needed to help with Scott's funeral, and she had her doctor's appointment to discuss her migraines.

Another yawn slipped from her mouth as a twinge of pain spiked in her forehead. "I need a nap first," she muttered. Mags watched the bus approach and boarded it. She leaned back in one of the seats, her eyelids fluttering. A snort emerging from her own mouth woke her and she shook her head. The last thing she wanted to do was fall asleep on the bus and miss her stop.

24

October 14th
5 p.m.

After meeting with Inspector Omani Woods for lunch, Juliette had remained mostly quiet during the rest of Monday. She and Wilt and Trann had been investigating the jewelry heist case that afternoon, but she had to admit, her mind wandered quite often during the interviews with witnesses.

Keep your head in the game, she told herself. *You still have a job to do.* But the prospect of working with Interpol kept slithering into her brain, getting her more and more excited. She and Woods were to meet up that evening after she finished work. He said he already had some new arson leads and would give her the files of the other fires they believed were Triad-related.

Now, Juliette watched her phone's clock change at last to the final minute of her shift. She grabbed her bag and jacket, said goodnight to everyone, and took off. Driving through the end-of-day Boston traffic, she followed her GPS to Woods' temporary headquarters in Newton. The thirty-minute drive gave her a little time to think.

One thing she'd decided to do was bring her prosthetic ear. Though not an arson matter, she thought Woods may want to know about it, so he could understand the complexity and tech-savvy-ness of the Triad groups. The arsonists sounded much sloppier. She had a feeling they weren't Triad members at all, but an outside party.

She'd also thought once again about calling Mags and having her look at the ear, but she just couldn't bring herself to bother her friend. When she'd arrived at her car right after her shift, she called to check in, but Mags didn't even answer. She was sure Mags must be completely overwhelmed with all the funeral proceedings.

Forcing herself away from her contemplations, Juliette pulled up to an average office building, with windowed glass and double doors. The building appeared to be about ten stories high, surrounded by several other similar buildings. The sun hung low in the sky, reflecting off the glass, creating a mirrored effect. Juliette found a parking spot and pulled in, noting that many employees were leaving the building, having just finished work for the day.

Entering, she found the suite number provided to her by Woods, and headed up to the fourth floor. After knocking, the door opened.

"Detective Tay. Brilliant, come on in." Juliette couldn't help admiring Woods' physique. He'd loosened his tie a bit and she could see his suit jacket lying over the back of a chair. His upper body filled out the men's dress shirt nicely.

Once fully inside, she noted three other people in the sparsely decorated space: two at computer terminals on the left and the third flipping through paperwork at a large, plastic fold out table in the center. On the right sat a large whiteboard, with a few papers taped on it and some scribbling underneath them she couldn't read. The shades had been half-drawn and the setting sun's light shone through the bottom of the windows, illuminating the lower half of the room. Overhead fluorescent lights lit up the rest of the space.

"I'd like you to meet the rest of our team," Woods said, gesturing to each person in turn. "This is Agent Xena Leeds," he said, indicating a tall brunette at one of the computers. The slim woman stood briefly, her red pencil skirt covering two rail-thin legs.

"No," Leeds said with a slight smile, "I'm not named after the 'warrior princess.' I was born before that show." An Australian lilt tinted her words.

Juliette smiled back. She had a feeling Leeds said that after every introduction.

Woods continued, pointing to the person at the other computer. "Inspector Jean De'leu."

A stocky man with a receding hairline and a bulbous nose sniffed at her. "Pleasure," De'leu said, his French accent rolling across the word. Juliette couldn't detect any actual pleasure in the word.

"And Detective Francine Franks."

Agent Franks briskly stood up from the table, reaching across to shake Juliette's hand. The handshake was brisk and firm. Her short, blonde hair bounced in tight curls around her face, like an adult peroxided-version of Shirley Temple.

"Please, call me Franny, would'ya?" Notes of an upper Midwest or possibly Canadian accent touched her words. "Francine makes me sound like my grandma."

"Sure thing," Juliette said, her smile widening.

"Welcome to the team," Woods concluded.

"I'm glad to be here," Juliette said, enthusiasm bubbling up inside her. "Where do I start?"

Woods waved her over to the documents on the table. "We've printed everything out for you about the past fires." He then pointed to a shorter stack. "Those are recent fires we believe may be connected."

Juliette glanced at the pages. "What makes you think so?"

"The fires have to do with seemingly random places. For example. . ." he said, picking up the first folder and flipping it open. "This one happened in Vermont two days ago. A car drove into a lake house and the engine combusted. The car had been rigged with accelerant to explode."

"Strange, granted, but—"

Woods interrupted her. "The woman who lived in the house, Betty Patrickson, aged fifty-three, died that same day. Not from the fire. She accidentally drowned in the lake behind her house before the explosion occurred."

Juliette paused. "So. . .someone set her house on fire by using a car *after* she'd already died?"

"Exactly."

Woods picked up the second file and continued. "We also have another Vermont incident from the same day. A motel about an hour south. A car exploded, blowing in the door on one of the rooms. No body was found inside and the occupant never checked out of the hotel or showed up later for questioning. When they searched for the occupant's ID information, the police discovered a 'Jenny Jones' who paid in cash."

Juliette found herself sliding into one of the chairs near Inspector De'leu. She felt like she'd just stumbled upon the most intricate puzzle. Adrenaline shot through her as she stared at all the cases in front of her. "Have we ID'd either of the vehicles?"

Woods held up a hand. "Hold on. First, you need to catch up on the past cases. Remember, we need your profiling expertise first. We have to have an idea of who we are looking for. Right now we are three steps behind, only noticing patterns after the fires happen. That has to change. We need to get in front of whoever this is, find out how they are determining the Triad agents or activity. If we can do that, we can not only catch this arsonist, but we can have a leg up on Triad patterns as well."

Juliette gave a few quick nods. "I understand."

Woods flashed her a grin. "Coffee is in the back corner and the loo's down the hall." He placed a hand on her shoulder. "Good to have you aboard, Detective."

25

October 14th
6:00 p.m.

Charlotte heard a rap at the door. Her eyes were already open, staring up at the vehicle's beige ceiling. She'd never been in a motor home before. The closest she'd ever come had been a full-sized van that she'd slept in as a child on a family vacation.

A fourth night in a new place. Her mind could hardly keep up. She missed her bed, her clock with large, blue numbers, her towels. She missed the privacy and the quiet.

Basically, the camper had everything they needed—a bathroom, small shower, sink, fold-out beds, a TV, and a small bolted-down couch next to two booth-like seats on either side of a table. The mobile home was currently stationed at a campground northwest of Boston. They had electricity and internet as well as access to food supplies and showers.

Charlotte had only been camping once before. She and her brother pitched a tent in their backyard in Seattle the year before he'd died. Her brother knew the best ghost stories and Charlotte had been fascinated by the way he could make her feel terrified and yet safe at the same time. The memory of him brought the sting of tears to her eyes, but the voices near the RV's open side door pulled her back to the present.

"It's done," Carla's sultry voice said. She stood just outside the doorway, tapping the edges of her shoes against the side of the makeshift steps, dislodging any dirt caked on their bottoms. Her long hair hung in bulbous curls, framing her face. Though she most likely hadn't gotten a lot of sleep, she still looked refreshed and energized. Charlotte admired that as she herself put a lot of stock in her physical appearance.

Then she remembered how Triad women prided themselves on physicality and felt a little ill at the idea of any resemblance to them.

"Any problems?" Isabella asked.

"None," Carla replied, tapping the edges of the doorway with her fingertips. "Although I found a listening device lodged in her bookcase and one under the lip of her nightstand."

Charlotte sat up at the words, nearly smacking her head on the low ceiling. She remembered that Carla had been sent back to her apartment to retrieve the Book and leave her phone. Someone had planted listening devices in her apartment?

"Did you disarm them?" Isabella asked.

"I thought it best to leave them undisturbed."

"Good idea. It may buy us some time."

"Some, but not much. They will soon realize she's not home."

"True." A pause. "We may have to speed up our timeline," Isabella continued.

"Agreed."

Isabella peered over at Charlotte. "I'm assuming you heard all of that?"

"Yes," she answered, hoping the fear in her heart wasn't evident in her voice.

"The good news is they were only listening. Nothing had been planted in the apartment to hurt you."

Charlotte swallowed. "What do you think they were listening for?"

Isabella shrugged as Carla finished entering the vehicle, placing a knapsack on the tiny table. "Could be a lot of things," Isabella said. "My guess? They were curious about you and wanted to know more. See if you really fit the Messiah lore or if you were a fake."

Charlotte rotated her legs off the bed, hunching over so as to not hit her head, and slid off. She'd been given the top bunk; the two beds folded down, much like sleeper cars on trains. She began to deftly braid her hair over one shoulder. "May I see this 'lore' on the Messiah?"

Isabella's eyes blinked a few times. "I don't see why not. We don't have a translation here, though."

Charlotte's shoulders sagged. "Ah, yes. I forgot the Book is not in English." She waited a few beats. "Can we get a translation?"

"Probably." Isabella looked over at Carla. "Where do you think the closest one would be?"

"Most likely the precinct that confiscated the Book in the first place. They had it in their possession for several months before the trial, in which translated pages were introduced as evidence."

Isabella tapped her fingers on the edge of the table. "What about Jordan? Would she have copies?"

Charlotte's ears perked up at the new name.

Carla nodded. "I believe so. I'll give her a call." Carla headed towards the front of the camper, pulling out her phone as she moved.

Isabella moved closer to Charlotte at the rear end. "Can I ask what you want the translations for?"

I want to know if it really is me, she thought to herself.

"I want to learn everything I can to be convincing," she said out loud. "The more I know about what constitutes this Messiah, the more I can use when speaking to the Triads."

"That's a really good idea." Isabella smiled. "I'm glad you're here, Charlotte."

"I do not have much of a choice," she replied, bitterness tinging her words.

"Maybe, but you did have one." Charlotte could see a glimmer in Isabella's eyes. "I really think we may be able to pull this off."

"I hope so," Charlotte said.

Carla came back over to them. "I just spoke with Jordan. She can get the translations and bring them to us tonight."

"Who is Jordan?" Charlotte automatically asked.

Isabella and Carla shared a look.

Carla gave a word of warning. "The less she knows, the better."

"I think it's too late for any more pretenses," Isabella said.

Charlotte could see Carla's face harden, but she didn't refute Isabella's statement.

Isabella faced Charlotte. "You've already met this associate. Jordan Parker."

Charlotte searched her mind for the semi-familiar name. Then it dawned on her. "The district attorney?"

Isabella nodded.

Shock coursed through Charlotte. She'd just seen the woman at Violet's trial, spoken to her to cover cross-examination questions. She would never have expected that woman to be involved in all this. And yet, that was their job, wasn't it? To blend in where needed, cover up what they had to, lie about themselves and their true intentions.

"That is not an easy position to fake one's way into," Charlotte said slowly.

"It's not fake. We got her hired. She was a district attorney out of Tennessee."

"But she lost the case against Violet."

"The outcome of the trial didn't matter. We would have dealt with Violet afterwards, regardless of where she ended up."

"What about you?" Charlotte asked. "Are you actually a student at the University?"

Isabella gave a grimaced smile. "No. My ID and email account were forged."

Charlotte ran a shaky hand along her braided hair.

Isabella's face pinched in concern. "The deceptions we make are not because we want to, Charlotte, it's because we have to. My ruse as a student allowed me access to you and your office and to Detective Trann and the precinct. We needed to assess the risk of exposure. You and the Boston P.D. are the first ones in a long time to break open and expose a Triad. We needed to be sure you wouldn't follow up on them."

"You already told me this," Charlotte mumbled.

"I know. And I really am sorry about the lies. I, *we,* just wanted to keep everyone safe."

Charlotte peered over at Carla. Even though the knowledge they had to deceive people was known to her, the positions of power these women held were tremendous. She wasn't sure why, but she somehow pictured them pretending to be servers at a fancy gathering or a "party girl" to get close to their mark. But a district attorney? A university student?

"And you?" Charlotte asked, nodding at Carla. "You're an assassin and you were allowed to be near all of us. What was your cover story?"

"Police counselor," Carla chimed in, holding Charlotte's stare.

A counselor? Charlotte shook with anger. "You took advantage of them in their vulnerable state. You planted things in their minds, messed up their emotions for your own agenda. A counselor and their patient need ultimate trust. You violated that."

"And I'd do it again in a heartbeat," Carla snapped.

Charlotte bristled.

Carla shifted her focus to Isabella. "She still doesn't

understand," she said. "She's not ready."

"It doesn't matter," Isabella replied. "We're out of time. We'll have to do the best we can."

"How?" Charlotte demanded. "How am I not ready? I am here, am I not? I am in this motor home, away from my home, my work, lying to my friends to protect them. . ." she trailed off.

"Exactly," Carla said. "Do you get it now? The deception is to protect them." She hesitated, cocking her head to the side. "If I hadn't left my Triad, if I hadn't made the decision to change my life, I could easily have been ordered to execute any one of you if my team believed we'd been exposed. And I would have done it. Without thinking, without caring, and without a trace." Carla moved towards Charlotte. Isabella took a brief step halfway between them, as if protecting Charlotte.

"We are trying to save lives," Carla seethed. "You can't doubt us anymore or we will all fail. And that doesn't mean the 'go back home and pout' kind of fail. It means we and the people we love and anyone else they believe knows about us will be removed from existence." Carla backed up. "I'm going to wait outside for Jordan," she muttered before exiting the RV.

"I'm sorry about her," Isabella said with a sigh. "She doesn't trust well. In fact, it took her a long time to believe in Jordan, even though she was the one who wanted to bring the district attorney on board."

Charlotte raised an eyebrow. "It must be difficult for her to live by both wanting help and not trusting help."

"When you lose what you love by those you trusted. . .yeah, it's pretty difficult."

Charlotte remembered what Isabella had told her about how

Carla had left the Triads after the murder of her husband. "You lost someone you loved as well. Do you have the same trust issues as Carla?"

Isabella chewed her bottom lip. "Truthfully? When it comes to other Triad members, I don't trust them. When it comes to outside help, I do. But then again, I've had more people help us along the way than Carla has." She patted Charlotte on the shoulder. "Jordan should also have more news than just about the Book. She'd been keeping an eye on those who were involved, making sure everyone is doing all right. Also, speaking of help, she says she has a backup plan in place."

"Backup plan?"

"If ours doesn't work, or even if it does but we find resistance, Jordan is working on a way to locate other Triad members."

Charlotte sat up straighter. "Really?"

Isabella nodded, then narrowed her eyes. "You *do* understand this isn't an alternative plan. It's only to be used if ours doesn't work. At any rate, it'll only be supplemental. We won't have as much luck reaching as many Triads as we will with you."

"I understand." A little part of her chest tightened. She supposed she still hoped somehow a change would occur to still allow her to get out of all this.

Isabella nodded towards the tiny table. "Why don't you eat something?" She eyed Charlotte. "Not that I'm sure you eat very much with your thin self."

"I eat what is appropriate for my body type, activity level, and health."

Isabella rolled her eyes. "That sounds. . .boring."

"Perhaps, but there are a variety of things out there that are delicious and still good for you."

"Well, I believe everything in moderation, no matter what it is. I don't know what I'd do if I couldn't eat Cheetos anymore." She winked.

Charlotte let out a laugh.

The two of them sat and ate a simple meal of bananas, a protein drink, and granola bars. Charlotte was sure she wouldn't be hungry since her appetite had all but disappeared the past two days, but Isabella once again made the environment comfortable and her stomach growled at the first bite of fruit.

An hour later, after finishing their meal and some small talk, Isabella tilted her head towards the door, like a bird hearing a noise. Her shoulders relaxed after a few moments of listening. Charlotte wondered if Isabella would ever be able to relax. Even if they somehow managed to disband all the Triads, her training and habit of constantly being on guard would be difficult, if not impossible, to break.

"Sounds like Jordan is here," she said. She motioned towards the door. "Care to meet her *not* as the district attorney?"

Charlotte nodded and swallowed against the lump in her throat. They headed outside onto the dirt drive, surrounded by trees. The brisk air smelled of lingering campfires and pine needles. Under different circumstances, this could look like a women's camping trip, with four friends meeting up to get away from their usual, city lives. The reality of what they were truly doing sliced through Charlotte's thoughts.

Charlotte eyed the district attorney, with her short

strawberry blonde hair and pale skin. She appeared to have come directly from her office, wearing a fitted dark grey suit and a lime green dress shirt underneath. The shirt brought out the green in her eyes.

"Evenin'," she said, her southern drawl kicking in. She handed over a large packet of papers to Isabella. "Here are the translations."

"Thanks, Jordan," Isabella said. She nodded over to Charlotte. "You remember Doctor Charlotte Salla."

"Of course. Pleased to see you again, Doctor Salla."

Charlotte couldn't respond. A feeling stole over her, like a light electric shock. This woman worked for the law and still chose to help killers kill other women.

Isabella cut through the tension. "Any luck with the addresses?"

"I manipulated my. . .contact," Jordan said, her eyes flickering towards Charlotte for a moment, "just as you suggested. She took the bait and offered to search through the files herself." Jordan paused. "I have to admit, it was harder than I thought it would be."

"To convince her?"

"No, to lie. I like her."

Isabella let out a small sigh. "I'm sure you do. But you know the rules."

"She may be willing to join up with us, if she knew what we do. I did." Jordan nodded at Charlotte. "*She* did."

"Your circumstances were unique, Jordan, you know that. And as for Charlotte?"

"I did not have a choice," Charlotte chimed in. "Well, not a good one."

Carla spoke up, her voice icy. "I doubt you'd have helped us otherwise."

Charlotte turned towards her. "Perhaps not. I suppose we will never know."

"Ladies," Isabella said, her tone soft. "The important thing is we are working together now. And we are as close as we can get to ending the Triads once and for all." She redirected her attention to Jordan. "How long on the addresses?"

"Not sure. Maybe a day or two."

"That'll do fine." She gave a curt nod. "We'll be in touch." She handed over a small slip of paper. "Here is my new number for the next three days. Also, the name of our next campground after tonight."

"Got it." Jordan pocketed the piece of paper.

"Take care and watch your back," Carla said.

"I always do." Jordan walked away, got in her car, and left.

"Who is her contact?" Charlotte asked, watching the car drive away, envious for a moment that Jordan got to return to her life.

"An outsider," Isabella answered vaguely as they both headed back into the RV.

Charlotte stopped for a moment outside the motor home door and frowned. "I thought you said I could know everything now."

"About us, yes. But we are in the business of protecting people. I won't put anyone else in danger and if something ever happened to you, the less you know, the better."

Charlotte realized by 'something' Isabella meant captured,

not killed. The idea that Triad women may keep her alive for information was less than comforting. She glanced at the translation in Isabella's hands and climbed into the camper.

"May I?"

Isabella handed the pages over. "I don't know who translated these."

Charlotte recognized the file names. "I do. I hired the linguist specialists myself, before I left on my trip around the world to search for other Triad groups." She ran her fingers over the stack of papers. "I believe they will be as accurate as we can get."

"Good. I'm going to chat with Carla for a bit. I'll leave you to it."

Charlotte took a seat at the table and began sifting through the translated text. "Let us see who this Messiah really is. . ."

26

October 14th
6 p.m.

Sean met up with Elaine after work at the same BWW they'd first run into each other two nights before, only this time without Millan there. Being a Monday night, the place wasn't overly crowded, but apparently that could change at any moment because of the football game coming on later which, according to their server, would bring in quite a number of people.

"Thanks for the heads up," Sean told the server, waiting until he moved out of earshot of their booth. "Okay, he said to Elaine, "so I checked in this afternoon with the officer heading the investigation on Gloria's murder. He said that as of right now, there are no witnesses and no leads."

"Figures," she grumbled.

Sean gathered his thoughts. "Then I remembered what you said, about the office fire that had also been a potential Triad-involved group. So, I contacted that local precinct and asked around. Turns out they believe it was arson as well. They discovered that acetone had been used as an accelerant."

Elaine's eyes widened. "That's what was used in Gloria's car!"

"Exactly. However, it is common in arson. It's also easy to obtain and easy to detect, so it doesn't really indicate a professional. Once I tracked down the lead investigator in the arson case at the office, she told me there hadn't been a clear ignition point."

"Meaning?"

Sean took a slug of beer. "Often there will be a barrel or a container that holds the accelerant. The fire can be ignited from a distance and that point is where the fire starts. It's a safety measure so that the arsonist has time to leave the area. But apparently, in the office fire, the acetone was splashed around everywhere, meaning the culprit most likely remained in the room, lit the fire, and then ran out. It's pretty dangerous."

"And what about Gloria's car?"

"Same thing. There were remnants of plastic on the engine, indicating small containers that held the acetone, but the ignition point of the fire was inside the car, and lit before it hit the house. Also..." he hesitated, knowing it would be hard for Elaine to hear. "Gloria hadn't been killed before the explosion happened. Looks like blunt trauma to the head, but the coroner determined she was still alive when the car rammed into the house, just unconscious."

Elaine's face puckered and paled.

"I'm really sorry, Elaine." Sean could see tears forming in her eyes and wondered if he should have told her that last part. As an officer, he believed people needed to know all these details when investigating. It helped sketch a profile. In this case, whoever had set the fire had no mercy, letting someone burn alive.

He watched Elaine look upwards and blink several times and could tell she was trying not to cry.

"I barely even knew her," she said, rubbing a fist into one of her eyes. "We'd only started working together about three months ago, putting our facts together about the Triads. We only met in person twice in the past couple weeks. She had this really silly giggle. . ."

Elaine shook her head and cleared her throat. Sean noted the hardness that stole over her face. "Well, at least we know that whoever is setting these fires doesn't care about hurting or killing people to cover their tracks. We seem to know how they are doing it and that they are targeting Triad-related people."

"Possibly."

"*Probably,*" Elaine insisted.

Sean tapped his fingers on the edge of the table. "You know, maybe we can make that into a 'definitely' somehow."

"What do you mean?"

"You know how you said you had a copy of the list of addresses that Charlotte and Mags used to search around the world for Triads?"

"Yeah?"

"What if we did what you did and checked out other address

areas, see if there were vacancies, new move-ins to other places nearby. See if there have been other fires or murders that may fit the MO."

"Most of the addresses were out of the country, although there were about four more in the states, if I remember correctly."

Sean frowned. "Okay, we'll have to focus on those." He paused in thought. "The moving from one place to another is one thing—that information could prove Triad activity. But what if we find other fires? I find it hard to believe that one person can be traveling to different states, causing these fires, and getting away with it."

"*We* got to the lake house within twenty-four hours."

"True, but we couldn't get to all other states in that time." He scratched his nose. "It's a long shot. We don't even know if there are other arson cases out there."

"But if there are?"

"We may be looking at more than one person setting these fires. And possibly, a coordinated group of people."

"Who would want to do such a thing?"

"I'm not sure." He wondered about talking to Tay, since she used to be a profiler. "Maybe I can get some answers that will help us." Their server could be seen halfway to their table, food in hand. "Until then, why don't you email me a copy of those addresses you have. We can both check them out and see what we can find."

"Sounds like a plan."

27

October 14th
6:15 p.m.

Mags woke up to the pinging of her phone alarm. She'd set it for half an hour before her scheduled doctor's appointment, just in case she forgot. She'd managed to squeeze into the last appointment slot available for the day. Rubbing her head, she turned over and silenced the alarm. The doctor's office was only about a ten-minute walk from her apartment, so she had some time to wake up.

Stretching out, she realized she'd fallen asleep on top of her covers. She sniffed, her nose feeling dry. Peering over, she noticed a few droplets of blood once again on her pillow.

A shot of fear spiked through her. This was the second time

there'd been blood on her pillow. Was something really wrong with her?

Mags furrowed her eyebrows. She also realized she couldn't remember how she'd gotten home after leaving Jordan's office. She remembered getting on the bus, but then. . . She guessed she must have fallen asleep and been groggy getting off at her stop and walking home. Perhaps another migraine had hit and she'd taken a pain pill and slumped into bed. Sometimes the pain pills made her dizzy and unable to think straight.

Either way, she was glad she had a doctor's appointment.

Forty-five minutes later Mags sat on the hard, plastic chair in the doctor's office as he scanned her chart. She'd been thoroughly examined and according to him, everything seemed normal so far.

"I am concerned though," he said, "about the nose bleeds and lost time combining with the head pain." He looked up from the computer. "I'd like to schedule you for a CT scan."

Mags gulped. "Really?"

"Unfortunately, these symptoms could be an indication of a bigger problem and the best way to find out for sure is to take some pictures of your brain."

Anxiety spiked through her, causing her hands to tingle and her chest to tighten. "What could it be?" she managed.

His face softened. "A lot of things. But it also could be nothing."

"What *could* it be?" she asked again.

The doctor pursed his lips for a moment. "A blot clot or tumor in your brain. Or excess fluid causing pressure. Nosebleeds do happen sometimes with migraines, but the lost time is what I'm worried about the most. It could also just be a reaction to your pain medication and could indicate you need to try a different kind."

"It's probably just the meds," Mags said, jumping on the least scary option.

The doctor's jaw tightened for a moment. "Could be, but I suggest you get it checked out. The sooner the better."

"When can I schedule the scan?"

"I can put a request through for tomorrow."

Mags' stomach dropped. *That soon?* The anxiety turned into full-blown fear and her breathing came in shallow puffs. "I can do tomorrow," she replied, her voice shaky, thankful she already had requested to take tomorrow off work as well.

"I know this may not help," he said, his eyes soft, "but checking this early is a good thing. If there is a problem, we can get ahead of it. Some people wait months before seeing a doctor. It's good you didn't wait."

She nodded, a buzzing in her ears.

"I'll send the scan request over right away. They should call you tomorrow morning with a time. Until then, try to do something relaxing. Stress may be aggravating your symptoms."

Mags snorted in response. Like she could relax after all this?

Mags left the office several minutes later and walked home, her feet heavy. The sun had already set and the streetlights shone down on her, their yellowish beams like little spotlights between each step in the darkness.

A blood clot. Or tumor. Please *let it just be a problem with the medication,* she prayed. She wasn't sure how much more she could handle. The only spots of joy in the past several days had been Payne waking up and the thought of working with Jordan. One gave her happiness that a man hadn't died because of her and the other a focus which gave her a sense of purpose during all this insanity.

What if there really is something wrong with me? she thought. *Then none of this will matter anyway...*

On the way, her phone rang.

"Hello?" she answered.

"Hello, dear, it's Kathryn."

A sense of dread settled over her chest. *Scott's mom. What now?*

"Oh, yeah, of course. Hi Kathryn."

"Margaret, we've scheduled the funeral for this Friday at two in the afternoon. You don't have to worry about any arrangements, but I do hope you'll come."

"Of course I'll be there."

"Well, with everything that happened between the two of you..."

"We still cared about each other," she insisted, "even if we did break up. I want to be there."

"Wonderful. Well, let us know if you need a ride or if you need anything else before then."

"A ride would be nice. Thank you. I'll give you a call Friday morning."

"Very well. Good night, dear."

"Night, Kathryn." Mags hung up, dragged herself up the few steps into her apartment building, stumbled inside, and fell on the couch. Somewhere in the midst of her sobs she fell asleep.

28

October 15th
9 a.m.

Juliette greeted Wilt and Trann as she walked into the precinct on Tuesday morning, noting that Mags was still absent.

I have to call her and check in, she thought. Guilt nibbled at her. *I'll call at lunch,* she promised herself. Her friend was going through so much and Juliette had allowed work to interfere with their friendship. She really didn't want that. Mags had become such an important person in her life. She needed, no *wanted,* to spend more time with her, especially during her grief.

And yet, she'd spent over four hours at the Interpol office the night before working through the arson files they'd provided, instead of spending time with Mags. By the time she'd left, she had a pretty clear profiling picture of their culprit, or she should say culprits, plural. The timelines and locations proved there had to be more than one person setting these fires.

As for who was setting them, Juliette compiled what she felt proved to be a pretty good profile: angry, vengeful, and non-professional.

"Honestly?" she'd said to Woods the previous evening. "This feels personal. Almost as though this group is punishing the Triad women."

Woods had dragged his hand over his shorn scalp. "That may make sense. Perhaps it *is* personal. For example, if this arson group believes in the Triads and members of said group had been targeted by these women, whether personally themselves or someone they know, they may be seeking revenge."

"But to what end? Why set all these fires? Why draw attention without claiming responsibility? What do they want?"

The two of them didn't have an answer, and when Juliette left, her head swam with ideas, all equally valid and just as equally unprovable. This morning, she had no new theories.

"Morning, Tay," Wilt replied, pulling Juliette from her thoughts. "You ready to question the manager's brother today?"

It took her a few moments to switch gears and realize he was referring to their current jewelry heist case.

"Of course," she said, slapping a grin on her face.

Trann moved over towards them. "Well then, let's go."

"I'll drive," Wilt said, heading towards the back exit where his car sat in the parking lot.

Juliette felt a gentle pull on her elbow and turned to see Trann with a questioning look in his eyes. They fell a few paces behind Wilt.

"What is it?" she asked.

"I have a quick question for you."

"Go for it."

"When you used to profile, did you deal with arsonists?"

A shock like touching an electric eel coursed through Juliette. Why was he asking about arsonists? "Yes," she began slowly, "they were my specialty."

"What do you think would be the reason behind group arson?"

Juliette's eyes flickered back and forth, searching Trann's gaze. He couldn't possibly be talking about the same fires, could he? How could he have found out? Should she let him know about Interpol? Except the case had been deemed classified so she couldn't.

Juliette formed her answer carefully. "Group arson is quite rare. In the few cases I've researched, the group dynamic revolved around a large concept, such as religiously-charged burnings or mob mentality-driven riots."

Trann's eyebrows contracted. "So, most often righteousness or hate-driven with others encouraging violence."

"Yes. And anger. Lots of anger."

"Would perceived injustice be a reason?"

Juliette's body tingled. This was one of the same reasons they'd wondered about in the Interpol meeting last night. "It could be, yes. . .?"

Trann must have heard the questioning in her last statement. He shook his head slightly and smiled. "Thanks."

"What's this all about?" she asked as they made their way

over to Wilt's car.

"Just covering some loose ends on a case," he said.

Juliette didn't fail to note the vagueness of his own response. She didn't want to say any more as they'd just come within earshot of Wilt, but she knew she wanted to talk to Woods about what had just occurred. If Trann was somehow onto the arson cases, he may prove a valuable asset after all.

29

October 15th
9:30 a.m.

Charlotte vaguely remembered the previous night when a hand jostled her awake from the RV's small table and led her back towards the bunks. She'd fallen asleep while poring over the Book translations. The past few days had ruined her normal routine so she'd had a hard time knowing when to sleep. She supposed it would probably be that way until she got to return home.

If she got to return home.

The thought of losing the life she knew invaded her restless slumber, creeping into her dreams. At one point, she'd found herself inside a video game where she had to collect enough "home-shaped" coins to make a house, but tiny ghostlike women kept stealing them just as she was about to grab them so she could never get enough coins to construct a home. She woke up with a start, relieved it had been a dream. Then a sadness stole through her when she realized she wasn't in her own apartment.

The motor home was currently empty and Charlotte relished the minutes she had to herself. Light from the sun lit up the backs of the closed shades, creating opaque windows of a dark orange color. It felt like being inside a carved-out pumpkin.

She got up, brushed her teeth and hair, and changed behind the "bedroom" curtain. Once done, she returned to the table. The translated pages remained where she'd left off, which she felt glad of, considering she'd been putting them into specific piles to keep organized.

Charlotte had to admit, if only to herself, how impressed she'd been at the contents of the Book.

According to the translators and linguists, the Book dated to a time before Sumerian writing, which was considered the first written language. Tests for precise dating had been scheduled for the Book itself, but they had to wait until after the Triad trial, since no one wanted to damage or misplace the evidence. Charlotte had been exceedingly excited to learn more about the Book's contents after she returned from her trip, but when she didn't discover any secret Triads around the world, her enthusiasm about the Book faded as well. On top of that, it had been stolen the day the trial started, so she hadn't given it much thought since.

Now, she had the tome in front of her, with translations of all its secrets. She once again found herself wondering about its origins. Who wrote it and why? The Book itself had been made of some sort of thinly pressed stone and resin pages, so they hadn't worn with age or handling. Though the Book weighed quite a bit, it wasn't much heavier than a normal volume of that size. The cover, bound with leather, ivory, and gold, looked exactly as Charlotte remembered when Truth had shown it to her six months ago in the underground bunker.

While reading the previous day, Charlotte became fascinated by the translated text. The Book predicted several world occurrences with eerie accuracy. It spoke of the over-population of humans, of climate change, of the destruction of natural resources, and, without using the term evolution, it referred to the balance of nature by keeping adaptive traits and eliminating unnecessary ones to keep the balance. It spoke of how humans would stray from their animal tendencies and follow their egotistical ones. How, as the top of the "food chain," they would eventually find the need to create gaps between themselves and other humans to create a new hierarchy in their own world, generating dissension amongst their neighbors, friends, even family.

The Book then spoke about imperfections in humans, which Charlotte knew referred to why women were allowed to kill others. It said that many traits would not be weeded out, in a natural manner. Humans would adapt the world to themselves and not the other way around, eventually making it inhospitable. The only way to keep the equilibrium was to change the dynamic between these traits and the environment.

Feeling a bit overwhelmed, Charlotte had stopped there and taken a short walk through the campground. She stared at the trees, heard the pitter-patter of wildlife before hibernation season arrived, watched the rays of the setting sun streak through the branches and leaves. In her field of study, she never felt like she had much inclination for nature. With her head down while reading her textbooks or pouring over a cadaver, she didn't take time like some of her colleagues did to go camping or skiing or swimming. She enjoyed city life and the hustle and bustle of her busy world.

But here, now, after reading the Book, being forced to slow down, and finding herself stuck in a miserable situation away from everything she loved, her heart ached for the natural world. She sat, back against a trunk, and let herself feel her surroundings. The scratchiness of the bark, the coolness of the ground, and the smell of crisped autumn leaves and dirt beneath her. As a scientist, she was fully aware of climate change and the hole in the ozone layer and pollution. But as someone who is a part of this Earth? She never gave it any thought except to recycle and to use non-chemical products when she could.

She couldn't believe how easily it happened to her without her noticing: being in the world, but not being a part of it.

After her walk, Charlotte returned, feeling ready to read the Messiah sections.

The words scared her.

She truly felt like she was reading about herself.

The three main requirements were:

1) marked across the body from birth, which will fade, as she represents the true beauty that lies underneath imperfection.

Charlotte recalled the strawberry birthmarks she had all over her body, which eventually faded away.

2) Isolated from others as her intellectual superiority and sense of rationality becomes a source of envy.

Charlotte had always felt removed from others because of her intelligence and logical nature.

3) She will be one with death—as comfortable with it as life itself.

Charlotte had always found a sense of purpose and commune while working with cadavers or on cases in the morgue.

To have these words written in a book from six thousand years ago. . .

This can be anyone, she'd thought. *Truth even said they'd searched and believed they'd found other Messiahs in the past. Those women must have also fit the parameters.*

But Charlotte had questioned Isabella last night, asking about any previous Messiahs.

"I don't have the information on all of them," Isabella had said. "The last one I heard of was about seventy-five years ago. Somewhere in China, I think."

"What happened to her?"

"She didn't complete the required tasks."

Charlotte perked up at this. "*What* required tasks?"

Isabella shrugged. "To be honest? I never really put that much stock in the whole 'Messiah' thing when I was part of my Triad, so I didn't really pay much attention to that part of the Book. When Truth revealed you, I researched the parameters, not the tasks. I'm sure they're in there somewhere."

"They better be," Charlotte said. "If I am pretending to be this Messiah, then many of these Triad women will expect me to fulfill these tasks. What if I cannot?"

Isabella had chewed her lip. "Um. . .I didn't think about that. You're right. Guess we better find them."

They'd then worked for several hours, flipping through more than two hundred pages of translations, but eventually Isabella called it a night and shortly afterwards, Charlotte had fallen asleep at the table.

Carla must have been the one to lead me to bed, Charlotte realized. The thought bothered her. She couldn't find any fault with Carla, but the two of them. . .didn't exactly mix well.

Charlotte pulled herself back to the present. She needed to find out about the tasks. . .

Half an hour later, with no success, the door to the camper opened and Carla entered.

"Hello," Charlotte said.

"*Buenos días,*" Carla answered. "How are you today?"

Charlotte could feel the stiffness in Carla's words, but had a feeling the woman was trying. She found it interesting that she could be a psychologist and yet be so standoffish with Charlotte.

"I slept, though not well."

"That seems to be a pattern for you lately."

"My mind is otherwise occupied."

"I bet." Carla sat across from her. "How's all this going?" she asked, gesturing to the pages on the table.

"Slowly. Have you read any of this?"

"Oh yeah. Front to back. Well, the translated version I had where I used to live."

"Really?" Charlotte straightened. "Do you remember anything about the tasks a Messiah must perform?"

"Of course."

Charlotte let out a short laugh.

"What's so funny?"

"I never thought to ask you. I mean, you did not arrive last night until late. I asked Isabella and she said she did not know. I assumed. . ." Charlotte paused.

"You assumed that because I chose to kill I would not have cared what was in the Book?"

That had been the crux of everything. Isabella had coordinated kills and Jordan helped discover Triad agents, but Carla actually murdered them. And wanted to, from the beginning. Charlotte had made the assumption that those choices made Carla a cold-blooded killer, someone who just wanted to kill for sport and not care about the reason behind it.

Charlotte let out a sigh. "I assumed wrong."

Carla shrugged, but Charlotte could see her shoulders relax.

"So, the tasks?" Charlotte prompted.

"Well, they are pretty straightforward. I mean, you already pass the requirements to *be* the Messiah and of course, you didn't die."

Charlotte cleared her throat as her hand automatically went to the right side of her chest. "Right."

"The tasks are basically the following," Carla said, ticking the points off on her fingers. "A—you must accept your role as the Messiah to all Triad members, B—you must guide all other Triads to a new path and C—you must meet every Triad member individually."

Charlotte coughed. "Wh-what?" she stuttered. "That final item cannot be correct. That would be impossible."

"I'm hoping that an internet video connection with everyone personally will cover that final task. Until the introduction of the internet, which split us into factions to begin with, we couldn't have a Messiah. But now, because you can have each person actually see you, you fit the task."

"That is a *big* gamble."

"Maybe. But the timing makes sense. 'Humans will divide through communication. They will become closer and further apart at the same time. This will also divide the Triads, but from this division, the Messiah will unite us.'"

Charlotte gawked at her. "What are you talking about?"

"It's at the end of the Book," Carla said, "about how the Messiah will come to be. It's how I knew it was you."

The words took a few moments to sink in. "Wait. . .*you* think I am the Messiah?"

"Of course."

No words came to her. The woman who'd stayed distant, who'd pushed back at Charlotte, who'd challenged her readiness, thought she *was* the Messiah?

Carla reached over to the bowl of grapes on the table and popped a few into her mouth.

"Can you. . ." Charlotte began, suddenly feeling timid. "Can you show me where that section is?"

"Sure."

Together, the two of them found all the passages pertaining to the Messiah. By the end of their chat, Charlotte's stomach grumbled. She hadn't eaten anything all day.

"We should take a break," Carla said.

Charlotte wanted to refuse, but when she leaned away from the table, the muscles in her shoulders and back protested from their continuous hunched-over position.

"Good idea," Charlotte concluded.

Suddenly, the door to the RV flew open and Isabella charged in. "We gotta go, now!" she exclaimed.

"What happened?" Carla asked as Isabella readied the vehicle to leave.

"Jordan got the list of addresses. She discovered something about her contact that may have compromised everything."

"Where are we going?" Charlotte called out, oblivious to the reason they were leaving, but fully feeling the fear and tension in the air.

"To the next campground," Isabella replied. "Although only for one night this time. We'll have to stay on the move from now on until we figure out what this means."

Charlotte caught Carla frowning. "What is it?" Charlotte asked her.

Carla replied, "It's just that Jordan said she trusted this contact, enough to suggest bringing her into our group. What could she have possibly discovered to change her mind?"

Isabella called out over her shoulder as she drove out of the campground. "She's going to contact us later and let us know. She just suggested we stay on the move and don't call her. She doesn't know if she's safe."

30

October 15th
10 a.m.

Mags laid flat on her back, dressed in a white papery gown, with soft, white booties on her feet. Headphones rested over her ears playing soft classical music.

Terror flooded through her. She was about to get a CT scan, to find out what might be wrong with her head.

Staring up at the dimly lit ceiling, she heard a disembodied voice call out to her through the headphones: "*We are going to move you into the machine now. Do your best to stay as still as possible while we take the photos. I can hear you speak so if you have any problems, just let me know. I will tell you before we take each set of pictures.*"

Mags nodded, then remembered she was supposed to stay still, so she said "Okay" instead. The conveyer belt she lay on moved automatically forward until the white, rounded machine enclosed her. If she rolled her eyes upward, she could just make out the wall behind her. A breath of relief escaped her. At least she wasn't completely closed in.

With her arms pinned to her sides and the top of the machine about five inches from her face, she mentally thanked the stars above that she didn't suffer from claustrophobia. Being in this white, plastic tunnel was hard enough with the anxiety shooting randomly through her body about the test results to come, but to add in a fear of small spaces? She wondered how people did it.

The voice came through again. *"Okay. Going to do the first set of pictures now. You'll hear a clanking metal noise. When it's done, that set of pictures is over."*

"How many sets of pictures will there be?"

"About twenty."

"Okay. I'm ready."

Mags closed her eyes and tried to focus on the soothing music when she heard the clanking around her head. It reminded her a bit of a train and she recalled the one she and Charlotte had taken when leaving Paris. The thought soothed her and she did her best to focus on it, but as the time passed by, so did her thoughts. They settled on the reason *why* they'd been in Europe—not for a vacation as one might imagine, but trying instead to locate invisible and unfindable Triads.

Mags had given up on the idea that other Triads existed well before Charlotte did. Even though they had 60 addresses to search, Mags had given up around the 10th. Still, she plodded forward with Charlotte and they finished the entire 60, with nothing to be found. Not until then did they return to Boston.

How ironic, she thought, *that I accepted there were no Triads and now I'm investigating that other Triads could exist.* She wondered how Charlotte would feel about the investigation. Probably pretty upset. But maybe she'd be glad? She had been pretty determined to discover the existence of other Triads.

Well if I find anything, then maybe I'll share it with her. Although, I wouldn't want to put her in danger, either...

Mags' mind drifted to the list of addresses she'd procured from the precinct. It hadn't been hard to get—she had access to precinct material anyway since they often had her work on email tracing and other IT evidence-related cases—and afterwards she sent an email copy of the list over to Jordan that same morning. Hopefully, between the two of them, they could break this "code" and actually find alternate Triad locations.

A buzzing initiated in Mags' head. She resisted the urge to scrunch up her face. The clanging sounds stopped, and the buzzing shortly after.

"Round one of pictures is complete. They turned out well. There will be fifteen seconds until the next round."

Mags let out a sigh and twitched her nose a bit. She glanced upwards again to view the tunnel opening. Her mind wandered over to the idea of the Triads in general. She couldn't imagine how someone would *want* to join such a group, and yet, people joined cults all the time. Still, there must be a pattern to the women chosen.

"Next set is starting shortly. Please stay as still as you can."

As soon as the clanging started, the buzzing began again. There wasn't pain; it felt more like she stood near a bees nest.

"Second round is done. Looks good. Going into round three in twenty seconds."

After this interruption, she continued to wonder about the Triads. The first and second positions she could almost understand, but the third? Giving up most of your life just so you could kill? She couldn't fathom being given the option of living in an alternate life, only to "awaken" as yourself once a month to murder a person. Who would ever choose that sort of existence?

"Third round starting." The clanging began. This time she could *feel* the buzzing. Her whole head felt like it was vibrating.

Is this normal? she thought.

"Third round is done. You're doing great. Next round starting soon."

Her teeth felt achy and her body on edge. When the fourth round started, she could *sense* her skin vibrating. She opened her mouth to say something when a flash of an image passed before her eyes, almost like a strange dream she was remembering.

The image appeared and disappeared very quickly, but she saw it with complete clarity: she was arguing with Scott outside the Lolita Back Bay restaurant in the alley. She could tell the location because they'd waited near that same alley to get into the place several times in the past.

"Fourth round done. Pictures look great. Fifth round starting soon."

Mags wanted to shake her head. Why was she remembering a time with Scott right now? She hadn't even been thinking about. . .

The fifth round began and Mags' whole body arced inside the machine.

"Holy shit!" she heard the voice through the headphones. The clanging metal stopped as the machine shut down. The music stopped. Mags could hear the voice in her ears.

"Are you okay? Miss, can you hear me?"

Mags blinked several times. "Yes," she answered. Her mouth tasted like pennies. She also felt a slight pain there as well and realized she must have bitten her tongue.

"I'm going to pull you out of there," the voice said. The conveyer belt began to move, shifting Mags out of the white tunnel, and back under the dimmed lights. They brightened and the assistant rushed in, telling her to sit up slowly.

Mags obeyed, half listening to the assistant's questions: can you move your feet and hands, do you have any pain, do you have any metal on you, do you have a history of seizures, etc.? Mags diligently answered all the questions, but her focus was on nothing in this room.

She couldn't stop thinking about the images that had just flashed through her mind during this last round of pictures.

She'd been standing in the alley again, arguing with Scott. He said something accusatory, his face twisted in anger. A rage overtook her, unlike anything she'd ever felt before. When he turned his back to her, she retrieved a knife from her pocket, and called out his name. He swiveled back around.

She then plunged the knife into his stomach.

Mags grasped her hands together to keep them from shaking. Her thoughts fluttered, calculating different options. Why did she have this memory if she didn't remember doing it? Why did it feel so real, the fury, the motion of stabbing Scott?

"Do you want to continue with the scan?" the assistant asked.

"No," she whispered. *It couldn't be.* Realization hit her. "I don't need a machine to tell me what's wrong with me."

Without another word to anyone, Mags left the room, got dressed, and fled from the hospital.

31

October 15th
4 p.m.

"See you later, Tay," Sean called out. She gave a wave as she left the precinct early, saying she had a doctor's appointment, and then planned to spend some time with Mags. Sean himself felt antsy to leave as well, seeing as how he'd arranged to meet up with Elaine again after work. They'd both tackled the address list and two of the places were located in Keene, New Hampshire, which was only about a two-hour drive with traffic. They'd planned to check out the locations, ask around, find out about details with the local precincts, and follow-up on both site changes in those areas and compare them to suspicious cases.

Sean flipped his phone over in his hand, watching the clock

on the wall as the minutes ticked by. The notion of talking to Charlotte flitted through his mind. He missed her. He wanted to discuss all of this, even though he knew it would be best not to. Hopefully she was getting good rest and they'd be able to spend some time together that weekend.

Sean's attention then switched over to Millan's office, whose door was once more closed. He'd arrived late again, but seemed less depressed than the previous morning. When Sean had entered his office and approached to say hello, Millan blurted out that his wife agreed to come over that evening to talk. Sean had wished him luck and really meant it. The guy deserved a break, although he still wished his sarge didn't have to retire to *get* that break.

Mulling over paperwork to use up the rest of his time, Sean at least felt pleased with their current case. The jewelry heist appeared to be a simple team fight-gone-wrong scenario. It had been performed by three people, according to the store's cameras, with one of the perpetrators killing the manager. However, this morning, one of the thieves, Randy, showed up at the precinct, asking for protection.

Randy told Sean there had been a huge argument over how to split the money and jewelry the night before, that the man who'd killed the manager had demanded a higher cut, since he needed to flee the country faster. The other refused and they'd fought. The killer murdered the other thief, then turned on Randy. Randy escaped and stayed at a friend's for the night. Before he got all the way home the next morning, he saw the killer sitting in a car in front of his apartment building, waiting. Fearing for his life, Randy went through the alley behind his place and came to the police for help.

So far, Randy hadn't ratted out the killer, but Sean knew it would only be a matter of time. They'd offered leniency if Randy gave up the information. A few nights in a holding cell for someone who'd never done any time would make him rethink how long he wanted to be in jail. Sean only hoped the killer wouldn't bolt before they could find out his name.

Finally, the clock ticked over, and Sean collected his things to leave for the evening. As he walked out of his office, he saw one of the other officers searching around the bullpen for someone. Sean recognized him as a new recruit who worked evenings, but couldn't place his name.

"Can I help you?" Sean asked.

The young man replied in a thick Boston accent. "Yeah. I'm looking for Detective Tay. Is she around?"

"She left for the day. Can I give her a message?"

"Sure. It's about that case from the weekend, about the mugging and murder of Scott Hamtion. Tay seemed wicked interested, so I thought I'd update her."

Sean perked up. "Oh yeah. I know she was following up on that case because our receptionist knows the vic."

"I know. Mags has stayed late a lot of days. I don't know her too well, but everyone seems to like her a lot around here."

Sean smiled.

The officer continued. "Anyway, I got the blood test results in and thought I'd pass them along to Tay."

Sean nodded towards her desk. "You can leave them there, in her inbox. I'm sure she'll be glad to see them first thing in the morning."

"Thanks." He strode over and plopped down the file. "Have a good night, Detective."

"You too, Officer."

The young man left and Sean shrugged into his jacket. He took two steps towards the door and paused. The file called to him. It wasn't exactly private, as the results were available to any detective, so he could *glance* at them, right? Besides, then he could call Tay right away if there were any significant findings and she could tell Mags tonight they had a lead instead of waiting for tomorrow. Sean knew if it were him, he'd want to be told everything possible right away if he knew the victim.

Sean moved towards Tay's desk and picked up the folder, thumbing through it. He read over the basics, which included the location of the homicide and victim's identification. A sense of strangeness washed over him when reading Scott's name. He still couldn't believe he and Mags had split, much less that he'd died. It fascinated Sean to see and work with these people every day and still know so little about them, especially as a detective.

Murmuring a little out loud while he read, he skimmed down to the forensics report.

Sean's heart skipped a beat.

"What?" he said out loud. He reread the words. There had been two blood samples recovered from the scene: one belonged to Scott himself and the other to a Margaret Stinson.

Mags' full name was Margaret Stinson.

"Why was her blood there?" he muttered. He flipped through the rest of the papers, but no other strange evidence showed up. Knife wound to the stomach, body left in the alley, no signs of struggle. No murder weapon. Nothing else found at the scene.

Sean wracked his brain for a reason why Mags' blood would have been on Scott's face, but he couldn't do anything except draw a blank.

A hollowness sucked at his soul. *This can't be happening,* he thought. *She can't have had anything to do with this.* And yet the detective part of him kicked in without his consent. The two of them had just broken up. Perhaps they went out to talk and things got out of hand. Maybe Mags followed Scott and saw him already with another woman. Maybe they'd both been attacked by the same mugger and she didn't report it for some reason. Each theory blew in and out on the thought that Mags could be involved in any way with a murder.

A hand fell on his shoulder and Sean jumped.

"Whoa! Didn't mean to scare you," Wilt said.

"Oh, uh, yeah," Sean said, closing the folder. "No problem, man."

"Done for the day?"

Sean ran a shaky hand through his hair. "Yeah, I'm just heading out."

"Taking some work home with you?" Wilt asked, gesturing to the file.

"What? Oh yeah, yeah. Something I gotta follow up on."

"Well don't work too hard. It's tough enough without Mags here and with Millan late all the time and now Tay leaving early. Feels like everyone's outside life is taking over."

Sean swallowed, hard. "Yeah. Don't worry, this won't take long. I just don't want to leave it until tomorrow."

"All right. Have a good night, Trann."

"You too, Wilt." Sean walked past him, the folder gripped tightly in his hand. As soon as he reached his car in the lot, he pulled out his cell to call Mags.

But then he paused. What was he going to say? Since the results just came in, had anyone reached out to her for questioning? Should he? Should he even be calling her at all and asking about it? Would that be against protocol?

The information he held felt like an armed bomb. He couldn't let Mags know he knew about her blood. He had to question her first, see if he could find an explanation.

I'm sure there is a perfectly good reason, he said without any real conviction. He knew internally he *hoped* there'd be an innocent clarification more than he believed there would be. He slid over to Wilt's number instead and called him.

"Hey, Trann, what's going on?"

"You still at the precinct?"

"Yeah, I'm just heading out to the parking lot. Why? Did you forget something?"

"I'll meet you at the door. I need your help with something." Sean hung up, exited his Jag, and jogged over to the exit just as Wilt came out. A chill bit into him and he snatched his jacket closed with his free hand.

"What do you need?" Wilt asked.

"I need someone else's eyes on what I just read. I got the file on Mags' ex-fiancé's case."

"About his mugging?"

Sean nodded. "I want to talk to Mags about it, since we know she saw him earlier that night."

Wilt frowned. "Didn't she already give her statement?"

"Yeah," he said, gripping the folder a bit tighter.

"What am I missing?"

Sean cleared his throat. He knew as soon as he said the words it would make the situation real. "They found Mags' blood at the scene."

Wilt blinked several times before speaking. "What?"

Sean handed over the file. "It was on Scott's face in the alley."

Wilt paged through the documents, the light shining down from the flood lamp above the door. "That can't be right. There's no way."

"You know we put her identification info on file after she started working for us. Fingerprints, DNA, the works. There's no mistake."

Wilt's face fell. "But how? Why? Was she there in that alley? Tay said Mags and Scott had a fight and he left. Did Mags follow him?"

"I don't know, man. I'm as freaked out as you are right now. But we should go question her. I want you there as backup." Sean motioned towards his car. "We can take mine."

"Good. I don't know if I want to drive right now."

The two of them climbed inside and left the lot, heading towards Mags' apartment. Sean stayed quiet while Wilt turned on his phone's flashlight and read over the paperwork. After several minutes, Wilt leaned backwards.

"This can't be real."

"There are a lot of reasons why he could have had her blood on him."

"Really?" Wilt retorted. "You know as well as I do that blood at any crime scene that isn't the victim's does not bode well."

Sean clenched his jaw. "I know."

"What the hell are we going to say to her?"

"We will ask her to go over her statement again and then ask why her blood was on his face."

"What if she doesn't have an answer?"

Sean shook his head, taking a right turn at the lights in front of him. "I don't know. She's not a suspect, not officially. We don't have any other evidence that she was there in that alley. There is nothing that connects her to the crime specifically."

They remained quiet for several more minutes until Sean pulled onto her street.

Wilt said softly, "Do you think she could have killed him?"

Sean remained silent. He didn't trust himself to say no, but couldn't bring himself to say he wasn't sure.

With quick motions, Sean parallel-parked outside her apartment. He remembered coming here once to drop off her purse she'd accidentally left at work. Since she took the bus, he'd offered to swing by on his way home. He hadn't planned to go in, but when she'd opened the door the smell of her infamous coffee hit his nose and he couldn't help himself. Though he only stayed for about an hour, he remembered noticing the funky colored throw pillows and beaded curtain separating the living room from the dining area. Mags' sense of style had not been limited to her unique wardrobe.

Dragging himself from the happy memory, he and Wilt got out of the car and walked over to her door.

"This is the worst," Wilt muttered.

"Yeah. . ." Sean rang the buzzer.

No answer.

He rang it again.

No response.

"Maybe she's not home?" Sean couldn't help but notice the uptick of hope in Wilt's voice, that if she wasn't there, they wouldn't have to question her.

"I'll call her and see where she is." He pulled out his cell and made the call. It went straight to voicemail. He didn't know what to say so he hung up.

"What about Tay?" Wilt asked. "Didn't she say she was leaving early to spend some time with Mags after her doctor's appointment?"

"Oh yeah. Hold on." Sean switched over to Tay's number and dialed it.

Tay answered after the second ring. "Hey, Trann."

"Hey, Tay. Listen, are you with Mags?"

"Yeah. Why?"

He gave a knowing nod to Wilt. "Where are you?"

"At the Beacon Inn. She was visiting with Scott's parents and then decided to stay the night at the hotel. Said she didn't feel like going back home. She had a bad day today."

Tension spiked through him. "Why? What happened?"

"She went in for a CAT scan and it went wrong. Bloody thing made her all shaky."

Sean frowned, not expecting that answer. "Is she all right?"

"She's still pretty shaken up. We were about to grab a bite to eat. Why? What's going on?"

Sean glanced over at Wilt. "Uh, Wilt and I need to see her. Can we meet you at the hotel?"

A moment of silence. "Trann, what's going on." It came out

as more of a demand than a question.

"Can she hear me?"

"No."

"Okay, look. Don't react, all right?"

A pause. "All right."

We got back the results from the blood tests done on Scott. You know, her ex?"

"Of course, I know. What did it say?"

"Promise you won't let her see you react to this."

Another moment. "Okay," Tay said, her voice neutral.

"It's Mags' blood."

A longer pause. "I see."

"We need to come talk to her. Officially."

"I understand. Not a problem."

Sean could hear the slight quaver in Tay's voice. He knew she understood the ramifications of what he'd just revealed. "Can you keep her from leaving? We can be there in about thirty minutes."

"Of course."

"All right. Sit tight." Sean hung up and he and Wilt got back into the car as Sean filled Wilt in on what had happened.

"I can't believe this," Wilt said.

"Me neither," Sean replied as he made the turn west towards the Beacon Inn.

32

October 15th
5:15 p.m.

Juliette hung up her phone and disconnected the call from Sean. A heaviness, like a bowling ball, dropped into her gut.

"Everything okay?" Mags asked from across the hotel room.

"I'm not sure," Juliette mumbled, staring over at her friend. The room, with its leaf-patterned wall paper, beautifully carved wooden furniture, and faux fireplace suddenly seemed a lot smaller. "I'm not feeling very well all of a sudden." Juliette definitely felt ill, but not because of some virus or bacteria. She could very well be staring at the face of a killer.

They'd gotten so close over the past six months, ever since they'd both been abducted by a Triad group. They'd spent time together, shared thoughts and feelings about their lives to one another. Bloody hell, they were about to be flatmates in two weeks! But now the woman sitting on the king-sized hotel bed appeared more like a stranger than a friend.

Get a hold of yourself, Juliette thought. *You know Mags. She isn't a murderer.* But Juliette knew that when she'd originally asked for the results from the blood work on Scott's case, she had a feeling it had been the killer's blood on his face. Could she push that notion aside just because she knew the possible perpetrator?

Mags frowned. "What's wrong? Stomach?"

Juliette swallowed hard. "Yes. I feel a bit nauseous."

Mags crossed her legs. "Oh no. Do you still want to go out to eat?"

"I think we should wait a little bit. I'm sure it's nothing major."

"No problem." Mags scooted backwards on the bed, leaning against the pillows and headrest.

Juliette stood ramrod straight next to the table between the bathroom and the front door, not moving. She knew she needed to act casual, but she couldn't bring herself to relax. There had to be an explanation for Mags' blood being on Scott's face. There *had* to be. This couldn't be happening. This couldn't be real.

"What do you want to do while we wait?" Mags asked. She grabbed and shook the remote. "We could watch a little TV."

Juliette nodded, then shook her head. The clock next to the bed clicked over. Still twenty-five minutes until Trann and Wilt showed up. Whether her own curiosity or her detective instinct, she couldn't wait to find out the truth. She needed to hear it from her friend. "Mags, can I ask you something? About the night

Scott died?"

Mags' face paled. "I guess. What is it?"

"Why do you think he went to that restaurant if it was a favorite of yours and his?"

Mags shrugged. "I must have asked myself that same question a hundred times. I know *I* don't feel like I could ever go there again, not without him. It was *our* place. But maybe he felt nostalgic or he was just hungry and was driving by. . .I don't know,"

"You didn't know he'd gone there though, right? He didn't tell you he was going there?"

"No. I didn't find out until you told me that's where the police found him."

"So. . .you didn't follow him there?"

Mags' eyebrows furrowed. "Of course not."

"You said you fought, though, at the apartment. Did it get physical?"

"No. Jewels, I told you this already. We only argued." She paused. "Why do I feel like you're interrogating me?"

Juliette bit the inside of her lip to focus herself on the pain, keep her composure. She needed to relax and wait for the two other detectives to show up. "Sorry. Just. . .some things don't add up. Thought I'd ask."

The clock ticked by another minute. Juliette could feel the prickling of perspiration under her arms. She felt so helpless, just waiting. Usually at a scene she felt in control. Questioning someone, whether a witness or possible suspect, always brought her closer to closure on a case. But this? Could her friend really have murdered her own fiancé, ex or not?

"Well maybe we can just get some food delivered. I think I saw some brochures on the table next to you." Mags stood, coming closer. Juliette couldn't stop herself and took a step back.

Mags froze. "What's going on? Why are you acting this way? Are you scared of me?"

Juliette glanced again at the clock on the nightstand. Trann and Wilt still wouldn't arrive for another twenty minutes or so. "Of course not," Juliette lied.

"Why did you back away?"

"Did I?" Why had she? She couldn't believe her friend would hurt her, could she? And yet she remembered how Mags had killed the woman in the bunker. Granted, it had been self-defense, but she *had* killed someone.

Mags' face tightened and she walked towards Juliette again, who automatically took another step back.

"You just did it again. What is going on?" Mags demanded, her hands on her hips.

Juliette held up her hands in a defensive manner. "Look, just stay calm. I'll explain everything."

Mags tapped her foot and crossed her arms. "I'm waiting."

She's your friend! Juliette thought to herself. *What if it were you? Talk to her like a friend.* "The truth is, we found out something about Scott's case. It doesn't look good for you. I promise I'm on your side, I just need to know what really happened."

Mags dropped her arms. "I *told* you what really happened. Why do you suddenly not believe me?"

Juliette took a deep breath. "They found your blood. At the scene. On Scott's face. Three droplets."

Mags stood there, completely silent. Juliette couldn't read

anything on her face.

"Mags?" Juliette asked softly.

Mags slowly lifted her hand to her own face, mumbling softly, and motioned as if wiping her nose.

"Mags?" Juliette asked again. "Are you okay?"

Mags sunk down onto the bed, her face ashen. "I'm afraid."

Juliette's heart went out to her friend. "Whatever happened, it's better if you tell me, so I can help."

"I saw flashes."

Juliette didn't understand. "Like lightning?"

"No. Memories. While in the CT scanner this morning. I saw flashes of Scott dying."

"What do you mean?"

Mags looked up, tears rimming her eyes, magnified behind her glasses. "I think I killed him."

Juliette sucked in a sharp breath. "What?"

"I saw it. I saw myself put the knife into his belly."

Holy shit, Juliette thought. *She's confessing!*

"But it wasn't me." A pleading tone saturated her words. "Jewels, I *swear*, it wasn't me."

"I don't understand what you're saying. Did you kill him or not?"

Mags' words came quick and clipped. "I think I did, but I don't think it was me. I don't remember doing it. Everything I told you about the argument with Scott at the apartment and the migraine after he left were true." She winced, whether from current cranial pain or remembered pain, Juliette couldn't tell.

Mags' words then came faster and faster as she spoke. "I'd been so upset and stressed from the breakup and the attack and

Payne in a coma, I could barely think straight. My head started hurting, really bad, and I went to the bathroom to get a pain pill. Next thing I knew I woke up in bed, blood on my pillow. My nose had been bleeding. I thought it was from the migraine. That's why I decided to set up an appointment with my doctor. But what if the blood got on Scott? What if those drops were from my bloody nose except I don't remember anything, I swear to GOD I don't remember!" Her voice had grown to a fevered pitch.

"It's okay," Juliette said, motioning with her hands to calm Mags down. "Just keep going. What else happened?"

Her words came so quickly they almost blurred together, as if she wanted to get them out of her as fast as possible. "During the scan I heard buzzing and then felt my body shaking. It was at that moment I saw flashes of killing him and I think maybe I did it but it wasn't me, it couldn't have been me, but I know I've been losing time during these migraines and oh God, Jewels, what if it was me but I just don't remember?" Mags gripped the blanket underneath her, knuckles white.

Juliette's mind spun with thoughts, all battling with each other to gain traction as her main focus, but she couldn't settle on any one notion. Instead, she focused on getting the situation under control. "Mags, take a deep breath. I'm here. I'm not going anywhere. I'm going to help you through this. We will figure it out, no problem. I promise."

Mags rolled her eyes and wiped the streaks of tears from her cheeks. "Help me how? Scott and I argued. I saw flashes of memory, of me stabbing him. My blood was on him. Isn't it obvious I killed him?"

"But why, Mags?" Juliette now moved closer, taking a seat at the small table. "Just because you argued? It doesn't make any sense. There isn't a mean bone in your body."

Mags returned her focus to Juliette. She looked terrified, with wide eyes and trembling lips. "Jewels, what if I'm not real?" she whispered.

Juliette didn't understand. "What? What does that mean?"

"What if I was. . .created? What if I'm just a personality construct? What if they made *me* to cover *her*?"

"I don't. . ." Juliette started, but then the realization sunk in. "You're talking about the Triads."

Mags nodded as she clasped her shaking hands together.

"That's impossible. The Triads are gone." Juliette said the words, but she knew them to be untrue. Her current work with Interpol showed that. However, she also didn't want Mags to panic anymore. It couldn't really be possible, could it? Could Mags somehow be a Triad agent and she didn't know?

Mags winced again and rubbed her forehead. "I don't think it's as impossible as you say. I've been looking into the Triads, with an outside. . .source. We think they may be real. I didn't want to tell you because it sounds crazy and we were just starting to put together proof. But I think they *are* real and Jewels, what if I'm one of them?"

"You're not," she said emphatically. But her mind started to whirl again. Mags had been looking into Triads, too? And who was this "outside source?" Could it be Trann? Is that why he'd asked her about the profile of arsonists?

"Well if I'm not someone they made me be, then I'm a killer all by myself." A batch of tears erupted from Mags and she put both hands up to her head. "I have to take a pain pill," she mumbled, and rushed to the bathroom, slamming the door behind her.

Juliette could hear her sobs and the shaking of pills inside the bottle through the door. Her heart broke, but what was she supposed to do with this situation? It was preposterous! Mags couldn't be a killer. She couldn't! And yet everything pointed to the fact she was. *It doesn't have to be a Triad,* she thought. *Maybe Mags just had a mental breakdown and a split personality arose?*

Was that any better of an outcome?

Tears stung her own eyes as she listened to the hiccupped sobs continue from the bathroom. She was glad Trann and Wilt were on their way. She didn't want to deal with this anymore on her own.

Juliette heard the crying in the bathroom stop. She guessed Mags had gotten herself under control.

"Mags?" Juliette called out, tentative. "You okay in there?" The words sounded empty, but she didn't know what else to say.

"I'm fine," she heard Mags reply. The doorknob to the bathroom jiggled. "The door is stuck. Can you help me open it?"

"Sure. Hold on." Juliette rose and moved to the door. She gripped the handle and tried to turn it, but it didn't move. "It's unlocked, right?"

"Yes."

"Okay, stand back. I'm going to try to push it with my shoulder."

"All right."

"Count of three. One. . .two—"

The door flung open with Juliette still holding onto the handle. She found herself pulled into the bathroom, off balance.

Before she could say anything, she felt pain rip across her throat. Letting go of the knob, she clung to her neck, feeling the hot wetness of blood spurt through her fingers. Her momentum continued and she fell, stumbling into the toilet, falling over it, and knocking her head against the edge of the tub. White spots danced before her eyes. She blinked and coughed, the feeling shooting new pain through her throat.

Turning her head, she saw Mags standing above her, fingers bloody, holding what appeared to be the cartridge to a razor blade.

Juliette tried to say Mags' name, but she couldn't speak. Her head swum. The lights dimmed in and out.

The last thing Juliette remembered was the look on Mags' face. Cold. Haunted. Full of rage.

That's not Mags, she thought before oblivion took her.

33

October 15th
5:30 p.m.

Sean flashed his badge at the bed and breakfast's front desk. "I need the room number for a Mags Stinton."

The owner's eyes widened before she nodded vigorously. "Of course. One moment." She typed on her computer, the keystrokes loud in Sean's ears. The car ride had been eerily silent as both men kept quiet. Sean figured Wilt felt the same way: surreal.

"She's in room fifteen," the owner said. "Third floor, to the right."

"Thank you."

"Is something wrong? Do I need to alert the other patrons?"

"No, ma'am. We just need to speak with her."

The woman behind the desk visibly sagged with relief.

Polished wood, flower-patterned wallpaper, and big throw rugs covered the lobby. The room smelled of something sweet Sean couldn't place. Sean, with Wilt closely behind, raced up the carpeted wooden staircase to the third floor, taking the steps two at a time. They approached the correct room. Sean heard Wilt let out a deep exhale.

Sean knocked. "It's us," he called out.

No response.

Sean knocked again, this time louder.

Still nothing.

"Maybe Juliette couldn't stop her from wanting to go out?" Wilt suggested.

Sean pulled out his phone. "I'll call and see where they are." Sean dialed Tay's number. Shortly after he heard it ring through his speaker, they heard a phone trilling inside the room. Both men looked at each other.

Sean pounded on the door. "Tay! You in there?"

Only the final rings of a phone answered through the door before it went to voicemail on Sean's end and became silent.

"I've got a bad feeling," Wilt said.

A rock formed in Sean's gut. "Me too. We gotta get in there."

"I'll run back down to the desk and get a key." Wilt bolted down the hallway to the stairs. Sean continued to bang on the door. A middle-aged couple in the room next door popped their heads out.

"Is everything okay?" the woman asked.

Sean flashed his badge. "Yes. Please, if you'll both just stay in your rooms—"

But the woman stepped out towards Sean and interrupted him. "That's Margaret's room. Is she all right?"

"You know Mags?"

The woman nodded. "She's my daughter-in-law. Well, almost."

Scott's parents, he thought. He remembered now that Tay had told him they were staying in this place until the funeral. "My name is Detective Trann. I'm trying to speak with Mags. Do you have a key to the room?"

The woman shook her head.

Sean heard the breathy run of Wilt from down the hall as he sprinted forward, the owner close behind. He waved the key and Sean stepped out of the way.

"Oh my God," Scott's mother said. "Is Margaret okay?"

"Please, ma'am, step back," Sean ordered. The woman took a few tentative steps towards her room, but craned her neck to keep viewing the action. Her husband came from behind her, placing a hand on her shoulder.

Wilt unlocked the door and burst inside, with Sean on his heels. At first glance, everything seemed in order. A woman's purse sat on the small table just inside the door with a coat hanging over the back of a chair. Just past the table, Sean noted a closed door, which he assumed must be the bathroom. He then noticed the wide-open window near the head of the bed across the room. Frilly curtains fluttered in the night breeze.

"I'll get the window," Sean said.

"I'll take the bathroom," Wilt said at the same time.

Sean bolted across the space and peered outside. He couldn't see anyone running below. He did note a smear of blood on the

windowsill, as if someone had placed a hand there to boost themselves over the edge.

Sean heard an animalistic cry of rage from behind him. He
whipped his head around and raced to the bathroom. The
woman and her husband stuck their heads inside the room.

"Out!" Sean yelled at them, and they pulled back. He
slammed the main door then peered into the bathroom.

The scene would be forever burned into his mind.

Wilt had dragged Tay's body to the middle of the floor, his
hands pressed against her chest, counting under his breath. Blood
still seeped a little from the slash on her throat, though much of
it had caked across her neck and shirt. A smeared blood stain ran
from the edge of the tub, across the floor, to the back of her head.
Her eyes stared, unblinking, at the ceiling.

Sean closed his own eyes for a moment, forcing himself to
regroup. He then opened them, pulled out his cell, and called for
an ambulance, reporting an "officer down."

"It's on its way," the 911 operator told him. "Tell him to
continue CPR."

Sean hung up. He opened the front door. All three people
still stood there. He addressed the owner. "An ambulance will be
here soon. Please direct them to this room."

The young woman took off, her beige flats silent across the
carpeted hallway. Scott's mother let out a howl.

"MARGARET!" she cried out, trying to bulldoze her way
past Sean in the doorway.

Sean held her steady. "Ma'am, calm down. It's not Mags.
Mags isn't in the room." He turned towards Scott's father.
"Please, take her to your room and stay there. I'll have some

questions for you shortly." The man nodded and Sean closed the door in their faces. He reentered the small bathroom, pulled a towel from the rack, and pressed it against Tay's neck to put pressure on the wound. Her skin felt clammy and she didn't respond to his touch.

"They're coming," Sean told Wilt. "The ambulance is on its way."

Wilt's eyes were wide and wild. He didn't respond. He just kept counting.

"The cavalry is on its way, Juliette," Sean whispered to Tay, remembering when she'd said those words six months ago. Then, she'd had a bullet in her belly and an ear shot off. She'd made it through that. She could make it through this.

"1...2...3...4...5..." Wilt counted, then paused. "1...2...3...4...5..."

Sean stared into her open eyes.

She'd been fine six months ago.

Everything would be fine.

34

October 15th
5:45 p.m.

Charlotte's head jerked towards the sound of a car approaching their RV. They'd moved to a new campground that afternoon after Isabella's frantic outburst, but none of them had left the motor home itself for the past several hours. There'd been no word from Jordan as to why they'd needed to flee so suddenly or if they were somehow still in danger.

Charlotte kept herself busy at the table by continuing to page through the Book's translated notes, but her stomach jolted each time a vehicle drove past their campsite. Isabella had taken a nap, then busied herself with cleaning the motor home, though eventually she stopped when Carla complained about the fumes.

As for Carla, she merely sat on the couch beside Charlotte, her stare fixated on the door. Charlotte was forcibly reminded of a large cat waiting for its prey to move before it pounced.

Now, with the sound of a car stopping right outside, Carla jumped to her feet and peered through the blinds. Isabella, having resorted to doing a crossword puzzle, perked up from the bed where she lay.

"It's Jordan," Carla said. She placed a hand on the doorknob, but waited.

"Is she alone?" Isabella asked.

A few heartbeats passed.

"Yes." Carla opened the door and exited. Charlotte heard Isabella give a sigh of relief. She left behind Carla, and Charlotte followed suit.

Jordan looked exhausted. Her face-framing hair was kinked on one side, as if she'd been halfway through straightening it and stopped. Though her clothes appeared clean, Charlotte recognized the outfit from when they'd seen her the day before.

Carla waited about three feet away from Jordan while Isabella ran up and gave the woman a hug.

"Are you all right?" Isabella asked.

"Yes," Jordan said. Her gaze flickered towards Charlotte. "But we may have been compromised."

Charlotte's heart thumped inside her chest.

Isabella released the hug. "That's what you said. What happened?"

Jordan leaned into her car and retrieved a set of papers. "This is the complete address list."

"You got that from your. . .contact?" Isabella asked, still

apparently keeping the name from Charlotte.

Jordan glanced over at Charlotte again. "It's okay. We have to tell her."

"Why?"

This time Jordan held Charlotte's eyeline. "Because Mags is a Triad agent."

All three women looked at Charlotte.

Mags? Charlotte's mouth went dry. "Agent? What does that mean exactly?" she asked, her heartbeat racing even faster.

"We should go in," Carla said. Charlotte didn't like the idea, since the fresh air and the stretching of her legs felt wonderful, but she knew by now it was better not to argue.

The four of them piled inside: two at the table, including Charlotte and Jordan, and the other two on the couch next to the table. Charlotte quickly scooted her own documents over so Jordan had a place to set hers.

"Start from the beginning," Isabella said.

Jordan took a breath. "Okay, as you both know. . .and now you'll know, Charlotte. . .I approached Mags a few days ago and broached the subject of her helpin' me. I convinced her that there had been a similar list of addresses back in my hometown and that I had suspicions that the Triads still existed. I persuaded her to want to help me look into them, to see if there was a code." She faced Charlotte directly. "We needed access to the list you and she retrieved from the underground bunker. I already know the code to decipher the addresses."

Isabella pointed at the papers. "It's obvious you got the list, but this is more than the sixty addresses Charlotte and Mags searched through around the world."

Jordan nodded. "Mags told me when she downloaded the original file from the bunker, it appeared to be damaged. She'd only been able to decipher sixty of the listed addresses. Except the files only *appeared* to be corrupted.

Charlotte's forehead furrowed in confusion. "We could have recovered more of the addresses?"

Isabella pursed her lips for a moment. "The corrupted data is an illusion. It's a backup safety precaution. Instead of deleting the file if found, which would have been easier to retrieve by someone with computer skills, a computer program had been specifically designed to create the appearance of damaged information."

"Then how'd they recover any information at all?" Carla asked.

"I think the system was shut down before it could complete the program to corrupt all the addresses," Jordan said. "Mags tapped into the precinct's database and got me the entire file. She couldn't separate the list she'd recovered from the original file, so she decided to send me the whole document. That way, according to her, we both had copies, in case someone came in and deleted the data from the precinct server."

"Smart girl," Carla said.

"I thought so, too," Jordan agreed. Her tone sobered. "At first."

"So were you able to open the whole file?" Isabella asked, an eagerness in her tone.

"Yes." Jordan gestured to the papers before her. "Now that I had the entire list for the three of us to use, I planned on 'not' figurin' out the code with Mags and eventually tellin' her I'd determined that the Triads weren't real. That way she wouldn't be involved any longer and be safe and we'd have the entire directory. Before that, though, I decoded all the addresses, to make sure the file was intact. I uncovered an address on the list I wasn't prepared for." She paused.

Carla's face tightened. "Mags' address."

Jordan gave a tight nod.

The three women quieted.

Charlotte had sat almost completely silent, listening to these three discuss Mags. She wasn't sure what to think or what to say. She'd been asked to cut off her own life, give up her phone, not be in touch with anyone for fear they could be targeted, and here these women were, bringing the same people she knew back in, putting them at risk. And now Mags' address was on a file as a Triad target? No, not Mags.

"We have to help her," Charlotte finally said. "We cannot let them hurt her."

Silence.

Isabella finally spoke. "Charlotte, I don't think you understand."

Charlotte continued, insistent. "Mags' address is in that file, which means the Triads will pursue her."

Isabella's face softened. "No. The list isn't targets, re-member? It's agents. Triad agents."

Charlotte scoffed. "Not a chance. That would mean—"

"Mags is a Triad agent."

They all sat there, staring at her. They were crazy. Mags? No way in hell. Mags would never be a Triad agent. She'd been there, flying around the world, helping Charlotte hunt the Triads down. She'd been kidnapped by Truth's Triad and held captive. If she were an agent, why would she let them do that? She couldn't be. She just couldn't.

A wave of anxiety hit Charlotte in the chest. She hadn't had a panic attack since the day she'd been stabbed in the back by a stalker. No, not a stalker, a rogue Triad agent. Another connection to these insane women.

The panic increased and Charlotte's breath became shallower. Isabella immediately rose and gently pushed Charlotte's head downwards.

"Breathe, Charlotte, just breathe."

Charlotte's head swam, but the breathing became easier. Her gaze remained locked for several moments on the camper's floor, its fake linoleum so benign in this unrealistic situation. She concentrated on one tile, which had a scratch in it. The shape reminded her of a scalpel. Her breathing slowed.

"That's it," she heard above her. "Now come up, slowly."

Charlotte rose, a bit dizzy, but her breathing had returned to normal. A heat rushed to her cheeks. Even though she knew she couldn't have prevented the anxiety attack, she still felt ashamed it had happened.

"I cannot believe it," she whispered, averting her eyes for a second from their stares. "Not Mags."

Charlotte returned her view to the women around her. She could see the compassion on Isabella's face, the determination on Carla's, and the tears in Jordan's eyes.

Jordan spoke up. "I didn't want to believe it, either. I really like Mags. I even wanted to recruit her to join our cause. But there is no other reason for her address to be on that list."

Isabella cleared her throat and asked, "Do we know what position she is?"

Charlotte could see Jordan swallow hard. "A third," she answered.

That means the executioner, Charlotte thought. *The one who kills the targets. Mags is a killer. Oh God...*

Carla's hands clenched into fists on her lap while Isabella just nodded.

"That's why you had us leave the campsite," Isabella said.

"Yes," Jordan answered. "I didn't know how much Mags knew about us. I didn't know if she had a plan, or if she was aware that we have Charlotte."

"Is there any indication she's after us?"

Jordan shrugged. "I don't even think she accessed the full list yet. She may not even think she's on it, if she believes it only contains the sixty addresses listed."

"Would she not know about the computer program in-stalled on the file?" Charlotte asked. "If she works for a Triad, would she not know about the codes for the addresses or the program that makes them appear corrupted?"

Isabella shook her head. "Only primaries know. Seconds and thirds don't have any informational access about other Triads."

"We need to find her," Carla said suddenly.

Charlotte could hear the heat in the woman's voice. "Absolutely not," Charlotte said, standing. "You are *not* going to kill Mags!"

Carla shot her a venomous look. "*Madre de Dios,* I didn't *say* kill her, I said *find* her. We need to know what she knows. We need to know her plan."

"I know this is a shock to you," Isabella said to Charlotte., "but Carla is right. We need to find her, learn what her goal is."

Charlotte quieted and sat back down, her body still tense. Her mind wanted to race into a thousand different thoughts, but she forced herself to focus on these women's words.

Jordan chimed in. "Isabella, I've been thinkin' a lot about this on the ride over here. I don't know if Mags *does* know."

Isabella raised her eyebrows. "A construct?"

Jordan nodded. "There was no indication that Mags was pursuin' anythin' from me. I had to convince *her* about the Triads."

"She could have been tricking you," Carla said.

"Maybe," Jordan answered, "but if she knew her address was on that list, I can't imagine she would have offered to give me a copy, at least without removin' herself from it."

"Except she thought the rest of the list was corrupted."

"Then why give it to me at all? Why work with me in the first place?"

Carla shrugged. "To see what you know, what your role is with the Triads?"

"Except, once again, I approached her, not the other way around."

"The truth is," Isabella cut in, "we don't know. We may have a rogue agent, we may have an agent with a specific agenda, or we may have a construct. Whatever the circumstances, Mags has to be caught and questioned." She turned towards Charlotte. "I know she's your friend, but we have to find her. Do you know where she might be, outside of work or her apartment?"

"Do you promise not to hurt her?"

"Of course," Isabella said.

Charlotte glared over at Carla, who, after a moment, gave a curt nod.

Charlotte opened her mouth, then gave an exasperated sigh. "I do not know very much about her. She is from Canada, but I do not know if she would flee the country." Charlotte paused. "She had a fiancé, though their relationship sounded rocky on our trip. I overhead her in heated arguments with him. He may know her whereabouts."

"Do you know his name?"

"Scott, I believe. I do not know his last name." She thought for another moment. "She also became quite close with Detective Tay, Juliette Tay. They bonded after their abduction into the underground bunker."

Jordan nodded. "Those are two good places to start. I can follow up with Detective Tay if I can't find Mags directly. I'll tell Tay. . .I'll tell her there was a form we lost that we need Mags to re-sign."

Carla said, "I'll look for the fiancé. Track him. See if they are still involved or in contact." She glanced at Jordan. "You'll call me if you find her first so I can secure her?"

"Of course."

"Check back in when you hear something. We'll be leaving in the morning to the next campground," Isabella said.

Jordan and Carla rose, said goodbye, and left.

Just like that. The decision happened and they'd already moved on it. So proficient. So well-oiled.

Charlotte felt sick. She hadn't moved since she'd sat back down. She couldn't think. She couldn't feel. Every part of her felt numb, except for her roiling stomach. These women had just moved forward with a plan as if this sort of thing happened every day.

But for them it does, she told herself. *These women are not surprised by anything Triad-related. They may not expect everyone to be involved, but they accept it readily if someone is. This is their life.* She paused in thought. *This is* my *life.*

"How are you?" Isabella asked, her eyes soft.

"I. . .I am not sure," Charlotte replied. "It is a difficult concept to digest, that Mags may be a Triad agent."

"I know you're still processing, but you have to accept there is little doubt she is an agent, based on that list," Isabella said, a gentleness in her tone. "However, she may not be aware of it. That's what we need to find out."

"So once a month, this whole time, she may have been killing people? But what about our three-month trip? She never snuck away. She did not have time to kill anyone."

"Not all Triads work the same. Triads can make exceptions for any circumstance," Isabella explained. "It doesn't have to be precise clockwork and most often it isn't. Things come up: weddings, funerals, surgeries, job changes, crises, etcetera. A Triad primary can keep the construct going through maintenance for a long time, if they are allowed to change back periodically into their natural state.."

A thought sprung into Charlotte's head. "How long?"

"As primaries, we learn that most constructs start to break down after about four or five months if they aren't maintained, but can be kept in their created personality for up to ten to twelve months at a time, if necessary. Meaning they don't revert back to their natural selves. It isn't recommended though."

A sense of hope bubbled inside her. "Why not? Individuals can take drugs for that extended amount of time, they can go to therapy and retrain their brains."

Isabella's face softened. "I know what you're thinking, but if Mags is in her construct persona, she can't stay in it forever."

"But with maintenance. . .?"

Isabella sighed. "Think of it like this. If you had a plant, but you wanted to reduce its natural size, you could keep it in a smaller pot, restrict its nutrients and water, and it will stay smaller." She paused. "For a while. Eventually, the plant will either grow and need more than what it's getting or die because it's not getting enough. Or become very sickly and it will be noticeably unhealthy.

"That's the same with these women," she continued. "If we don't switch them back to their original forms for tune-ups, maintenance, drug testing, etcetera, you will be keeping them in a restricted pot with poor nutrients, where they will become sick or die. Or have to keep giving them more and more medication to balance them out, which results in permanent damage."

Charlotte's shoulders slumped. She'd been so sure that Mags could stay Mags. She didn't believe for one second that she could be a killer the way she was. But then again, she hadn't expected it from Isabella. How could she trust anyone she knew anymore?

The urge to call Sean tugged at her heart. She felt so alone in all this and wanted nothing more than to simply hear his voice, even if he couldn't help. But that avenue had been cut off as well.

"How are you feeling about your research on the Book?" Isabella asked, changing the subject.

Charlotte dragged her thoughts to the new topic. "I believe I have what I need about the Messiah and the Triads to counter any arguments."

"Wonderful. We'll rehearse what you'll say tonight and record it tomorrow."

Charlotte started. "Tomorrow? So soon?"

"Unless there is a reason you want to wait? Plus, with the revelation of Mags as a Triad member, she may try to find you."

Fear slunk through her. "Find me?"

"She's had access to you for a long time. She may have been the one to bug your apartment or blow up your car at the motel. We can't take any chances now."

Charlotte felt her head nod, though she hardly registered the agreement behind the motion. Six months ago, she'd known nothing of Triads. Three months ago, she'd set out with Mags around the world to find more Triads. And four days ago, when Violet's trial ended, she thought she'd be done with Triads forever.

Now Mags was a Triad agent and she was preparing to claim herself their Messiah.

35

October 15th
6:30 p.m.

Forensics came through the hotel room, taking pictures, collecting evidence. They did a thorough sweep and informed Sean they'd let him know when they got the results back on DNA and fingerprints. They assured him they'd make this top priority.

Sean simply stood there. His hands felt dry from the caked blood on them. He hadn't washed them yet. He hadn't done anything since the ambulance arrived fifteen minutes ago.

Tay's body lay on a stretcher in front of him. But not one with EMT workers hustling around her, strapping an oxygen mask to her face, or checking her vitals.

The EMT workers had left.

They wouldn't stay for the dead.

Instead, the stretcher on which she lay was being rolled methodically out of the room by the coroner's team. Tay's body was completely covered, not by a white sheet while someone tried to revive her, but wrapped in a black plastic bag, zipped over her head. The strangest thing was that her prosthetic ear hadn't been there. Had Mags removed it? Why?

A force had taken over Sean's body. It filled him from the top of his head to the tips of his toes. A sunken, sucking, sense of despair. He could only stand and stare as everyone else scurried around the room.

Wilt had screamed at the EMT's when they'd arrived. They'd spoken to him about blood loss and blunt trauma to Tay's head, but he yelled over them, shoving one of them, ordering them to save Juliette's life, demanding they take her to the hospital.

They wouldn't.

They don't take the dead.

Now, Wilt sat on the edge of the other bed, peering past the bloody smear near the window, gazing out at the night. Cold wind whipped through the room, blowing around the frilly curtains and the flyers for the hotel's local food delivery services. Wilt didn't watch as they took Tay's body from the room.

Sean couldn't tear his eyes away.

The scene reminded him of a movie. He'd seen it a thousand times. The people in the scene can never believe someone they know or care about is gone. Hell, as a cop he'd *witnessed* it countless times in others. He always thought that if it happened to someone he knew, he'd understand that death was inevitable, that we lose loved ones, that bad things happen to good people.

But this?

Tay killed by Mags?

After everything he'd been through the past six months, this was the worst. Losing an officer in the line of duty can be part of the job, but having one be murdered by her best friend and his coworker?

Because that was the only conclusion. There was no sign of Mags. No sign of a struggle. No sign of forced entry. Only a little blood smeared on the windowsill, blood Sean knew would match Tay's.

A head peeked into the hotel room, dragging Sean from his thoughts. It was the woman from next door, Scott's mom.

"I don't mean to interrupt," she said, her eyes red, "but please, will you tell me what's going on? Was that. . .was that Margaret they took out of the room?"

Sean wanted to answer, *needed* to answer her, but he didn't know what he could say.

"No," he finally managed, the word guttural in his throat. "It wasn't Mags."

"Where is she then? Is she all right?"

"I. . .I don't know. She's not here. I'm sorry, but this is now a police investigation. I can't answer any more questions."

The woman broke into tears. Sean felt for her—she'd just lost her son. And now her almost daughter-in-law was not only on the run for killing Tay, but also Scott. Except at this moment the woman didn't even know that.

I can't tell her, he said. *Not right now. It'll be too much for her. Too much for me.* The thought put a sense of authority back into him. He moved over towards her, his body feeling stiff, as if he hadn't moved in days.

"Why don't you give me your contact information. I'll have someone follow up with you when we know more. We may also have some questions." He knew he should ask her something now, but he couldn't think of anything pertinent. His mind had gone blank.

"I would appreciate that. I'll grab a pen and paper from my room." She returned shortly, her name and number on the page.

"If you hear from her," he said, pulling his own card out of his pocket, "give me a call."

"Of course," she replied. She left, clutching the card in her hand.

Sean turned around, staring at the scene. The room was now empty. There was nothing else to do. "We have to leave," he said to Wilt on the bed.

Wilt said nothing.

Sean didn't know how to console him. He didn't know if he could.

A shaky breath wheezed out of Wilt's mouth. "She can't be gone. Not Juliette."

Sean heard the pain in Wilt's words and it made his chest hurt. "I know, man, I know."

The two remained silent for several more minutes. Finally, Sean heard Wilt sigh.

"Why would Mags have done this?"

"I don't know," Sean answered.

Wilt faced Sean. His voice cracked. "She can't be gone."

Sean didn't trust himself to speak.

Finally, as if pulling himself from a vat of tar, Wilt stood, walked past Sean, and exited into the hallway.

Sean took one last look around. He didn't understand the world anymore. In his job, he often saw the worst of the worst of people.

But not people like Mags. She was one of the best.

Releasing a shuddering breath, he left, locked the door behind him with the key provided by the owner, and attached the yellow *Crime Scene Do Not Cross* tape across the door.

36

October 16th
10:30 a.m.

A quiet unrest filled the precinct Wednesday morning. Sean arrived a little late, having only gotten about two hours of sleep the night before, but he knew no one would care. Wilt acknowledged his entrance with a look containing nothing except a reflection of his own sorrow. Millan's office remained dark, the door closed. Sean wondered if he'd heard the news yet about Tay and Mags. He couldn't imagine how this would affect the already despairing man.

When he'd left the hotel yesterday, Sean automatically called Charlotte, but the call went straight to voicemail. He'd forgotten that her phone no longer worked. He'd thought about stopping by her place to let her know what had happened, but even the idea of showing up on her doorstep at night with such terrible news sapped the rest of the energy from him. He wanted to go to her for comfort, but he knew she'd be hurt as well. Besides, there were more things to do that night for the case.

They'd issued an APB for Mags. The announcement had made Sean sick to his stomach. So far there hadn't been any sightings of her. Since they knew she didn't have a car, they assumed she hadn't left the city. Alerts had also been posted at bus and train stations, as well as car rental locations and the airport. Everything went like clockwork, since Sean and the precinct had done this sort of thing many times before with other fugitives, but Sean's brain still didn't want to process who they currently searched for.

Mags.

Her apartment had been thoroughly explored. There'd been no sign that she'd returned or packed anything up. A patrol car remained on lookout at her place overnight, just in case. But the worst part had been the items found underneath her mattress: Scott's credit cards, phone, and keys.

Her desk area and locker at work had also been examined. There wasn't much there, as she usually just brought in a purse, but they found a few personal effects, including a small canister of her famous coffee.

The sight of the coffee had bothered Sean more than anything so far. He'd excused himself, stepped outside to the parking lot, and stood with hands clenched, taking in and letting out deep breaths to calm himself.

What had happened? How could Mags, of all people, be a

killer? And how could she have murdered Tay?

He wasn't sure how he'd made it through the day. Time simply. . .kept moving. That night he'd tossed and turned, expecting his phone to ring any minute, informing him that they'd caught her or found her dead, but a call never came. He'd finally dozed off around five in the morning and groggily woke to his alarm two hours later to start another day.

Now, he simply felt deflated.

Sean entered his office and took a seat behind his desk. His tired, grainy eyes surveyed the area. Files lay in his inbox, waiting to be read. Most likely new cases, but Sean couldn't seem to care. He wanted to, knew he had to continue on with his job, but he couldn't seem to make his hands move to lift the papers. His computer stayed dark, most likely containing emails to reply to, but he enjoyed the silence for as long as he could. Starting up his computer meant starting his day. This day. He didn't want to face it yet.

A commotion at the front of the precinct brought him out of his stupor. Standing, he went to the door of his office and peered towards the front of the room.

Payne had just entered.

Thoughts and emotions battered their way around inside Sean, between joy at seeing his partner up and moving about, to fear at having to tell him what happened to Tay and Mags. He knew how much Payne had fallen for Mags and he couldn't imagine how this would break the man's heart.

"Hey Trann," Payne said, walking over. He moved a bit slowly, as if someone not quite sure of their balance.

"Wow. Payne. I didn't know you were cleared to come back to work."

"Technically, I'm not, but I left my stuff here the day I got clonked in the head. My apartment and car keys are in my locker."

"Of course. You'd only been walking Mags to her car when…" Sean trailed off. He'd already forgotten that Payne had saved Mags' life. Something acidic sat in the back of his throat. If Payne hadn't saved Mags, not only would he *not* have ended up almost dying in the hospital, but Tay would still be alive. Although Mags would've probably been killed, but since she was a murderer, maybe that would have been better?

Sean chastised himself at the thought, but he couldn't help it.

"Speaking of that she-devil," Payne said with a grin, "is she not coming in today? I saw Judy at the front desk."

Sean clenched his jaw. He had to tell Payne. "We should sit for a minute. A lot has happened since you've been away."

Ten minutes later, Sean finished his recap. Payne hadn't said anything the whole time, just letting Sean speak.

Finally, Sean could hear a grinding noise issuing from Payne's jaw.

"This is bullshit," he said.

"I get it, Payne, but this is what happened."

"Mags wouldn't do this."

"I agree, but—"

"Someone's setting her up," he interrupted. He stood, knocking over his chair. "She wouldn't do this."

"Payne, I—"

"This is BULLSHIT!" Payne shoved the table and stormed out of the precinct.

Sean let him go, and hoped to God that Payne could somehow be right.

37

October 16ᵗʰ
11:30 a.m.

Charlotte woke up with a sense of both excitement and fear mixing in her belly.

Today she would proclaim herself the Messiah for the Triads.

The feelings quickly dissipated, turning into nausea. Charlotte stumbled to the RV's tiny bathroom and threw up in the toilet. This was the second time she'd ever thrown up in her life. She hoped it wasn't going to become a habit.

Exiting the bathroom after cleaning up her face and mouth, Charlotte found Isabella sitting at the camper's tiny table, holding a tablet.

"Morning," she said.

Charlotte merely nodded, not trusting herself to speak.

"Nervous?"

Charlotte nodded again.

"Not surprised." Isabella pointed at the tablet. "I'm going to record you on this. We can re-record your speech until we feel comfortable with it before I send it out to all the Triad members."

Her chest tightened. "I am really doing this," Charlotte said.

Isabella paused. "You don't have to."

Charlotte laughed, the sound harsh and crass. "Oh, *now* I do not have to."

Isabella patted the table's surface across from her and Charlotte took a seat on the other side of the booth. "Listen, you always have a choice, even if it's not a good one."

"If I do not do this, these women will keep killing, they will keep coming after me, and I will never be free. Or possibly still alive. If I *do* do this, I will immerse myself in this Triad-world, proclaim myself in a position of power, and become a completely different type of target."

"Like I said, it's not always a good choice, but you do have one."

Charlotte sighed. "I am not sure if I can do this."

Isabella chewed her bottom lip for a moment. "Tell you what. Let's just make the recording. I won't send anything out until you're ready and *you* can push the button to send it. Until that moment, nothing has changed and you still have a choice. One step at a time."

Charlotte took in a deep breath. "All right."

"Okay. I think we got your speech fully prepared. Let's run

through it for a test."

Charlotte picked up the paper with the words they'd worked on the night before. Her hand shook.

"We'll make sure the paper doesn't show in the shot," Isabella reassured her.

Charlotte nodded and cleared her throat.

Isabella took up a position behind the table and held up the tablet. "Okay. . .recording."

Charlotte began.

"Triad members. You may have heard of me by now. My name is Charlotte Salla. Truth, the primary of a Boston Triad, claimed me as the Messiah six months ago." She swallowed, hard. "I am here to—"

Isabella's ringing phone interrupted them.

"Sorry," Isabella said, placing the tablet on the table. "There must an update." She answered her phone. "Hey, Carla. What's going on?" A few moments of silence passed. Isabella's eyes flitted over to Charlotte. "Yes," she said. More silence. "*What?*"

Charlotte heard the shock in the word. "What happened?" she said through her teeth.

Isabella held up a finger. "You're sure?. . .Suspect?. . .wow. . . All right. I'll let Charlotte know. Are you coming back or. . .yeah, I get it. Contact me when you can. Bye." Isabella hung up.

"What is it?" Charlotte asked, her heart pounding.

"Carla went to track down Scott, Mags' ex." She paused. "He's dead."

The words didn't register for a moment. Why would Scott be dead? "What? How?"

"The police think it was a mugging gone wrong."

"Oh my. . ."

Isabella cleared her throat. "Charlotte. . .it may have been Mags."

The idea was preposterous. Mags would never kill Scott. "Not possible."

Isabella's face softened. "I know this is new to you, but after what we learned yesterday, Mags is a killer, or possibly in a killer's body. Besides, there is evidence of her involvement. Carla accessed the police file on him. Mags' blood was found at the scene. *On* Scott's body."

"How. . .?" Charlotte composed herself. Logic would help her explain all this. "Okay, first, how did Carla access those files?"

"We've had access to the precinct's files for months, pretty much since Truth's Triad was exposed. It was how Carla was able to get such good intel on the officers involved, beyond just what she learned during counseling sessions. Carla's not as good as Mags at hacking, but she'd been granted access to their personal and professional files for her work, and, once in the system, she managed to get full access to everything else. It was also the only way to keep track of any other cases that may have involved the Triad."

Charlotte shook her head, once again amazed at the depths these women had gone to infiltrate the precinct. "All right, then second, why would Mags kill Scott?"

"I don't know, but it is a strong enough suspicion that the police have put out an APB for her arrest."

"Does that mean they know she is in a Triad?"

"Unlikely. I'd imagine they think it's a lovers' quarrel. Carla is staying in Boston to find out what else she can learn, and to see how the case is progressing. She hopes to get to Mags before they do and bring her to us."

"I do not know if I can take much more," Charlotte said, pulse racing. "I spent months with Mags. If she is in a Triad, why did she not come after me while we were alone?"

"Like I said before, she may be stuck in her construct, or flitting back and forth. She may have been ordered to keep close to you, monitor you, not kill you." Isabella hesitated. "Do you remember that woman who stabbed you in the back in the parking garage?"

Charlotte snorted. "It is not something you easily forget."

"Joslyn, or Jasmine as the public knew her, was a broken Triad agent. A third."

"What?" The notion slammed into Charlotte like a runaway bus.

Isabella nodded. "She'd been left off maintenance by her primary, we believe for about six months. The timeline fits with the trial. I think. . .now this isn't fact, just an idea. . .that other Triads may have done this as well."

"Done what?"

"Abandoned their positions, their connection to the Triads, and possibly their agents after the trial."

A brief sense of compassion filled her. "Abandoned? They left those women to fend for themselves, unaware that they are not real, unaware that they are killers?"

Isabella shook her head. "You don't understand, Charlotte. The exposure created by Truth's Triad has only happened maybe once or twice in the history of the Triads."

"In all their history?"

"On this scale, yes. There have always been conspiracy theories or some random connection inside one Triad group, but never this type of revelation about the existence of all Triads. This reveal *scared* these women. Their devotion to the Book is not unwavering. Just like any religion or scientific doctrine, if it's broken open, only the true 'believers' continue on. Whether they're right or wrong doesn't matter—they trust in their faith.

"From this," Isabella continued, "I believe a lot of Triads abandoned their posts when they learned of the exposure six months ago. The cleanest method is for the primary to kill the second and third, then cover up any lingering traces of their crimes, but most primaries aren't killers, not directly at least. There is a reason they are picked to stay behind the scenes. Joslyn wasn't the first abandoned Triad agent we've found. And if Mags is one, she will be very confused, losing time, and eventually, her real persona will break back through and the construct will be gone. Forever."

"But you could put the personality back on her again, right? Remake Mags, so to speak, even if she gets erased?"

Isabella's forehead furrowed, her eyes sad. "The construct is like creating a child. Even if the base is the same, like in identical twins, there will still be differences and variations in the end result. We could use the same building blocks, assuming we could find them from her Triad primary, but she still wouldn't quite be Mags ever again."

"So, she will die."

"In a sense, yes."

Charlotte felt the sting of tears in her eyes. "I like Mags. I do not want to see her vanish."

"She's not real," Isabella said. "The killer in her is. You have to remember that."

Charlotte couldn't accept that. She knew Mags, had confided in her on their trip, had shared meals and hotel rooms. She. . .was. . .real. She had to be.

Overwhelmed, Charlotte excused herself and stepped outside the RV for some fresh air. Construct or not, Mags had made a life for herself, a life that this killer-personality would destroy if they couldn't find her.

So much loss. Too much.

A sense of determination filled her. She wouldn't lose Mags, no matter what Isabella said. There'd already been too much pain. She would use her Messiah status and find a way to save Mags, to save her friend. She couldn't lose anyone else.

The door to the motor home opened behind her, startling her from her thoughts. A look of horror covered Isabella's face.

"What?" Charlotte asked, crossing her arms as if protecting herself from the next blow. How could things get any worse?

"I'm so sorry, Charlotte. I'm so sorry."

Her stomach clenched and her throat felt tight. "What is it?"

"I just heard from Jordan," Isabella said, her eyes glistening.

It cannot be good if Isabella wants to cry. "What. . .is. . .it?" Charlotte repeated in a whisper, squeezing her arms around herself.

"She just saw the news. There is a bulletin from the police about Mags. They are searching for her."

"You told me that. Because of her connection to Scott's death."

Isabella stepped outside. "It's not Scott. It's worse." Isabella's face pinched. "Mags killed someone else."

Charlotte's heart skipped a beat. "Who?" The word barely made any sound.

"Detective Juliette Tay."

38

October 16th
Noon

Mags awoke to some strange jangling noise in the background. *A phone?* It sounded like a computerized trill more than an actual ring. She forced her eyes open and blinked repeatedly at the fuzziness of her surroundings.

Glasses, she thought.

She groped around, feeling like her bed was *way* too big, while the noise continued. Finally, she found the nightstand with her glasses on it and put them on.

The room came into clarity, but any semblance of recognition was lost to her.

Where am I?

She sat up, a shot of adrenaline rushing through her body.

Definitely a hotel room, but not the Beacon Inn where she last remembered being. The minty green bedspread and oceanic pictures on the walls told her nothing about her current location, although perhaps she may be someplace seaside based on the décor.

I've lost time again. The knowledge both terrified and re-assured her because at least she knew what was going on. She forced herself to think, to recall what happened before now. She'd been at the bed and breakfast with Scott's parents. Juliette had come over. They were going to go out to eat. And then...

The shock hit her and her whole body shuddered. Juliette had told her that they'd found her blood on Scott's body. That Mags was a suspect.

Tears coursed down her cheeks. The images she'd seen in the CT machine must have been true. She had killed Scott.

She felt sick. Running to the hotel's bathroom, she pitched forward over the toilet and threw up the nothing in her stomach. Dry heaves continued for several minutes until her body tired. Mags sat on the floor, clutching her aching belly, clearing her sore throat. What she'd told Juliette must be true. She must be a Triad agent.

Mags dragged herself up and stood at the sink. She rinsed out her mouth and then peered at herself in the mirror.

Who am I? she thought at the face reflected back at her. *Who are you?* She recalled what she'd learned about the Triads. They worked as a set of three, so which position was she? A first, who chose the victims who needed to die? A second, who chose the way they would die? Or a third, who killed them? Then she remembered—only thirds were given a fake personality.

You're not a murderer, she thought at her own image.

Or was she?

Fresh tears filled her eyes. She was. She'd killed Scott. She must be a third. She was a woman found by the Triad, then convinced to help them kill others, and, finally, put into a brainwashing program to create a false, innocent persona the killer could hide within.

Which meant "Mags" wasn't real.

"You," she said out loud at the mirror. "You're not real. They made you." Her hands curled into fists. "Who are you? *What* are you? You're not real!" She pounded her fists against the glass. Her reflection merely pounded back.

Rage coursed through her. She was nothing. She didn't exist. She'd been created to hide a monster.

"Come out," she yelled at her own face. "Come out of there! Show yourself!" She didn't know if she expected her face to contort or speak back at her, but it remained the same: crying, angry, frustrated, and tired.

Mags ran from the bathroom and flung herself onto the bed. The tears came and she let them. She cried for herself, for how much she was tired of crying, for Scott, for her own life, real or otherwise.

Eventually nothing remained inside her and she simply lay there, exhausted. She didn't want to think or feel anymore. She just wanted to go to sleep and wake up and find this was all a dream.

The electronic jangling began again.

"What is that?" she muttered. Sifting through the covers, she found a laptop. Not really thinking, she flipped it open. The screen lit up, revealing a steely-eyed man with short blond hair and a chiseled jaw.

"Mae, you all right?" he asked. His brow furrowed. "You look like hell."

Mags blinked. *Who is Mae?* Realization hit her, hard. The Triad members all had code names. This man thought she was her counterpart, the killer.

"I'm fine," Mags replied.

"Why are your eyes all red?"

"Shampoo," she lied, her mind putting forth the first thought that entered it. "Just got out of the shower."

"Too bad we have to stay apart. I could have joined you." He winked.

Mags gave a weak smile. Either they were involved or this man was merely a shameless flirt. *Just tell him you have to finish washing the shampoo from your eyes and get the hell off this call!* But the rest of her brain didn't listen. Ideas streamed through her head, similar to the times when she would work through a computer program or break a code. Puzzle pieces whirled around faster than she could keep up. If she were fake, this "Mae" would eventually return and kill again. Perhaps she could learn more from this man about her other self? Or maybe acquire more information about her next target? As a man, though, he couldn't work for the Triads, right?

First things first. Information.

"What's going on?" she asked, ignoring his comment about the shower.

His eyes softened. "I've been worried. I saw the news this

morning."

Was she supposed to have seen the news, too? She didn't want to give anything away about herself so that he might realize she wasn't this "Mae" person. "What did you think of the report?" she asked, trying to keep her question neutral.

"Well, I was surprised to see your face on it, naturally." Sarcasm dripped off his words.

Was he talking about her killing Scott? Was she on the run from the law? And now how should she respond? Was her alternate self aggressive? A pushover? She had no clue.

Easy does it, she thought.

"Anything else?" she said calmly. She noticed he lowered his eyes a bit. *Submissive,* she thought.

"I didn't think we were ready to be exposed," he said. "You didn't let anyone in the Coalition know."

So, she was in charge of some group called the Coalition, and apparently, there were others. *Better start acting like a leader.* She clenched her hands in her lap where he couldn't see them, trying to keep herself steady.

"Circumstances changed," she replied. "No one can control everything."

He reestablished his gaze. "I know, Mae, but this? You killed a cop. That's not going to go over well."

His words hit her like a lead pipe to her gut. *Who the hell did I kill?* Her hands tightened, the tips of her nails digging into her palms. She couldn't let him see her shock.

"Couldn't be helped," she said, hoping her voice sounded steady.

"All right. Well, we can talk about it tomorrow night at our meeting. Maybe it's a good thing? Maybe it's time we came forward anyway."

"It'll be discussed." She paused. She needed to get him to tell her about the meeting. "Is everything ready for tomorrow? Everyone confirmed for the meeting?"

The man nodded. "Yep. Set for eight. Just make sure you aren't in the bathroom when the call comes through." He grinned.

Mags allowed herself a small smile. "I'll do my best."

"Talk to you later, Mae. Love you."

Those were *not* just flirting words. Her response came thick in her mouth. "Love you, too." She ended the call by closing the laptop. Pain stung her hand and she looked down. Her hands had been balled so tightly that her nails had cut into her skin. Little lines of red were slitted across her palms.

She went to the bathroom to rinse off her hands, her mind full of thoughts.

Mags couldn't keep track of all the notions racing through her head. She currently inhabited the body of a killer. She'd just had an online meeting with a man with whom she was romantically involved. She was apparently the leader of a group called the Coalition. And they'd planned another online meeting tomorrow night with others.

Was she supposed to initiate the meeting? No, he said she shouldn't be in the bathroom again, so presumably he would be calling her.

If nothing else, it appeared that her alternate self was planning something major. The man hadn't thought they were ready to be "exposed" yet. Were they planning to announce themselves somehow? For what reason? And about what?

Too many questions.

One thing seemed clear: her alternate self had *not* predicted Mags' return. Perhaps she knew a way to keep Mags sedated, so to speak. Or, she realized the time losses were more and more often and believed Mags wouldn't reemerge. According to the clock, Mags hadn't been herself for over twelve hours. She'd never lost more than about three hours of time.

Mags stared at her reflection in the mirror. "Think, Mags, THINK," she said. Her first inkling was to call Juliette or Sean, let them know where she was. But then what? Could she explain her situation? No, she needed more information first. Something concrete to help them find this Coalition and stop whatever it had planned.

Before she made any move, she needed to watch the news, find out what happened, and just how bad the situation was. Being a fugitive couldn't be a good thing.

Mags returned to the bedroom and turned on the TV. She flipped through several channels until she saw her face plastered on the screen. Insides numb, she sunk onto the bed while she watched.

Margaret Stinton is still at large and considered dangerous. If seen, the police urge you not to approach her and to call the hotline listed below immediately. We've received word that she is currently a suspect in two murders: her fiancé Scott Hamtion and co-worker Detective Juliette Tay of the Boston P.D. Details will be—

Mags muted the television.

Juliette.

Juliette was dead.

She'd killed her best friend.

It wasn't me, she argued with herself.

Bullshit, her mind replied. *It's who you really are, a murderer.*

Her hand shook as she lifted it to cover her mouth. How could Juliette be gone? She'd just seen her at the bed and breakfast. They'd been talking. Mags had confessed and Juliette said she'd help her and then. . .

. . .then her head began to hurt. She'd gone into the bathroom and. . .

. . .and nothing. Blackness until waking up here.

Mags forced a breath in and out of her. Somehow stress was triggering her migraines and those were causing her to switch back into the alternate persona. She needed to keep herself under control or she'd switch back again.

I can use it as a warning sign, she thought. *If the pain starts to come, I'll know I'm switching. I can. . .*

She could what? Handcuff herself to something until she switched back? Tell someone so they could lock her up? Who would believe her? Maybe Juliette would have, but she was dead. And what if she never came back again? What if she remained Mae and convinced others to let her go and then killed again?

I could end things, here, right now. If I kill myself, she'll die, too.

But then Mags remembered the meeting tomorrow tonight. If she died, those people would still continue on with their plan, whatever it was.

Mags closed her eyes, suddenly exhausted. But she didn't want to sleep. She didn't trust that Mae wouldn't return when she woke.

Was there anyone else who might believe her? What about Sean? Or Millan? Or Payne? They all knew about the Triads. Would they believe her? Even if they did, could they help her?

"I don't want to disappear," she said out loud, tears forming in her eyes. "This isn't fair. This isn't right!" A few tears slid down her cheeks and she rubbed them away with her knuckles.

Focus, she thought. *You don't know what's going to happen in the future. All you can control is what you do in this moment.* The words from her adopted father rang through her mind. He'd shared that thought with her when she'd found out she had a genius level of intelligence and that she had to leave her school and friends to go to college early.

But did that girl even exist? How much had been reality and how much had been programmed into her mind by someone else?

And why was she switching between personalities to begin with? Was she faulty? Forgotten by her Triad? A reject? Or had this been someone's plan all along?

The thoughts in her head overlapped each other and she couldn't think straight. She tried to refocus, but they came faster and faster, crowding each other out. Her body felt achy and her chest tight. Then the pain in her head began.

"No," she said out loud. Mags scrambled to find a pain pill, but the items in the room weren't hers. A purse held a wallet with a fake ID inside, belonging to a Hannah Sims. A wad of cash and a passport under the same name lay inside as well as other normal items like a hairbrush, toothbrush, deodorant, lipstick, keys, and phone.

A phone! But who to call?

A sharp pain caused her to wince and slap a hand to her forehead.

Sean. It had to be Sean. He'd seen his ex, Angellica, switch back and forth between personalities. He'd believe her. He HAD to.

Another sharp pain, this one accompanied by a roll of nausea.

Mags slid down the side of the bed to the floor, opening the phone, trying to see the contact list.

But Sean's number wasn't in the phone. Because it wasn't her phone.

A sense of absolute terror overtook her as the pain in her head increased. She was going to disappear. She knew it. What if she never came back?

Blackness silenced any more of her thoughts without giving her an answer.

39

October 16th
12:30 p.m.

The precinct didn't remain quiet. Once word got out about Tay's death and Mags being a suspect, reporters swarmed the station and clogged the phone lines, asking questions about how one of their own employees could have killed one of their own officers. Millan fielded the press, his face even more haggard than usual. He'd heard the news on the radio on his way into the station and called Sean and Wilt into his office as soon as he'd arrived that morning.

"How *dare* you not let anyone know what was going on?" he barked. "You thought Mags was a suspect and went on your own to meet her at the hotel? You should have informed someone!"

"We were only going to talk to her," Wilt said weakly. "And Tay was there as well."

"Well we all know how *that* turned out!"

Sean chimed in. "Sarge, Mags wasn't officially a suspect. Her blood was found at the scene. We were following up. We had no idea what would happen."

"You should have seen it coming!" Millan shouted, his eyes bulging. "You should have seen the signs in Mags, that she. . ." he trailed off, merely pacing.

"None of us saw anything," Sean said. "Obviously Tay didn't either, otherwise she would have said something when we called. This hit everyone out of the blue."

"Unacceptable," Millan snapped. "That's why I'm leaving this precinct. None of you can do your jobs. Now get out!"

Sean and Wilt had left, closing the office door behind them.

"I've never seen him like that," Wilt said, tucking his hair behind his ears. "And what did he mean he's leaving the precinct?"

Considering that Millan had just revealed his own secret, Sean felt he could tell Wilt. "Millan told me two days ago that he'd put in his notice to retire. He hadn't planned on telling anyone until next week and asked me not to say anything."

Wilt had stopped in his tracks. "What? He's leaving? Why?"

Sean chose his words carefully. He still didn't want to disclose Millan's private life issues. "Everything for the past six months, I suppose. The Triad mess, the trial, losing his daughter. . . I guess it got to him."

"And now to lose Mags and Tay, on his watch." Wilt shook his head. "Trann, what the hell is going on, man? Everything is falling apart. Juliette's dead. She's fucking *dead*. And Mags did it? This is insanity. Complete insanity." Wilt had walked away to his own desk, leaving Sean alone.

That had been three hours ago. None of the "Mags sighting" leads had gone anywhere, the press wouldn't leave them alone, and Sean still felt like he'd somehow ended up in a strange surreal dream.

A knock on his office door brought him out of his reverie.

"Yes?" Sean asked, greeting a tall, black man in his doorway.

"Detective Trann?" A British accent accentuated the name.

Sean stood. "Yes. Can I help you?"

"The receptionist sent me your way. I'd like to speak with you, if I may?" Sean waved him in. The man entered and held up his identification. "My name is Inspector Omani Woods. I'm a detective from London and I work with Interpol."

Sean's curiosity rose. He gestured for the man to sit. "Interpol? What are you doing here?"

Woods took a seat. "Long story short, we'd been working with Detective Juliette Tay, up until her unfortunate demise."

Sean's forehead furrowed. "Working with her? She never mentioned that."

"Our cases had been deemed classified. However, she did highly recommend that you could help us as well. I had my doubts. . .but she is, uh, was, very convincing."

Sean smiled a little. "Not surprising."

"It is a shame I won't get to work with her any longer. We only met a few times, yesterday afternoon being the most recent. She was. . .very driven. I admired that about her."

Afternoon. The thought stuck in Sean's head. "She left early from work yesterday. Said she had a doctor's appointment."

"Apparently covering so as not to disclose the classified information."

The idea that Tay had been meeting with Interpol in secret bothered Sean more than he wanted to admit. He understood the idea of "classified," but there had been too many secrets from the people he thought he knew, the people he trusted.

Woods cleared his throat. "Well, the reason I'm here is that I'd like to invite you to replace her efforts."

A sense of wary rolled through him. "With what?"

"If you don't mind?" Woods asked, pointing towards the door. Sean nodded. Woods leaned backwards, caught the door with the tips of his long fingers, and nudged it closed. He returned his focus to Sean. "We have been tracking arson movement all over the world for the past three years. Lately, there has been an increase in cases. We believe these fires are connected to Triad activity."

Sean remained still.

"You don't seem surprised," Woods said.

"Actually," Sean began slowly, "I have been pursuing a similar avenue myself."

Woods raised his eyebrows. "You have? Did Detective Tay know?"

Sean shook his head. "I don't think so, although I asked her about some profiling regarding arsonists on Monday, so maybe she had an idea. Either way, she didn't say anything about it to me."

"Fascinating. . ." Woods tapped his knuckles against each other. "If I may be blunt, I know that your surroundings must be intense with everything that's occurred, but I'd like you to come help us. It seems as though Detective Tay was right—if you've already discovered some arson connections, you could be very helpful in taking down the Triads."

Thoughts swarmed through Sean's mind. This man proved that, internationally, Triad movement was well documented. But did he want to get involved? And was Interpol on the right track? "Do you think the Triads are responsible for the fires?" he asked.

Woods shook his head.

Sean let out a breath. "I don't either."

Woods smiled without showing any teeth. "Making sure we're on the same page?"

"Making sure what I'm thinking isn't crazy."

"I can understand that."

Sean treaded cautiously. "So how would this work?"

"If you could, tonight, I'd like you to meet the rest of the team." He handed Sean a card. "Here's the address. Seven p.m. If you are unable, perhaps we can meet another time. There is no obligation, of course, but I am following Detective Tay's instinct by inviting you. I hope you'll help us."

Sean took the card. "I think I can manage to meet tonight, but I can't promise anything. I have my hands full as it is."

"I understand." He stood. "If there's any information you have that you'd like to bring tonight, I would appreciate it. If we pool all our resources, perhaps we can determine how these people are deciding where to set the fires and in doing so, connect them to the Triads."

Sean thought about all the information he'd discovered with Elaine. He wanted to uphold her anonymity, but he figured he could bring any facts they'd discovered tonight without involving her. "Sounds like a plan."

"Thank you for your time." Woods paused at the office door. "And again, Detective, this is classified."

"I understand."

40

October 16th
1 p.m.

Charlotte ran.

She ignored Isabella calling after her to stop. She disregarded the voice in her head telling her she wasn't safe out in the open. Her legs didn't care. They took her away from the RV, through the trees, further into the campground. All she cared about was putting as much distance from what she'd just heard come out of Isabella's lips.

Detective Juliette Tay was dead. Killed by Mags.

Too much. Too much information, too much pain, too much loss. Charlotte had never fled from a problem in her life until now. And at this moment she ran with all the strength she had. Sweat pooled under her arms and trickles wetted the sides of her face. Branches whipped her, their leaves a myriad of golds and oranges and reds, as if she ran through a kaleidoscope of autumn. The ground felt sturdy under her feet, an assurance she could sprint without fear of falling. So, she pushed herself, further, faster, escaping from the world.

A stitch formed in her side and Charlotte gasped at the pain. She slowed to a stop, pressing her hand into the sharpness, gasping for air.

None of this could be real. It just couldn't.

Wake up, she demanded inside her own mind. *WAKE UP!*

The birds continued to chirp. The breeze continued to blow. The leaves continued to fall.

Charlotte felt completely out of control. She sat, hard, crunching into some fallen leaves. The smell of the earth soothed her, though it didn't provide any relief from the truth.

Mags had killed Juliette and Juliette was dead.

Something hard dug into her hip bone and Charlotte fished the burner phone she'd been given out of her jeans pocket. Flipping it open, the non-internet phone stared back at her, as if daring her to do what she currently wanted to do.

Rashly, Charlotte dialed a number she'd memorized a few days earlier. The phone on the other end went straight to voice-mail.

This is Detective Sean Trann's phone. Leave a message.

Just those few words in his own voice made her heart melt. She wanted him here so badly. She was in way over her head. He could help. Somehow, he could make this right.

But when she opened her mouth, nothing came out.

What could she say? He'd want to see her, she knew, as much as she wanted to see him. But she was supposed to be recovering from her injuries. If she told him she'd heard about Juliette, he'd want to find solace in her, as much as she did him. And if she started talking right now, she knew she would tell him everything: about the Triads, about her involvement, about her plan to claim herself their Messiah. And then what? Would he arrest her? Shut down their operation? Or worse, be killed to cover up Triad exposure?

Charlotte hung up the phone. There had been so much grief, so much death. She couldn't be responsible for this. She couldn't handle losing him, too.

Charlotte heard a light knocking, as if someone rapped on a tree. She glanced up from the ground, but didn't see anyone amongst the trunks.

"Hello?" she called out.

Isabella peeked her head out from behind an oak. "Hey," she said.

Charlotte let out a sigh. "I should have known you would follow me."

"It wasn't easy," she said, coming fully into the light. "You ran for almost an hour. And you're fast."

"I ran track in high school," Charlotte replied.

Isabella took a seat next to her and leaned against the same tree. "I never liked running until my Triad training."

Charlotte glanced over at her. "Training? I thought you were a primary and only found victims?"

Isabella lifted a leaf and twirled it between her fingers. "We may not go into the field, but health and safety are high concerns.

We go through rigorous training, physical, mental, and emotional, to make sure we are fit to lead a Triad. I used to be about forty pounds heavier."

"I thought Triads valued physical beauty above all else? I am surprised they chose you if you were overweight."

"Remember, not all Triads are the same. And I wasn't unhealthy, just a little heavier. The exercise simply sloughed off the extra weight."

Charlotte returned her gaze to the trees. "Under different circumstances, I would find this fascinating. If it did not lead to death and destruction, that is."

"You see the value in what the Book says, don't you?"

Charlotte remained quiet for a long time. The truth was, she *did* see it had value. And she agreed with almost everything it said. Not the principals, but the facts. Humans *didn't* know how to balance themselves with their surroundings. They treated this planet as if they owned it, instead of being a part of it. But she couldn't say that it warranted murder.

"I did not finish reading its contents. I stuck mostly to the references to the Messiah."

"So, you didn't read about when to kill?"

"No."

"Maybe you should."

Charlotte thought about it. "Isabella, how did this all start? I mean, who wrote the Book? The accuracy in predicting human nature is alarmingly precise."

"It's a long story. I'd be glad to tell it to you sometime. But right now, I think we should head back."

Charlotte felt the shift in the breeze turn from chilly to frigid as the sun slipped behind a cloud. Her breath formed as a fog in front of her face.

"Or you can keep running, if you want. I promise, I won't chase you."

Charlotte stared into Isabella's eyes. She could see the desire, the yearning for Charlotte to follow, but her will holding her back, letting Charlotte make the choice for herself. Charlotte had already forgotten for a moment that this woman had also lost someone she loved. Yes, Isabella had gotten involved in the Triads, but when she learned of their deceit, she made it her goal to stop them. She wanted to protect their victims and end the Triads.

Suddenly, the thought of running away slithered from Charlotte's mind like a wisp of smoke escaping from the top of a chimney. She didn't need it anymore. The power to help end this, to protect others from more destruction, belonged to her. Her voice, her face, her existence could change the world of Triads, forever.

Charlotte pushed off the ground and stood, wiping any dirt from her pants, then turned towards Isabella. "I cannot escape from this. None of us can. I cannot protect those I care about, like Mags or Juliette, even Sean, by running. These women will keep on coming if they are not stopped." She let out a deep breath. "I will no longer run."

Isabella touched the back of Charlotte's hand for a moment. "Thank you."

The two of them headed back. Even at a brisk walk, it took them almost two hours to return. Charlotte absorbed as much of the beautiful surroundings as she could, much like a prisoner marching down to the gallows. She knew her life would never be the same once she returned to the motor home. And she'd chosen her fate.

Finally content with her decision, the fear in her chest diminished, her steps became lighter. She could do this.

Once they arrived, they went inside the camper and sat at the table.

"Are you ready?" Isabella asked.

Charlotte nodded this time, steadily holding the piece of paper with her speech in her hand. "Yes, I am ready."

Isabella held up the tablet. The little red light lit up, indicating the recording had begun. "Go ahead."

Charlotte looked at the device and spoke.

"Triad members. You may have heard of me by now. My name is Charlotte Salla. Truth, the primary of a Boston Triad, claimed me as the Messiah six months ago.

"I am here to confirm her claim. I am the Triad Messiah.

"I fulfill all the personal requirements and will complete all the tasks found in the Book, which I possess." She held up the Book. "The three personal requirements: One—I was marked across my body from birth, the marks then faded, representing the true beauty that lies underneath imperfection. Two—I was isolated for my intellectual superiority, and my sense of rationality became a source of envy for others. And three—I am one with death, as comfortable with it as life itself. These instances are all documented, but I confirm them for you now.

"As for the tasks," she continued. "I have accepted my role as the Messiah, I will guide the Triads to a new path, and through this means of communication, I am individually meeting every

Triad member."

She paused, lowered the paper, and veered off script for a moment.

"And for anyone who questions my validity to this claim, three Triad members attempted to kill me on separate occasions. The Book states that you cannot kill the Messiah. They did not succeed. I survived. I am alive."

Charlotte's gaze flickered over towards Isabella's face and saw the glimmer of tears in her eyes.

She resumed reading from the paper. "I am here to announce myself. It is time to change the Triads. It is clear that there is dissension in the sects and loss of focus. We need a new path, a clear path. I tell you this now to prepare yourselves. Alert all your agents. Show them this message. Let them see that their efforts, and the efforts of those before, have not been in vain. But the time has come for a united front. Moving forward, I will provide a new direction for the Triads.

"This, therefore, is the conclusion the Book speaks of," she finished up, "that the Messiah will reunite the Triads, which have divided 'due to communication.' The Internet has done this. Though it increased our ability to communicate, it fractured the Triads. I will rectify this. I will broadcast again within a week with my instructions. Until then, remain in secrecy as always."

Charlotte watched the red light on the tablet turn off and heard a sniff from Isabella.

"Should we record it again?" Charlotte asked.

"No, I think we got it." Isabella waited a beat. "That was. . . incredible." She placed the tablet on the table. "Whenever you're ready, let me know. We will have to leave right after we transmit the message, so that we aren't in the same location if anyone tracks the signal."

"You believe there will be a backlash."

"Definitely. I know this is the right step. It will stop so many of the Triads, the ones who don't want to believe in the Book anymore, but the die-hard followers? They will come after you." She cocked her head. "The addition of you not dying was a good touch, though. It gives you a lot more credibility."

"But not enough."

Isabella shrugged. "You can't convince everyone, even if all the facts are in front of them. Humans by themselves are an indication of that. They will often hold onto their beliefs, even when proof shows them otherwise. The Triad women are still human."

Charlotte stared down at the tablet. "Waiting to send this declaration out will not help."

Isabella raised her eyebrows.

"The terrible things keep continuing," Charlotte went on. "I just learned of two losses of people I care about, one to death and one to the Triads. I will not be responsible for more devastation if my message can stop any of it at all."

Isabella gave an encouraging nod. "I'm ready, then, if you are."

Before Charlotte confirmed she asked, "What exactly happens next?"

"We leave this campsite, record our next message, and send that. At that point, we will have a tracer system to locate the IP address locations of anyone who opens the message. We will then systematically assess how many Triad members are left, how many respond positively to the message, and track down the rest."

"What if we cannot track them?"

"That's what the address list is for that Jordan has. Backup."

Charlotte shook her head. "It is still an impossible situation. You have no idea how many Triads are out there. You will not be able to stop them all."

Isabella's face hardened. "Every one of them we do stop will prevent more deaths. Every one of them that learns their Triad may be under observation won't risk exposing themselves by killing. Even if we only stop one woman of the three, we've saved all the people she may target, decide how they will die, or kill. If this isn't worth it to you, I told you, you still have a choice until I send this message."

"I know." Charlotte wished she could say no, but she'd been through all the arguments in her head already. This would be the best route to stopping the Triads; no matter how many get stopped, it would make a difference. "Can I have a few minutes by myself first?"

"Of course. I'll head over to the front desk and let them know we are checking out. Be back soon."

Once Isabella left and Charlotte could see her figure move out of sight, she pulled out her burner phone and redialed Sean's number. Once again it went straight to voicemail, except this time she cleared her throat and began to speak.

"Hey, Sean, it is Charlotte. . ."

She spoke for a few minutes before hanging up, then reviewed the video she'd just recorded. It seemed sound, strong, commanding, yet reassuring. Isabella was right, it didn't need a second take.

This is really happening, she thought. No tears reached her eyes, nor did panic settle in her chest. This time she only felt a sense of release. The only way back to her own life lay ahead, and the only way to help stop these murderers lay resting in her hands, on this tablet.

The door to the RV swung open and Isabella entered, carrying a receipt.

"We are all set to leave, whenever you're ready."

Charlotte set her jaw. "I am ready."

Isabella waited for a beat in the doorway. "Are you sure? This is your last chance."

Charlotte held the memory of Juliette, Mags, Sean, Payne, Officer Eth, and her brother in her mind. "I am ready," she repeated.

Isabella picked up the tablet, tapped it several times, then glanced up.

"It's done. Congratulations, Messiah." She headed to the driver's seat, started the engine, and they drove out of the camp-ground.

While they moved, Charlotte stared at the tablet, which had transmitted her message. A flash of her previous dream punctured her mind and she pictured threads of light streaking out from the tablet across the world via the Internet, arriving at the computers of Triad members everywhere. A giant spider's web, in the middle of which she sat as their Messiah.

Their queen.

41

October 16th
7:30 p.m.

Sean drove up to a non-descript ten-story building, a yawn slipping from his mouth. He got out, went to the appropriate room, and entered. Inspector Woods greeted him. He noted the sparse furniture: one table covered with papers and folders, four plastic chairs, a whiteboard, and two desks with computers. It definitely looked like a temporary operation. One other person occupied the room, sitting at one of the computers. A stocky man with a nose like a turkey baster bulb.

"Glad you could make it, Detective," Woods said, crossing the room in a few strides. He stuck out his hand, which Sean shook. "Welcome to our little operation."

Sean noted his British tones again and something stirred in his stomach. He sounded like Tay. He'd never hear her smart-ass jokes or her telling Wilt not to make her repeat herself again. "I'm sorry I'm late. No one could get out of work on time, with everything happening."

"I can understand. Unfortunately, our other two agents left already, so you'll be working with me and Inspector Jean De'leu."

"Let's 'ope 'e lasts longer zan ze last detective," De'leu said, derision coating his words.

Anger boiled in Sean's gut and he made a move towards the speaker. Woods stood in his way, blocking him.

"De'leu!" Woods snapped over his shoulder. "That's enough!"

The French man muttered something under his breath and then hunched back over his station, eyes on the monitor, ignoring the two other men.

"I apologize for him," Woods continued. "Losing Detective Tay is not easy, for any of us. I know. De'leu. . .he doesn't deal well with loss."

"And you told Tay *I* would be unprofessional?" Sean said through bared teeth.

Woods' gaze flickered over to the French man. "De'leu had been opposed to bringing in help outside Interpol for a long time. We've lost. . .others. . .in the past. To lose Detective Tay so quickly. . .we're worried it's not a coincidence. There was a lot of debate as well about whether or not to invite you."

Sean clenched down on his anger. "What do you mean, not a coincidence?"

Woods gestured for Sean to take a seat. "In pursuing the

Triads, we've come up against many obstacles. One of which is that they seem to be able to infiltrate government organizations. We believe several agents may in fact exist inside governments, authority groups, and influential positions around the world, both in the scientific and technological communities."

Sean slid into a chair and Woods sat down across from him, clearing his throat before continuing.

"We are also now aware of their technological abilities." He pulled something from a briefcase at the end of the table.

Sean's breath caught in his throat. Tay's prosthetic ear.

"How did you get that?" he demanded.

"She gave it to me, yesterday, when we met. She explained about how she'd discovered a musical device inserted inside, which burned away after the song ended. We planned to begin an investigation in order to uncover who controlled the device and who implanted it in the first place."

Sean remembered the inconsistencies surrounding the incident with her ear. The precinct believed the woman, Jasmine, who'd been confused and believed she was a Triad member, had assaulted Tay in her garage and installed the device into her prosthetic ear at that point. But Tay had insisted there'd been two attackers and that the timeline for Jasmine didn't fit. Sean had planned to look into it, but somehow in the chaos of the past few days, he'd forgotten. Apparently Tay hadn't, which is why she'd given it to Woods.

"We've managed to keep our main group down to about ten people total," Woods went on, "four of which, including myself and De'Leu, are currently stationed in Boston. This core group has been able to stay under the radar for the past three years, but we've had issues when bringing in outside help. The less people involved, the better."

"I understand." Sean immediately thought of Elaine and how the Triads or Triad-related people had gotten to Gloria. He decided to keep her name out of the current conversation to protect her when he spoke to Woods about the evidence they'd uncovered.

"I spent a lot of time considering both you and Detective Tay to assist us before approaching her. It wasn't an easy decision to invite her to join, and to have lost her so soon. . ." He rubbed his hand over his shorn scalp. "It seems strange and highly co-incidental to have one of your coworkers go rogue and murder her mere days after we invited her to our group and began investigating Triads here in Boston."

A sense of accusation hung in the air. Sean blinked several times. "Wait a minute. . .you think *Mags* has something to do with the Triads?"

"We aren't sure. We don't have any proof, it merely seems too coincidental. We are investigating the matter as we speak, which is where we'd like your help as well. Any information on Mags' whereabouts *before* the police find her would be im-mensely helpful."

"Why before? What are you planning to do with her? Interpol can't arrest people. And you're a little out of your jurisdiction as an Inspector."

"We just want to talk with her before she's processed by the local police. See if she has a relationship to the Triads or not. We can't publicly do so. You've seen how the Triads have tried to cover up exposure. And now with an arsonist group out there torching locations related to Triad members? Who knows if that extends to anyone who merely *knows* about Triads?”

“I get it,” Sean said slowly. “I also have some possible evidence related to the arsons.”

Woods perked up and Sean noticed De’leu’s clacking keyboard had gone silent.

“You do?” Woods said.

Sean placed the folder he’d been carrying on the table. “I have an. . .informant. . .that I’ve been working with regarding the Triad groups. We didn’t know anything about the fires until this weekend.” He opened the folder and handed a few sheets of paper to Woods. Woods read through them and then Sean continued. “My informant noticed a pattern in real estate movement about six months ago based on the partial list of addresses received by my precinct found in the underground Triad bunker. We tracked the movement in two different places in Vermont: one office space, one lake home. Fairly recently, the office space had burned to the ground with two female bodies inside it. The lake home had a female resident. A car was driven into the house with accelerant in the engine and it ignited the house.”

“That sounds familiar. The resident wasn’t in the home, correct?”

“Yep. That’s the strange part. She’d drowned in the lake near her dock.”

“Hm.” Woods read on for a few moments. “There are more details in here than what we have. The vehicle, for instance. . . rigged to explode or suicide bombing?”

“Rigged, but there was also someone in the driver’s seat. Female. Unconscious, but not dead before the car blew.”

"So definitely not an accident."

"Exactly." Sean rubbed his eyes, suddenly very tired. He didn't even know what time it was. He felt like he'd been awake for twenty-four hours. Pulling his phone from his pocket, he triggered it on to check the time, noticing three missed messages and one voicemail. He'd forgotten he'd silenced the device while in the second meeting with Millan at the end of the day, right before he left to meet Woods.

The backlit clock numbers indicated he *had* been up for over twenty-four hours. "Listen, I want to work with you," he said, "mostly because I think if we work together, we can figure some things out. But I need to head home and get some sleep. I've got another long day tomorrow, including reassignment of Tay's current cases." He nodded to the folder. "That has copies of everything I've collected so far. Feel free to keep it and finish thumbing through it. I can meet up with you all again tomorrow after work."

"Brilliant. I think your information will help us." Woods hesitated. "I can't give you copies of what we've done so far to take with you, for security reasons, but you're welcome to read through them before you go, or look at the data tomorrow when you return."

Sean's eyes watered when he glanced down at the pages. "Tomorrow would be better, I think."

Woods crossed his arms. "And Mags?"

Sean hesitated. "I'll do my best to let you know if I hear of any leads. It'll be tricky to get her to you without anyone knowing, and without putting my job in jeopardy. But..." he said, stopping Woods from speaking, "...I'll do what I can. That's all I can promise right now."

Woods' jaw muscle twitched for a moment, but he only responded with a curt nod.

Sean pushed his seat back and stood. "All right. I'll be here about six tomorrow."

"Anything new, call me at that number on the card I gave you."

"Same to you, call me on my cell." He scribbled down the number. "Also, if you find her first, you can't talk to Mags without me knowing. We have to be in this together."

Sean noticed out of the corner of his eye that De'leu peered up from his screen and over at Woods. Woods tapped his knuckles together. "Deal."

Sean gave a nod in return and left the room. He headed down to his car and turned his phone off silent. He looked again at the calls and messages he'd missed.

Voicemail or messages first? he thought. *Well, messages were quicker.* Sean skimmed through the typed words. All three were from Elaine, marked *URGENT.* They said she'd found some new information and to call her ASAP. He decided to call her before listening to the voicemail, since it was probably from her as well, asking him to get back to her. She picked up after the first ring.

"Where have you been?" she demanded.

Sean scowled at her tone. "In case you hadn't noticed," he said, "I've been busy at the precinct. I'm sure you've seen the news."

A few beats of silence passed. "I'm sorry, Sean, really I am. I did see the news. It's horrible about that other detective. Did you know her well?"

"Yes," he said curtly, not really wanting to talk about it. "And just to be clear, this conversation is off the record."

"Oh, of course. I was just asking to ask. I mean it. My station has been on us to get whatever info we can, but I would never use you as a source unless you wanted me to interview you. You trusted me to help with all this Triad stuff. I'm not going to jeopardize that."

Sean relaxed. "That's good to hear. What is so urgent?"

"I. . .gosh this is going to be harder than I thought. I, of course, didn't tell my boss about it because I don't know what to do about it."

"What is it?" he asked, yawning.

"I'm going to send you an audio clip, but let me explain where it's coming from first. See, one of the other things I've been doing is monitoring sites, online that is, and blogs about the Triads. They popped up right after the Triad trial six months ago. Conspiracy theorists, people who want to join the Triads, even those who think they might be Triad sleeper agents."

"We got similar notes and calls from people back then as well. Everyone jumps on a bandwagon to make themselves feel special." Sean rubbed his eyes.

"Well most of them seemed pretty cheesy, kind of like the ghost hunter and UFO sighting sites, but two caught my eye and I've been keeping tabs on them. The first one had been established over two years ago, so it piqued my interest, cuz it didn't just seem like a fad after the trial. It seemed to be monitoring possible Triad murders. It didn't actually use the word 'Triad' until six months ago, but it's all about unexplained deaths and rumors of women acting strange. There were examples of women who'd been in prison or mental institutions claiming amnesia. And finally what constituted a 'Most Wanted' list of women to 'watch out' for."

"Their own list of women they thought belonged to Triads?"

"Yes. I looked into it, and though they have a list of, like, one hundred, three of them had been incarcerated for murder *after* the post was made."

"Are they still around? Maybe we can talk to them." Sean yawned again. He couldn't seem to get excited about this new information. Maybe he should chat with her tomorrow instead, after some sleep.

Elaine continued, "They're all dead. They were all killed within about three months of being in prison. All three had different types of deaths."

The words piqued a little bit of curiosity and Sean thought for a minute. "This blog, it may have a list of *actual* agents?"

"Maybe. Or maybe they just got lucky. Seems a bit coincidental to me, but I think it'll be worth checking out."

Coincidence. That word keeps popping up.

Sean debated whether or not to tell her about his new connection with Interpol. She'd risked her neck, and had even lost the life of someone she knew, to be a part of all this. He wondered if he should tell her about his plan to share their research with Woods. On the other hand, part of him wanted he and Elaine to check out these websites on their own a bit first, to see if their information was worth mentioning to Woods at all.

A third yawn reminded him to turn his brain off instead.

"Well, that all sounds like great and solid leads, Elaine, but I don't know why you made it seem like it was so urgent."

A long pause.

"Elaine?"

"I'm here."

A chill crept up his spine and the tone of those two words. "What is it?"

A long sigh. "The second website. It seemed, at first, the same as all the others, except someone posted an audio clip. The clip seems damaged or corrupted or. . .like they retrieved some of it, but the signal was degraded. Maybe the file was encrypted or something. I don't know. It's patchy, at best, but I knew you would want to hear it."

"Send it over." Sean put the phone on speakerphone and clicked through until he could open the file she sent. The clip was only four seconds long. He played it. It crackled and hissed and the voice sounded distorted, like the sounds had been layered over themselves several times.

"*. . .confirm her claim. I am the Triad Messiah.*"

Sean couldn't speak. He recognized the voice. Even through the distortion, there was no question.

It was Charlotte.

"See?" he heard Elaine say through his speaker. "Someone is claiming to be some sort of 'Messiah' of the Triads. This proves they are real! Or, at least, someone is asserting that they are. We need to find out who is on this clip and where they recorded it. It's our first real lead, Sean! Can you believe it. . ."

"This is great, Elaine," he lied, talking over her, "but I have to run. Someone's coming to talk to me. I'll be in touch tomorrow."

"But—!"

Sean hung up. His finger trembled over the "play" button. He hit it again.

"...confirm her claim. I am the Triad Messiah."

How? How could this be?

Sean stared at his phone as if it were a monster who'd just devoured his heart. He couldn't take anymore. Mags a killer. Tay dead. Charlotte a Messiah.

His phone beeped at him, reminding him that he still had a voicemail to listen to. Assuming it was from Elaine, he methodically played it so he could immediately erase it.

"Hey, Sean. It is Charlotte."

A pain like a lance of fire drove into his chest at the sound of her words.

"I wish I could hear your voice. I could use your strength. I am involved in something. . .confidential. . .in which I am scared of the outcome. I find you soothing and it made me miss you.

"I will be away from my apartment for. . .quite some time," she went on. "I will let you know when I return. It will depend on how things go on this. . .case I am working on. It keeps me from you during this dark and difficult time. I am so sorry to hear about Juliette and Mags. I am with you in spirit."

Sean heard her let out a big sigh before she continued her voicemail.

"I also want to apologize for deceiving you about where I have been, but it was necessary. I am not allowed to discuss the case. I do believe, though, that I am doing the right thing. I believe I will contribute to make the world a better place. As someone who spends his life trying to help others, I hope you can understand this someday.

"*My heart belonged to you that night we were together,*" she concluded. "*It still does. I needed to let you know that. I do not know the outcome of this case, but if something happens to me, I needed you to know. Take care, Sean.*"

Sean sat in his front seat, turned off his phone, and stared out into the blackness of the night.

ABOUT THE AUTHOR

Christa Yelich-Koth is an award-winning author (2016 Novel of Excellence for Science Fiction for ILLUSION from Author's Circle Awards) of the Amazon Bestselling novels, ILLUSION and IDENTITY. Her third book in the *Eomix Galaxy Novel* collection is COILED VENGEANCE.

Christa has also moved into the world of detective fiction with her international bestselling novel, SPIDER'S TRUTH, the first in the *Detective Trann series*.

Looking for something Young Adult? Try the YA fantasy *Land of Iyah* trilogy, starting with book 1: THE JADE CASTLE.

Aside from her novels, Christa has also authored a graphic novel, HOLLOW, and 6-issue follow-up comic book series HOLLOW'S PRISM from Green-Eyed Unicorn Comics. (with illustrator Conrad Teves.)

Originally from Milwaukee, WI, Christa was exposed to many different things through her education, including an elementary Spanish immersion program, a vocal/opera program in high school, and her eventual B.S. in Biology. Her love of entomology and marine biology helped while writing her science fiction/ fantasy aliens/creatures.

As for why she writes, Christa had this to say: "I write because I have a story that needs to come out. I write because I can't NOT write. I write because I love creating something that pulls me out of my own world and lets me for a little while get lost inside someone or someplace else. And I write because I HAVE to know how the story ends."

You can find more about Christa and her other books at:
www.ChristaYelichKoth.com